T0061650

THE
MIRROR
OF
SIMPLE
SOULS

aline kiner

TRANSLATED FROM THE FRENCH
BY SUSAN EMANUEL

Pushkin Press

Pushkin Press
Somerset House, Strand
London WC2R ILA

Copyright © Editions Liana Levi 2017
English translation © Susan Emanuel 2023

The Mirror of Simple Souls was first published as *La nuit
des béguines* by Editions Liana Levi in Paris, 2017

First published by Pushkin Press in 2023
This edition published in 2024

This book is supported by the Institut français (Royaume-
Uni) as part of the Burgess programme

1 3 5 7 9 8 6 4 2

ISBN 13: 978-1-78227-832-0

All quotations from Marguerite Porete's book taken from *The Mirror of
Simple Souls*, translated & introduced by Ellen Babinsky, Paulist Press, 1999

Map hand-drawn by Neil Gower
Designed and typeset by Tetragon, London
Printed and bound in the United Kingdom by Clays Ltd, Elcograf S.p.A.

www.pushkinpress.com

PUSHKIN PRESS

Praise for

ThE
MIRROR
OF
SIMPLE
SOULS

'A remarkable evocation of hidden aspects of the medieval world…
Kiner blends unfamiliar history with a compelling account of
women struggling in a society determined to shackle them'

Sunday Times, Historical Fiction
Book of the Month

'A rich, surprising and devastating story of
a female institution long-forgotten'

Marj Charlier, author of *The Rebel Nun*

'An intimate, heartbreaking tale of female friendship and betrayal
in the royal Beguinage of Paris… Highly recommended'

Candace Robb, bestselling author of
the Owen Archer mysteries

'Brilliantly juggles history and fiction'

Le Figaro

'Sensitive and subtle in substance, carnal and
poetic in form… A luminous novel'

Huffingtonpost.fr

'Leads us with brio into a little-known Middle Ages of
strong, erudite, supportive, and generous women'

Page des libraires

ALINE KINER (1959–2019) was born in Moselle, France. She later moved to Paris where she became editor-in-chief of special issues of the magazine *Sciences et Avenir*. *The Mirror of Simple Souls* was the fruit of three years of research and writing on the beguines of Paris. It was a bestseller in France and won the Prix Culture et Bibliothèques.

SUSAN EMANUEL (SUSAN BOYD-BOWMAN) has been a French-to-English translator of academic and general audience books and articles for forty years. In 2022 she received an award from the French-American Foundation for two works of non-fiction. This is her first literary translation.

For my father, always

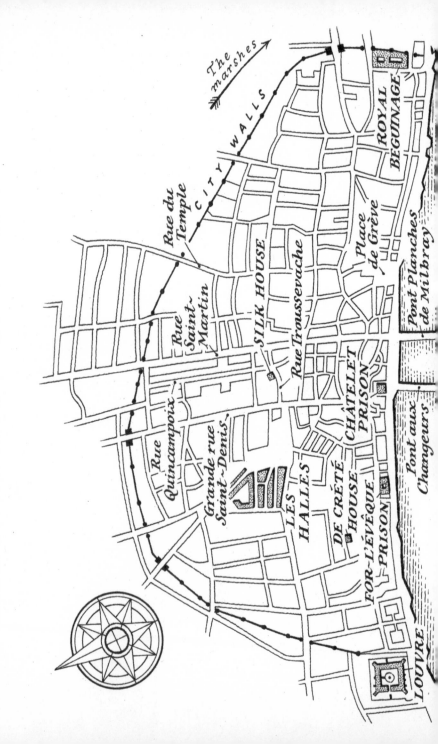

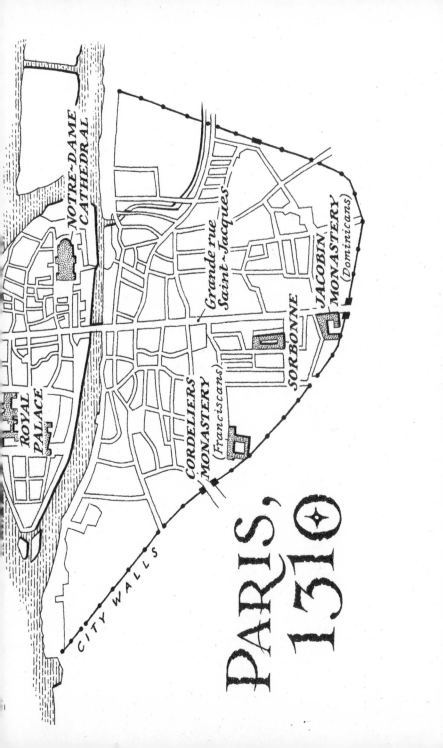

PARIS, 1310

NOTRE-DAME CATHEDRAL

ROYAL PALACE

CITY WALLS

CORDELIERS MONASTERY (Franciscans)

Grande rue Saint-Jacques

SORBONNE

JACOBIN MONASTERY (Dominicans)

CAST OF CHARACTERS

Beguines

MARGUERITE DE PORETE, a beguine from Valenciennes, author of *The Mirror of Simple Souls*

YSABEL, a herbalist and hospitaller at the Beguinage

MAHEUT, a redheaded girl found outside the Beguinage gates one morning

ADE, a pious and educated widow residing at the Beguinage

AGNES, YSABEL's assistant in the infirmary. Her cousin GEOFFROY is a prominent Dominican.

PERRENELLE LA CHANEVACIÈRE, the mistress of the Beguinage; succeeded by JEANNE LA BRICHARDE and then ARMELLE

GUILLAUMETTE, gatekeeper

CLÉMENCE, daughter of bourgeois PIERRE and ALICE DE CRÉTÉ

JEANNE DU FAUT, merchant and mistress of the Silk House

BÉATRICE LA GRANDE, her assistant

JULIOTTE, a mute girl employed in the Silk House

AMELINE, embroiderer

THOMASSE, servant at the Silk House

MARIE OSANNE, another notions dealer in rue Troussevache

BASILE, weaver engaged in sharp practices

9

Others

PHILIP THE FAIR, King of France, grandson of St Louis IX who founded the Beguinage. His daughter, Isabelle, married the King of England and his three sons also made important alliances, though the Valois dynasty was notoriously cursed.

GRÉGOIRE, the supervising canon, a Dominican

GUILLAUME DE NOGARET, Chancellor to King Philip

CLEMENT V, pope

JACQUES DE MOLAY, Grandmaster of the Knights Templar

WILLIAM OF PARIS, Inquisitor General

HUMBERT, a Franciscan monk from Valenciennes, former student at the Sorbonne

JEAN DE QUEYRAN, Franciscan master at Valenciennes monastery, defender of MARGUERITE

GUILLEBERT, husband to MAHEUT

BROTHER GEOFFROY, AGNES's cousin and Dominican prelate

ROBERT DE SORBON, theologian under Louis IX and defender of the beguines

PIERRE DE CRÉTÉ, burgomaster, silk dealer, and patron of the Beguinage, married to DAME ALICE

MASTER GIACOMO, a merchant from Lombardy

BERNARD, fellow student of HUMBERT, syphilitic clerk

HÉLOISE, ADE's sister-in-law

PREFACE

I N THE AREA OF PARIS called the Marais rises a broken
tower, at the corner of the rue Charlemagne and the rue des
Jardins-Saint-Paul. It marks the northern edge of an ancient
wall more than eighty yards long that is punctuated by a second
tower. These are the vestiges of the enclosure built at the end
of the twelfth century by King Philip Augustus, a curtain wall
to protect the city. Centuries later, the buildings of the Lycée
Charlemagne were erected upon this souvenir of medieval wars.
At its southern border, the wall joins the rue de l'Ave-Maria,
named after the convent that occupied the site long before the
school. But in the fourteenth century this street had another
name: it was called 'rue des Beguines'.

Surrounded by grey-paved alleyways, this quadrilateral now
muffles the sounds of the city, leaving the air free for the trills of
birds, the cries of children playing ball, the laughter of adolescent
girls and boys mingling their uninhibited voices. But few people
are aware that this site once contained an institution which was
unique in France: the Great Beguinage of Paris that was founded
by King Louis IX, known as Saint Louis.

For almost a hundred years in the Middle Ages, a succession
of remarkable women lived on this site and in its surroundings.
Unclassifiable and hard to categorize, these women had refused
both marriage and the nun's cloister. Here they prayed, worked,
studied, and had a haven from which they could roam the town

as they pleased, hosting some friends and travelling to visit others, disposing of their wealth as they wished, and even being allowed to bequeath it to their sisters. They had a freedom and independence that women in the Middle Ages had not known before—and would not know again for centuries. At the time, not all of them were aware of how special this freedom was, but some fought hard to preserve it.

For years I walked the streets of the Marais looking for the traces they had left behind. Day after day, they came back to me. I saw their shadows on the ground—now strong, now faint—I heard their laughter and their songs, the sound of their footsteps on the cobblestones, I felt on my skin the same sun that once warmed them, breathed the scents of the nearby Seine. We dreamt, trembled and strolled alongside each other, like companions whom time has separated but whose desires, fears and rebellions come together in a single echo.

Prologue

1st June 1310

I F NOT FOR THE SILENCE, you might think it was a festival day.

There is a crowd in the Place de Grève on this Monday before Ascension. All the people of the city are here. Merchants and clerks, citizens and craftsmen, schoolchildren and clerics, rakes and vagabonds, those who will do anything for the smallest coin and labourers who come to sell their manpower at the port. The heat of bodies pressed together, their smell. Grimy skin and fetid breaths mingle their exhalations with stenches from the street belonging to the tanners and slimy odours from the river. At the balcony windows of the fine dwellings around the square stand ladies and gentlemen dressed in vivid colours.

Shouts and cries, the shanties sung by boatmen and porters, all suddenly lapse into silence in a long wave rippling out from the riverbank. All that can be heard above the murmuring of the spectators are the bang of wood on stone as boat keels clatter against the quay, and the anxious lapping of the Seine.

Everyone's eyes are trained on the centre of the square, where stands a pyre similar to those that have been erected on the same site for carnivals and for the Feast of Saint-Jean. But instead of masked dancers and young apprentices jumping through the bonfire flames, now you see only a woman walking up the pyre, her bare feet stepping over the faggot bundles, with black hair and a long chemise stuck to her body.

She is tall but also frail, her gnarled neck protruding from the pierced sailcloth they have stuck over her head. She stands erect, unchanged by the long months of captivity, the many interrogations, the silence she has maintained. The authorities took this for arrogance. But she simply had nothing to say, or anyway, nothing they could understand.

A little further off is a second pyre. Tied to the stake, a man with a battered face is sagging on his legs, a Jew accused of having spat on images of the Virgin.

But *she* is the one everybody is watching.

Humbert finds himself a few yards away from her, his broad shoulders towering above the crowd. He wants to get closer, close enough to see the shut eyelids of the condemned woman and her knees showing below the shroud covering her. He jostles the shoulder of the matron pressed against him and slips between spectators whose unconscious surges bring them to the heart of the square.

Suddenly, on his right, he notices another figure pushing forward through the press. A slender silhouette enveloped in a grey cape eases its way between the spectators.

Now both of them are a few steps from the pyre.

The executioner is waiting, torch in hand. Close by stands a Dominican in his white robe and black mantle: William of Paris, the Inquisitor. Another man is wearing a sword and feathered cap; the provost steps forward and places a book on the straw at the woman's feet. She bends her head slightly, opens her eyes wide, as if in surprise. At that moment a breeze sweeps up the river. The silhouetted figure that was advancing in parallel to Humbert pushes back the crowd, advances resolutely to the pyre and lets her hood fall.

A mass of red hair tumbles over the dark cape, ruffled by the breeze.

The tormented woman turns her head. She seems to gaze at the young girl who has just revealed herself and to recognize her.

Humbert also stares at the girl, stupefied. Never would he have expected to find her here, nor in that habit.

The executioner takes a step towards the stake. Humbert lowers his head and turns away. He follows the redhead with his eyes as she covers her head with the hood again; another girl, similarly garbed, grabs her by the hand and pulls her away. Then he shoulders his way back to the wharf.

Soon the smell of wood and of flesh being consumed overcomes all other odours. And the cries of the crowd, excited and compassionate, cover the cries of the man at the stake. Perhaps also the cry of the woman who is being burned alive. For nobody could expect her to remain silent until the end.

Part One

January to June 1310

Among us are women—we do not know whether to call them seculars or nuns, since they live neither in the world nor outside it.

GILBERT DE TOURNAI

(1200–1284)

1

LEONOR, HER GRANDMOTHER, had said it would be so. Watching the farmsteads in the surrounding villages being abandoned one by one, children with torn clothes and empty bellies leaving their families and parishes for the town, she had told Ysabel, 'A day will come when the shape of our world will be transformed to the point that people my age will no longer recognize it. I will be gone soon, but you, keep your eyes open.'

This January morning of 1310, Ysabel rises when the first glimmer filters through the window of her room. She dresses warmly and, as she does every day, goes to her garden. Here she kneels beside a bed enclosed by low fences woven of hazel branches, her palms planted on the soil. She contemplates the new decade that is beginning and wonders what her grandmother would have made of it. Her grandmother whose bones must long have been picked clean in the earth where she wanted to be buried.

Has the world changed? Ysabel herself does not know what to think. She has known three kings. Louis IX died well before her second husband, and before she decided to enter the Great Beguinage. Louis's successor Philip III, 'the Bold', died in his turn. So on 6th January 1286, under the rose window that had just been installed in the Cathedral of Reims, the archbishop anointed with holy oil a strikingly handsome youth's head, breast and back. Ever since, Philip (known as 'the Fair' for his good looks) has ruled the kingdom. He is a horseman, a hunter who even in the most grave and solemn moments (such as during the birth of his son Charles) continues to chase game and run his hounds in the forests of Orleans and every other hunting domain in the north of his realm. He is opinionated and efficient, and has been raised to worship his grandfather, a venerated figure who is on his way to being canonized as Saint Louis.

With such a sovereign, and under the protection of such an ancestor, the kingdom has seemed more powerful than ever. Full of energy. The towns bristling with spires and pointed gables, the rivers and seas plied by barges and ships, their holds full of wine, salt and cloth. For decades now, French lands have experienced no great war, suffered no plague or famine. What ill could befall them?

And yet…

Since the jubilee of 1300, a year that the pope had declared holy—a time of pardon and jubilation, with a plenary indulgence promised to every believer—the more keen-eyed amongst the king's subjects have begun to see signs in the heavens.

The winters have become steadily harsher. In 1303, a frost scorched the earth. In the summer of 1305, drought withered the crops in their fields. In 1308, on the first Saturday after Ascension, a snowstorm made more destructive by huge hailstones devastated the region around Paris. The wheat harvest was lost, and grapes died along with their vines. And on 30th October 1309, a wind blew for an hour that was so strong it made the stone arches of Saint-Denis cathedral tremble.

That same year, on the last day of January, in the early afternoon, the sun conjugated with the moon in the twentieth degree of Aquarius. The eclipse lasted more than two hours before disappearing. Ysabel saw the air above her garden tinged with red and saffron hues.

What to make of these signs? The old woman sighs. Under her fingers, the topsoil is cracked, hardened by the frost. She scratches the cold crust, thrusts her hand into the earth, pulls up a clod and kneads it until the soil is soft and warm once more. Crumbled between her fingers, it gives off the fine smell of the manure she spread long before the first frost, cowpats supplied by a peasant from the marshes, and rotten straw to mix with them. As long as spring comes, she thinks, the land will be generous. In this little world where she has chosen to live, no change seems likely to take hold.

She lingers a moment to sniff the earth's spicy tang. Finally she puts her hands on her thighs and stands, feeling the stiffness in her leg joints.

The garden is laid out on the southern flank of the chapel. She turns the corner of the chunky limestone building in no hurry—there is still time before the morning office—and reaches the courtyard about which her sisters' dwellings are squeezed. Through open shutters, she glimpses the halos of oil lamps and candlesticks and moving silhouettes, and hears the clinks of pots and basins.

Here in the Beguinage all is so peaceful. She has not forgotten her astonishment when she pushed open this gate for the first time. Exhausted by a ten-day trip from her native Burgundy, aching from the juddering of the cart and nights spent in bad inns, dazed by her journey across Paris. In those days, the only town she knew was Autun, where one of her relatives lived. Paris had seemed a monster, an ogre in a shimmering robe, filled with vitality and vigour but with a heavy, crushing tread and fetid breath. The crowds in the narrow streets made even darker by the buildings' corbels, porticoes and suspended balconies, the calls of shopkeepers, the cries of waffle and wafer sellers, cobblers, milliners, vendors of frippery, their stalls crowding the street along with spitted joints of roasting meat, everywhere goods being carried hither and thither in bundles on men's backs or loaded onto carts, the animals that jostled you, horses and pigs and stray dogs, the mud, the slops and detritus, the frightful smell of the chamber pots emptied from windows practically onto the heads of those in the street below. When the gate of the Beguinage finally closed behind her, her head still ringing, it was as if Ysabel had plunged into a pool of water, so deep was the calm that reigned inside the compound.

An oasis in the heart of the city, a secure enclave. Abutting the city wall to the east, sheltered to the north by the lofty houses of the rue des Poulies-Saint-Paul, protected to the west by the buildings of the rue du Fauconnier, where the entrance lay, shielded from the river and its traffic to the south by the fortified Barbeau tower, whose defensive chains stretched across the Seine to the Château de la Tournelle on the other bank. A stronghold, but there were no virile voices here. A citadel for women, not a prison.

She had heard a rustling of wings—a tit landing on a house gable—and a young girl's laughter spilling through an open window... She remembers having raised her hands in thanksgiving to the luminous sky above.

*

Now she stands shivering in the middle of the courtyard. Even within the shelter of the walls, the cold is sharp and the wind whistles along stones glistening with frost. Jerked out of her reverie, Ysabel pulls her woollen cloak around her and tells herself it is time to prepare for the morning office in the chapel. A cry from the street stops her.

'My milk, buy my good milk!'

The first cry of the morning, to be followed by the cries of the bathhouses and the wine sellers, then of the sellers of fruit and broad beans. The song of the city. Ysabel hesitates for a moment, then makes for the gate. A bowl of creamy milk, fresh from the udder. That should ease the nostalgia for the countryside that usually grips her on leaving her garden.

The gatekeeper is in her little house near the entrance. The old beguine knocks on the door. Guillaumette appears, her bust rolling over her thick hips.

'I am going to buy a little milk. Would you like some?'

Guillaumette smiles, pushes the key into the lock. The door resists so she leans her shoulder into it, bumping into a figure lying on the ground against the doorjamb.

A thin child, dressed in a dirty cape, her face hidden by the hood, no doubt a beggar hoping for charity from the good women of the Beguinage.

Guillaumette is about to shoo her away, but Ysabel stops her.

Under the pointed chin that the child presses down into her neck dangles a lock of hair. Long and red.

Ysabel bends over and puts her hand on the hunched body.

'Come, little one, you must be frozen in this cold.'

2

THE WIDOWER CAME ALONE to the morning office and knelt in the first row. Facing him, the young girls form a tight group, their eyes fixed on the choir-mistress. The clacking of footsteps on the stone floor, the rustling of stiff clothing. Throats cleared. Silence. One voice rises, alone and vibrant.

'O, fighters for the flower, borne on a thornless branch,
you are the voice of the world.'

Ade closes her eyes. A gust of cold air slips beneath her dress, gives her goosepimples despite her woollen stockings, chills her feet stiff. With aching muscles and head gripped with fatigue, she tries to follow the singing, to slip into the throbbing rhythm of the long-drawn-out syllables, so elaborately modulated. But the words of the letter she received the day before still echo in her head.

Her eyes are closed, but she feels the presence of the man in front of her, his body heavily bundled in a cloak lined with squirrel fur. She knows him. He is one of the most generous donors to the Beguinage, an alderman of the city who has just lost his young wife in childbirth. He has asked the choir to remain after the service to sing in her memory the antiphons she loved so much. All of them were moved by this request, and Ade ought to be too. But the proximity of the widower prevents her from concentrating on the singing. Even under the sweet perfume of the wax flowing from the candles, he seems to give off a musky odour that emanates from his coat, or perhaps from his beard, which she knows is thick and black.

A brief pause. The soloist's voice hangs in the air. Then the choir in turn picks up the verses. The young voices roll out in harmony; a pure line rises up to the chapel's vaults.

Ade concentrates on the voices. She remembers others that lulled her during hours of rest in the convent, where as a child she was sent in order to complete her education. The echo of the nuns' sung prayers in the convent had slipped through the walls of her cell, more luminous than the rays filtering through the small skylight.

Had she been aware, back then, of the peace that the orderly world of the convent gave her? The silent processions of the nuns through the cloister's galleries. The five daily offices and the chanting of the psalms that ordered time, marking out the daytime and night-time hours. The peaceful mornings spent in the scriptorium perfecting her Latin, as she wielded the goosequill or watched the copyists working from dictation, attentive to the voices of the readers, to the scratching of pens on vellum, the metallic smell of the ink.

She would love to return to that place; without understanding why, she was happy there. The Beguinage is a compromise. A temporary home. She knows that she lives on the margins of this world that hums with laughter, prayer and daily routine. Her home is set apart from the rest, against the outer wall, and there she spends her long silent days, sharing the housekeeping tasks with a young and discreet servant girl. The rest of the time she spends in reading and silent contemplation. But it is difficult to be truly alone here, where hundreds of women live without the harmony imposed by the rules of a convent. They are all so different from each other.

The choir falls silent. A solitary voice rises: 'For I am surrounded by a pack of dogs...'

'… A horde of evildoers assails me,' the choir responds.

'They pierce my hands and my feet…' the voice continues.

'… I can no longer count my bones.'

Antiphons and responses alternate; the poignant song of the soloist in dialogue with the sharper tones of the girls. Most of them learnt the art of song at the Beguinage's school. Its choir is famous throughout Paris. Many gentlemen and merchant donors mention it in their wills, asking in return for prayers and vigils for the repose of their souls.

'Deliver my soul from the sword, O God…'

'… and my only one from the power of the dog.'

'Save me from the lion's mouth.'

'…and my lowness from the horns of the unicorns.'

Humility… Ade's brother thinks that as a widow she lacks it. She is already twenty-five years old. How many new husbands will she continue to refuse? He is impatient. Every sentence in his last letter was tense with this impatience. He does not understand her pain.

The man in front of her stirs heavily on his prie-dieu. The wood groans. He is fat, although still young, one of those merchants who spends all his time seated at tables handling either money or food. It was because of men like him that her husband died. Thrown onto the muddy ground and beaten like a swine.

Ade crosses her arms and clenches her fists against her belly.

'Oh, fighters for the flower, born on a thornless branch, you are the voice of the world…'

The choir reprises the opening of the song. Their voices open up now, the singers' throats are warmed up, liberated by the vibrant intonations that are born down in their bellies with each breath and rise to spill forth from their lips.

'… encircling the regions of wandering souls…'

The syllables flow after each other, sketching broad, continuous spirals in the air above, overlapping, curling like vines around the columns of the chapel, rising ever higher.

But Ade's body remains heavy, her soul bitter.

3

A DAY AND A NIGHT have passed, and all this time the little girl has lain curled up on her bed in the infirmary. Ysabel tried to undress her with the help of her assistant, Agnes. The child was sweating and feverish. The miasmas exuded by her damp rags would only further weaken her body. But she struggled, resisting Ysabel's attempts with all the strength of her wiry frame.

We have been clumsy, the beguine reproaches herself. Too hasty. Sitting at the table in her kitchen, she breaks pieces of plane and willow bark into little fragments, throws them into a pot of water—two portions of willow for one of plane—adds a sprig of agrimony, before stirring the mixture and putting it on the fire. This is a sure remedy for fever. But for anger? For it is anger that troubles the girl just as much as fear.

Ysabel has asked for a curtain to be hung about the girl's bed in the infirmary's great hall, to calm and reassure her, and to reassure the other patients too. For the patients in the neighbouring beds have seen what the child was hiding under her hood. The band that held back her hair had come undone as she fought off any attempts to comfort her. Her hair had spilt out over her shoulders. A thick mass, fire-red.

In the hearth, Ysabel's concoction quickly comes to the boil, turning a yellowish colour. The herbalist raises the rack and pinion, letting the liquid simmer while she thinks. A sovereign remedy against fever—but what against anger...? For it is indeed anger that troubles the girl, as much as fear...

Lifting the hem of her robe, she climbs the wooden stairs to the floor above. The door at the top of the staircase opens into a single room serving as both living and sleeping quarters. She has no fireplace, but the conduit from the chimney runs along the wall, bringing enough heat even in the cold spells to make the infirmary liveable.

Near the bed is a trunk of dark oak, with forged iron locks in the shape of stylized stems, the only possession Ysabel brought with her when she came here, a gift from her first husband. Ysabel raises the lid, and rummages beneath linen shirts and woollen tunics to pull out a stitch-worked case from the bottom of the chest. Inside is the jewellery she has not worn for years. But this is not what she is looking for. Her fingers feel among the rings and bracelets, until they recognize the angular hardness of the object they seek.

*

Outside it is even colder than it has been recently. The ground is slippery with ice, the sky frozen solid. The beguine examines the heavens for a moment. It will not snow; the temperature has dropped too low. The bailiffs will be gathering up new cadavers from the abandoned hovels and waste grounds of the city, unless the stray dogs find them first.

Like the herb and the vegetable gardens, the infirmary is situated between the south side of the chapel and the rampart, sheltered from the comings and goings of outsiders. It is flanked by a dozen two-storey dwellings, aligned in two rows, which are granted primarily to the older companion-sisters or to those who want more solitude to devote to prayer. Here, for convenience, is where Ysabel lives. On the other side of the chapel, which more or less splits the Beguinage in two, is the great courtyard around which are crowded most of the lodgings, including that of the mistress, and the communal hall where the youngest and the least well-off of the sisters are lodged.

As she skirts the long, low building where the sick are cared for, the old beguine imagines the look of worry on Agnes's face. Despite her best efforts, rumours are starting to circulate in the dormitory, fears to spread, amplified by the weakness of sick bodies and spirits, by pain and sleepless nights.

Rufus, the redhead! The monks fling this insult at each other when they quarrel. Red, the cursed colour, the colour of the traitor. The red hair of Judas and Cain, of Esau who sold his inheritance to his brother for a plate of lentils, of Ganelon who sent Roland and his companions to be massacred. The colour of the flames of hell that burn without illuminating. Of Satan and his evil spells. Of children who are conceived during their mother's menstruation. A few days ago, the abbot of Sainte-Genevieve expelled a girl from the town, her only sin that of being born with flaming red hair. But being cast out from her home with no resource but her young body would lead her to damnation more surely than the colour of her hair, thought Ysabel.

If red was so bad a colour, why had God put it on the flanks of the beautiful horses she once rode on the lands of her estate? And on the necks of the does that glow in the rays of the sun when they bend tenderly to their newborn fawns?

*

From the herbalist's belt hangs a pouch that never leaves her side. Inside it is the gift for her young patient, a gourd full of the draught made from barks and flowers, and another flacon containing a thick wine mixed with a paste of poppy seeds. Only a few drops of the latter. But before the girl will accept the offered remedies, Ysabel must speak with her.

She pushes open the door of the dormitory. It is well-heated, a fire burns in the hearth, maintained by the young girls who assist Agnes. The straw mattresses are lined up either side of a central walkway, covered with white cotton sheets that have been bleached with soap and ashes. Fumigations of fennel and anise are performed several times a day and give the air an aniseed smell. Ysabel is satisfied. Of course the beguines' infirmary is infinitely more modest than the Hotel-Dieu hospital, but it is well maintained.

Currently a dozen beds are occupied by elderly sisters and poor women from the neighbourhood. Many are suffering from the cold, and one is recovering with difficulty from childbirth. There is no husband and the infant has been given to a neighbour. The beguine hopes the mother will recover, but the poor woman has lost a lot of blood and will not eat.

Ysabel passes between the beds, glancing to either side, lingering a moment near old Cathau, whose condition has been worsening for several days. Her eyes are closed, but at least she has stopped moaning. Her breathing barely lifts the two blankets laid on top of her. Ysabel adjusts the cloth tied around her head, gazing tenderly at the face on which new hollows have been etched. Then walks on to meet Agnes, who suddenly appears from behind the curtain put up for the new arrival at the end of the dormitory.

'She still hasn't eaten anything,' Agnes whispers.

'Has she drunk a little water?'

'She refuses everything we bring her.'

'Leave a goblet at the foot of her bed and a plate of food so she can eat when she is alone.'

'That is what I have done!' Agnes's expression stiffens. Her sour face is a renunciation. The deep lines at the corners of her mouth, the wrinkles and folds in her skin, all seem to pull her face down as if a hand wanted to wipe it clean of features. Only her pointed nose sticks out, and her dark, arched eyebrows.

'Go and rest, Agnes,' suggests Ysabel. 'I will take care of her—and the others.'

*

The girl is still dressed in her soiled cape, the hood drawn down over her face. All that Ysabel can see of her are a sharp chin and a bony knee poking through her tattered breeches.

On the ground beside the cot, a bowl of soup has gone cold, the good chicken fat clotted in circles atop the golden broth.

Ysabel keeps still. She has noticed, from a small stiffening in her body, that the child is aware of her presence. She sits calmly at the foot of the bed and remains silent.

A ray of blurred light falls into the room through the oilcloth stretched across the window and onto the girl's back and shoulders. Ysabel rests a hand lightly on the sheet. On the other side of the curtain around the bed one woman clears her throat. Another breaks into a coughing fit. Then silence falls again, disturbed only by the crackling of the wood in the fireplace. Little by little, from the slight movements of the sheet under her palm, Ysabel feels the girl relax.

She waits a little longer, then starts to tell a story.

'As a child,' she says, 'I was unruly. A strong character. I liked nothing so much as galloping in the woods.'

On the bed, the girl stiffens again. The storyteller pauses, then carries on, her voice low and steady to begin with. She knows that the rhythm of her words—the force or softness she puts into them, the silences that she places between them—is just as important as their meaning.

'My father's estate was a few miles from Autun. We had meadows and forests, soil that grew wheat as high as you wished, hardy vines that hung heavy with grapes. At the end of every summer, I would ride my horse through the fields alongside my brothers. We would watch the ears ripen and yellow until our father gave the order for the harvest.'

The child is paying attention now. Ysabel can feel it. This attention must be the thread that guides her story.

'And then I grew up. I was asked to stay in the house to learn what young girls should know. But spending my days sitting down, with my embroidery frame between my hands instead of the reins of my mare, made my blood boil. My vivacity turned to anger. I did not understand why I was being deprived of what I loved, the outdoors, the wind on my cheeks, the smell of my mount after the gallop.

'This anger began to devour me. It was like a fire. My guts were twisted, my throat burned from spitting out angry words that should not be spoken, my head clamouring with thoughts that find no escape. Then one day, I slammed the door in the face of my governess and ran to get my horse from the stables. My older brother came after me and tore the reins from my hands, and—I don't know what came over me, but I fought him.'

This time, the girl moves, imperceptibly, as if to come closer to the source of the voice. Her hood slips, revealing the curve of her chin.

'My brother punished me. Hard. He struck me with his whip until my dress was torn, my skin bloody and bruised, and then I was locked in my room.'

Ysabel pauses again. With bated breath, she approaches the wild child lying on the straw mattress.

'But that is only the beginning of the story. What is important comes later. One evening, while everybody in the house was asleep, my grandmother came secretly to my bedside. She spoke to me. She said that anger, the anger of the heart and the mouth, the anger of the limbs, would destroy the body and the soul. But since I was still a child who did not yet have the strength and wisdom to fight this, she would give me a present...'

Ysabel rises, slips her hand into her pouch, and places the stone in the sunlight beside the girl's face. The carved crystal captures the light and tints it a pale blue, almost transparent.

'This is an aquamarine, a drop from the sea. You have only to hold it in your hand and look at it for the anger to dissolve. It has often helped me. I give it to you for as long as you need it.'

4

THE GIRL DID NOT react right away. The ray of light slowly slid across the bed, playing with the angular facets of the aquamarine, bringing forth turquoise and green watery sparkles, which then faded into sudden opalescence. Then the light left the stone in shadow, where it lost brilliance but gained in depth, like the surface of the ocean when the sun goes behind a cloud.

Then her hand shot out of her sleeve and closed around the gift.

She has fine white skin, so fine and so white that one can see the blueish veins under it. This is not the skin of a vagabond or pauper.

On the other side of the hanging curtain, the old woman begins to cough again. Ysabel stands up carefully and beckons over one of the girls. She hands her the gourd containing the draught and tells her to give a gobletful to the cough-racked woman. She is going to have to make a tour of the dormitory and examine each patient in turn. But the one right here still needs her.

The beguine moves closer to the child, whose fingers are gripping the stone from the sea. 'Don't be afraid,' she says softly, 'it's me again. I did not tell you my name. It is Ysabel. And you don't have to tell me your own. But since I gave you a gift, I would like you to give me one in return. I brought you a soothing drink.

I am going to put it near you. Take three sips. This will do you good, as much as the stone.'

She puts the goblet of wine on the ground alongside the cold broth, and withdraws.

*

It takes the poppy some time to act. As long as it takes Ysabel to do her round of the infirmary. When she comes back to the redheaded girl, her limbs have relaxed and she is dozing.

Agnes gazes at her in relief.

'We shall give her a bath,' says Ysabel. 'I will carry her. You can go to the steam room and heat the water.'

As her assistant goes away, Ysabel bends to take the child in her arms. She is still strong, her body muscled by the horseback riding of former times and now her work in the garden. But the child seems heavier than she thought. Taller, too. Until now, she has only seen her curled up.

In the room off the dormitory with the tub, the hearth glows red with embers and spreads a good heat. The old beguine lowers her onto a trunk placed against a wall and begins gently to undress her.

'Don't make the water too hot,' she tells Agnes. 'No warmer than the palm of your hand. We have to bring the fever down.'

First, she takes off the shoes, revealing small feet with swollen toes. Then the cape. Agnes's gaze weighs on her as she runs her fingers through the grime-stiffened hair to untangle it.

Under the cape, the child wears a linen shift. Docilely she lets her arms be raised so Ysabel can lift it off.

She is not only bigger than the beguine imagined, but older too. Under the chemise she wears next to her skin can be seen the shape of high, round breasts. Those of a girl soon to become a woman, if she is not one already.

But their curves are not the only source of the beguine's astonishment. Once again, the whiteness of the skin and its smoothness surprise her. And also the quality of the chemise, woven from a supple, light wool.

Behind her, Agnes empties the warm water from the fire into the tub.

'Wait for me, child,' whispers Ysabel to her patient, who lies back limply with eyes closed.

On some shelves set in a recess in the wall sit a number of varnished earthenware pots. Without hesitating, Ysabel picks up three in turn, plunges her hand inside and sprinkles handfuls of dry herbs and flower petals onto the warm water.

'White rose to purify the passions, mugwort to chase away bad thoughts, sage to cure anything, the panacea of panaceas.'

This silent prayer accompanies each of her handfuls in turn. Not really a prayer, perhaps, but God alone knows what it is. Her grandmother Leonor did the same thing to strengthen the power of plants. No doubt she slipped in other words from her homeland of Berry too, but that was her secret.

Since she was a noble lady, nobody had dared to call Leonor a 'healer'. Nor an apothecary, since she was only a woman. But everybody, from relatives to peasants, would ask for her help. When she visited a sick person, she needed only to examine the whites of their eyes, to press her fingers to their forehead and wrist, in order to know what imbalance they were suffering from and what concoctions to prescribe in order to re-establish the harmony of humours. She had taught Ysabel the remedies that took care of stomach troubles and fevers, those that purged or fought poison, the poultices that stopped bleeding, and herbs that relieved women of the pain of menstruation—and sometimes even of the burden of an infant. She had taught her the plants of God and those of the devil, about ferns capable of keeping evil spirits away and the strange plants containing the foam of elements with which Satan liked to meddle. In the fields and woods as they walked together, she had shown her the pulmonaria, whose leaves were spotted with white like the lungs to treat tubercular patients, *chelidonium* with yellow sap like bile that relieved liver troubles, nuts with kernels like lobes of the brain to treat sickness of the mind, and dragon's arum, with skin like a serpent's, which protected people from snakebite.

The Earth knows us better than we know ourselves, she used to say. She is benevolent and talkative. In each of Nature's works there are a multitude of signs. You must learn to pay attention to them.

*

The white rose petals spread across the surface of the water in the tub. The room fills with fragrant steam. Ysabel turns to Agnes.

'Add a little cold water, I pray you. Then you may go and take care of the other patients.'

The assistant raises her eyes in surprise.

'Don't worry,' whispers Ysabel, 'I know how to care for her.'

Agnes acquiesces with a slight nod of her head and, her task completed, departs with an abrupt swish of her grey robe.

Alone now, Ysabel tests the water temperature with her hand, then turns to the young woman, who has not moved all this time. She seems to have woken from her stupor, but she is still calm.

'I am going to get you out of your chemise, my child. Then bathe you.'

She pulls the light wool over the girl's head. She stands naked now, arms at her sides, the palms of her hands turned towards Ysabel, her head lowered.

White, yes, so very white. That creamy white of redheads. The body long and well-shaped, firm, the muscular thighs of a youth, narrow hips, the breasts are two delicate mounds on a delicate bust, the shoulders a little wide but delicate and responsive, as is the neck on which her face inclines. Splashes of freckles on her neck and arms. But other marks, too, larger, of dark blue tinged with red. On her ribs and lower back, and inside her thighs near her pubic hair.

Ysabel sighs, her heart tightening.

The girl has been raped.

She holds out her hand like a mother taking her child to the bath, helps her over the wooden edge of the tub, settles her down in the tepid water, then eases her back on the linen cloth that has been doubled over the wood to protect her skin from splinters. And until the hour of compline, she gently washes her with soap made from olive oil, kneads her hair, passes a clean cloth into the smallest crevices of the skin, between each finger and each toe, and finally into the intimate places, the most hidden, to cleanse them of all dirt and evil.

5

Y SABEL'S FIRST HUSBAND, Hugues, had been a faithful
companion of Louis IX. He had joined him in 1248 on his
disastrous Crusade, and it was only due to a fever that he had
not taken part in the Battle of Fariskur in Egypt, when the king's
army, overcome with fatigue and devastated by dysentery, had
been massacred by the Muslims; the king, to his great shame,
had been taken prisoner. Louis became convinced he was being
divinely punished.

Hugues had again accompanied the king in 1270 when for the
second time Louis took up the pilgrim's staff and the banner of
Saint Denis, and led another Crusade as expiation after a great
purification of the kingdom—Jews condemned to be broken on
the wheel, and blasphemers, prostitutes, criminals and scoundrels
implacably hunted down. Hugues was also near Louis when the
king died at Carthage, calling in his faltering voice upon the help
of the two saints to whom he was sworn, Jacques and Denis.

There followed a shameful quarrel over the corpse of the dead
sovereign, a precious relic that would attract glory and protection to whoever possessed it. Charles of Anjou wanted to keep
his brother's body in his kingdom of Sicily rather than ceding
it to his nephew Philip, the king's son and successor. However,
despite his youth, Philip the Fair won the right—once the body
was treated against putrefaction—to conserve the noble and hard
parts, the skeleton, whereas his uncle had to be content with the

flesh and entrails in all their softness. The king's chamberlains dismembered the cadaver of their master and cured it so long in a mixture of wine and water that the bones fell white and clean from the skin, so that there was no need to use force in the partition of the corpse.

Hugues had reported all these details to his wife—still so young. He also told her of the strange convoy that had crossed the Mediterranean, then all of Italy, over the Alps at Mont-Cenis to climb the valley of Maurienne, passing Lyon, Cluny, Châlons and Troyes, before the procession reached Paris. The small wooden coffin containing the remains of Louis IX was carried on the back of a horse. The corpse of his son Jean Tristan came behind him, followed in turn by the body of his chaplain, Pierre de Villebéon, who had also died during the voyage. Then a tragic stopover in Trapani added to the cortege the bier of Louis's son-in-law Theobald II of Navarre and, finally, after a fifth and double bereavement, came the body of the new queen of France, Isabelle of Aragon, wife of Philip III, who had fallen from a horse when crossing a river in flood and died at the age of twenty-four after delivering a stillborn infant.

Hugues had not gone on to the end of the voyage. He had abandoned the cortege after Lyon to rejoin his wife at his Burgundian estate. Nor did he attend the funeral of the sovereign at Saint-Denis. Exhausted by battles and fevers, he left this world a few weeks after his return.

This first husband, with whom she had lived only four interrupted years amid long absences, Ysabel had deeply loved. She had been fifteen when they wed, he twenty years older, but he was as virile as a youth. And so he remained in her memory. After his death she had married a good man who gave her a son, Robin, and much affection, and with whom for seventeen years she had shared bed and table, but this part of her existence seems to have evaporated—not so much disappeared as snuffed out, like a dream that lost its colour upon your awakening. By contrast, the rare moments spent with Hugues came back to her, vivid and clear. Their rides. Their laughter. Her tears when he went away. And that gesture he'd made when he left, hand outstretched with open palm, like an offering and a promise. She saw it only last night in her dreams.

Maybe it is age that pushes me towards these old memories, she thinks as she leaves her house in the morning. She has noticed this at the bedsides of the sick, shortly before they die—the nearness of death seems to gather up time. But the particular atmosphere of the Beguinage and the memory that inhabited it, that of the king whom her husband had loved to the point of following him on the most dangerous paths of salvation, probably had something to do with it as well.

Some used to mock the sovereign for his ostentatious piety. After the humiliating defeat of the First Crusade, it is true, he was seen to take pleasure in a life of privation, abandoning ermine and furs, luxurious robes, golden chains and spurs, to dress sombrely, eat simple dishes, and dilute his wine with water. Today, though, all must admit that during his life Louis tried to approach, as much as possible for any man in his incompleteness, the example of Christ. He supported the mendicant orders, founded hospitals for the poor, and encouraged the aspirations of women who wanted to practise their religion without falling under the yoke of the ecclesiastical authorities. Under his protection, small communities of beguines were established all over the kingdom: in Senlis, Tours, Orleans, Rouen, Caen, Verneuil. And in the capital Louis personally invested in the construction of the Beguinage, modelled after Saint Elizabeth in Ghent which he had once visited.

The king created the Great Beguinage as a home for pious women, so many of whom had been left alone in those times.

Knights' wives condemned to widowhood by Crusades and private wars, young noblewomen who could neither marry nor enter the costly convents for lack of a dowry. And those poorer still—the women who worked as carders or weavers in the surrounding wool workshops and who would be reassured each night to be able to come back to the shelter of its high walls.

'Are you really going to be happy among those good souls?' her son had joked when Ysabel had announced her intention to retire there. 'You, my mother, who gallops cross-country and speaks her mind, sparing neither man nor beast her tongue!'

'I will master my tongue, and old age will do the same for my impatience,' was her simple reply.

Robin had been married for one year. She left him the management of her estate and gave the keys to her house to her daughter-in-law. He did not understand that she was going away. He had been born into a world that seemed self-evident to him, while she had learnt that time had transformed its boundaries and its contours.

At the Beguinage she found more than she was hoping for. She immediately threw herself into the life of the community. At first she prepared medicines for the infirmary, then when the supervisor of the infirmary died, she agreed to succeed her in that office. She is also part of the council of four wise women—'Me, wise? How Robin would laugh!'—who advise the mistress and help administer the institution.

Sometimes she misses the green of the meadows in spring, the leaves crunching under the shoes of her horse in the autumn, the dusty odour of the threshed wheat stocked in the barn in winter. But she does not regret a thing. She welcomes the dreams that visit her. And repays what she was given.

Today, though, she is the one who needs help.

6

THE HOME OF Perrenelle la Chanevacière is undoubtedly the finest and now the most agreeable in the Beguinage. Some were surprised when she arrived to see her choose a house set back behind the garden and in need of some repairs. Coming from a family of rich drapers who were influential in the city—her father had once been cloth furnisher to Robert II, Count of Artois—she was said to enjoy a hefty income. But no other dwelling was available and Perrenelle was not inclined to wait. She had the roof and woodwork restored, the interior walls whitewashed, had a double bay window set in the first-floor walls which she had filled at great expense with clear glass from Sainte-Menehould rather than the oilcloth used in most houses of the enclosure. Two months after deciding to join the community, Perrenelle had moved in. A year later, she would replace the mistress of the Great Beguinage, who left to spend her last years with her family. Perrenelle preferred to remain in her current residence rather than move to the larger one that went with the office; she entrusted its use to one of the wise women on the council, who kept the ground floor for their meetings.

Stepping into Perrenelle's home, Ysabel immediately feels the sense of well-being she has each time she visits. The furnishings are sober, as they should be. The only concession to the luxury to which Perrenelle was once accustomed is a tapestry finely woven of silk that covers a wall on the north side. Its bright colours, the red of madder root and the sunny yellow of weld, radiate throughout the room, seeming to embrace and energize all that is in it. As does Perrenelle herself.

She is sitting at her table under the window that looks out on the garden. Rounded shoulders, a heavy face, red-veined cheeks. Like a peasant returning from labouring in the fields. The canon is seated opposite her, and despite his height and the majesty of his robe, he appears insignificant in comparison. A thick leather-bound book lies open on the table between them.

'Dame Ysabel, enter, I pray you, and take a seat,' says Perrenelle, looking up briefly. Brother Grégoire and I will soon have finished.'

The canon smiles, resumes his task, his index finger placed on the lined sheet to guide his reading. Ysabel knows him well. He comes every fourth Tuesday to examine the Beguinage accounts. King Louis had decreed that the earnings of the institution be deposited in sealed sacks in the treasury of Sainte-Chapelle. The very place he had built to house his precious relics—fragments of both the Holy Cross and the Crown of Thorns—and where since 1306 his body has also lain. It was the canons who received and managed the pensions granted by the sovereign to the community for its running and the upkeep of its buildings, but also, more personally, to a certain number of beguines, noble ladies in need of assistance. After the death of the sainted king, the grant to the beguines was maintained by Philip the Bold, then by Philip the Fair, in memory of their ancestor.

'Fourteen livres and six sous for Dame Emeline. Sixteen livres and nineteen sous for Dame Alice, and forty annually for her clothing...'

The man comes to the end of his list. He has the serene face of someone who has accomplished a task with little difficulty. The Beguinage is rich, possessing many goods and houses in the city. Apart from the king, many benefactors, both nobles and merchants, give it gifts or name it in their testaments and wills, as much to be associated with the favour of the sovereign as to benefit from the prayers of the pious women. Dame Perrenelle wisely administers this money, taking particular care of the buildings. Regularly rented or sold to new beguines, the houses have to remain in good condition. Some lodgings are offered to ladies without resources, and then maintained at the expense of the community.

'There,' concludes Grégoire. 'As agreed, I will send you the necessary sum for cleaning the well and repairing the house roofs.'

The canon closes his book. Perrenelle rises, fetches a carafe and three cups from the sideboard. She puts them in the middle of the table and pours a full-bodied wine that is delivered to her by her family each autumn. The servant has put more logs in the hearth. The fire crackles softly and gives off a fragrant warmth.

'Speak to us a little of what is happening in the city,' she asks, turning to Grégoire.

He takes his time savouring the wine before answering. He is about fifty years old, with a round face and fresh skin.

'What can I tell you? All the talk is of the Templars. The pontifical commission gathered again this morning at the Abbaye Sainte-Geneviève to hear possible defenders, but none were forthcoming.'

'But it is said that Templars have arrived in Paris in their hundreds,' exclaims Ysabel. 'Determined to testify to the innocence of their Order.'

'Hundreds, yes, maybe, but they are all being held in the prisons across the capital,' remarks Perrenelle, 'which makes it somewhat difficult for them to appear before the commission...'

'What arguments could they advance, anyway?' retorts Grégoire. 'The devil himself would have to plead the case!'

*

It is true that since the arrest of the Templars, the most frightening rumours have been circulating. Heresy, sorcery, sodomy... As
the investigations progresses, the list of their crimes grows ever
longer. The warrior monks suffer from an original sin: claiming
the right to bear arms and to spill blood while still remaining
monks. This status, which contravenes the strict division between
clerics and the laity within the community of the faithful, and
therefore the social order desired by God himself, has exposed
them to suspicion of every deviance imaginable. It is said that
they urinate on the cross. That during their initiation ceremony—
which takes place in the greatest secrecy, with lookouts on the
roofs to chase away undesirables—the novices kiss the celebrants
on the lips, the navel, the anus, the base of the spine—sometimes
even on the penis. That the brothers of the Order know each
other carnally and honour idols, that alongside the Saviour they
worship a mysterious head with a face covered by the bristling
hair of a dog. It is even said that they perform murders for him,
sacrificing infants born to a brother and a virgin, cremating the
remains and then using the fat to anoint the idol.

Though Ysabel knows the wickedness of the human soul, she
finds it hard to believe these stories.

'It seems that King Philip is at the end of his patience,'
Grégoire goes on. 'The pope's delays have wasted a lot of time.
But he can rely on Chancellor Nogaret.'

'That man's no fool,' agrees Perrenelle.

Silence falls in the room. Ysabel tilts her cup towards the
hearth, contemplating the reddish glimmers awoken by the
flames in the dark wine. Nobody around the table has forgotten the brutality of the chancellor, who did not hesitate
to confront two popes for his king's sake. The first was the
ambitious Boniface VIII, who thought himself God's deputy

on Earth and claimed a universal power superior to that of King Philip. But Nogaret had the nerve to bring an accusation of heresy against him, and present it to the Royal Council at the Louvre. He even went with a troop of armed men to arrest Boniface at the door of his palace at Agnani, where he held him captive several days. It is said that during this captivity the pope was slapped, the supreme humiliation. And that he died of shame a month later.

The second pope Nogaret turned into an enemy was the current pontiff Clement V, and this time the Templars were at the heart of their dispute. The episode that triggered Clement's punishment is fresh in people's memories. Nobody could have imagined such cynical manipulation! It was three years ago. The Templars were being increasingly criticized, accused of being corrupted by greed, of looking after the Order's money and possessions rather than fighting the infidels. The most serious accusations began to multiply. Philip the Fair demanded a major investigation by the pope, while the Order, anxious to defend itself, asked for the same. Clement was not inclined to proceed with the case, however, so the French king—with the help of his chancellor—decided to give History a helping hand.

The affair was managed with incredible skill. Instructions were sent in great secrecy to officers of justice and bailiffs all over France. For several days, the Templars were kept under observation on the pretext of a royal tax on their revenues. Then at dawn on 13th October, to everyone's surprise, and without the slightest forewarning of the Order despite the many messengers who might have tipped them off, every one of them was arrested, including Jacques de Molay, the Grand Master.

Only the previous day, Molay had occupied the seat of honour among the court nobles at the funeral of the king's sister-in-law, Catherine de Courtenay...

Since then, Philip has managed to appease Clement's anger with his subtle manoeuvring. Lacking space in his own prisons, Clement agreed to leave the Templars in the custody of the King's Guard. But his habitual prevarication has meant constant delays bringing the matter to court. And so for three years, hundreds of the soldier monks have languished in jails all over the country while the pontifical commissions charged with questioning and judging them deliberate.

'I have heard it said that Guillaume de Nogaret himself took part in the interrogation of the grand master,' resumes Grégoire. 'And that he unsettled Jacques de Molay to the point that he renounced his defence of the Order.'

'How did he manage that?' asks Perrenelle.

'I don't know. I am not sure of anything.'

As if he regrets having said too much, the canon brings his cup to his lips. The heat of the fire and the wine have turned his fine face rosy red.

'May I fill your cup?' asks Perrenelle.

'No, thank you. It is time for me to be going. Other duties await me at the Sainte Chapelle.'

He rubs his hands busily, pushes back his chair, and gathers his cape around him.

When he has left, the two women sit for a moment without speaking. Ysabel is troubled. She has little sympathy for the soldier-monks, but these drawn-out trials hang like heavy clouds over the kingdom.

'What do you make of all this, Dame Perrenelle? Are the Templars as depraved as they say?'

The mistress smiles. Ysabel knows the flame that dances in her eyes.

'They were questioned very rigorously. According to the Inquisitor General, this is a reliable method for reaching the truth. I will not permit myself to contradict him, but the truth obtained that way is often precisely the one you seek.'

She leans forward to reach the jug of wine and fills their two cups.

'This winter is cold and you seem tired. I saw you working in the garden despite the icy wind. You spare no effort! These grapes ripened in your beautiful Burgundy should help give you your strength back.'

Ysabel thanks her with a smile. She is sometimes aware of Perrenelle watching her when she is at work in the herb garden. It does not bother her, for she knows the gaze is full of curiosity and pleasure. Their sympathy with each other is also fed by the smell of the soil and the greenness of the plants that grow in it.

She raises the goblet. The wine pours into her throat, as thick as broth.

'You haven't answered me. Do the Templars merit such accusations?'

'The Templars are rich and powerful. In the eyes of our sovereign, their power and their fortune are certainly sins as serious as any others they might have committed.'

She laughs.

'These are very audacious words for a beguine mistress! But we are friends, are we not?'

She leans towards Ysabel. In a second, the malicious flame in her eyes dies, replaced by a look of affectionate interest.

'Let us talk of other things. Tell me why you came to see me.'

'I wanted to ask your advice about a young girl we brought in three days ago. She was found at the door of the Beguinage, early in the morning. Exhausted and sick.'

'The Redhead?'

Perrenelle knows, of course.

'Agnes told me about her,' explains the mistress, seeing her companion frown.

'She ought not to have done so. I am in charge of the infirmary.'

Perrenelle puts her hand on Ysabel's.

'Do not be impatient. You know that we must be understanding with Agnes. Let's go back to the girl. Did you learn where she comes from, who she is?'

'She says her name is Maheut… Refuses to tell us anything else. To tell the truth, she has spoken barely a dozen words since she found herself among us.'

'Is she feeling better?'

'A little. But she is still weak and feverish.'

'That is not what worries you, it seems. So what is it?'

'From her clothing and her skin, I think she is a girl of noble lineage.'

'So she must have run away from home?'

'Maybe. There is something else.'

'Yes?'

'She was raped.'

Perrenelle's look hardens.

'We will take care of her,' Ysabel goes on. 'But what then? I don't have the heart to send her back.'

Perrenelle crosses her hands on her lap. What should she do? The Beguinage is not a hospice; people come here by choice. It is her role to accept or deny the requests of new postulants, judging them according to their family, their honour, their means of support, but also, for the most forsaken, according to what she surmises about them: the quality of their faith, their honesty, their capacity to share the communal life. The good functioning of the Beguinage and its reputation depend on her choices. She is keenly aware of the responsibility. It would take only a few incidents for the Jacobins at the monastery to come meddling in the Beguinage's affairs. A few years ago, to protect the institution's reputation, Philip the Fair saw fit to place it under the patronage of these Parisian Dominicans on the Grande rue Saint-Jacques. For the time being, they are respecting its autonomy, and she wants to keep it that way.

'What do you think of the girl? According to Agnes, she has caused much worry and rumour at the infirmary.'

'I see Agnes was not content to merely communicate her presence to you.'

'Don't be angry, Ysabel. Just tell me your opinion.'

The old woman sighs and shakes her head.

'I would be lying if I told you I had been able to form one. But she is alone and vulnerable, and threatened by I know not what, or rather I know not whom.'

'What do you suggest we do?'

'We could keep her with us a while. Until we find out who she is. She could board with one of our sisters, help with her work. She'd be no burden on the community. If she misbehaves, we can always send her away.'

Perrenelle turns her head to the window. The dull light of the evening spreads over the heavy lines of her face, lending her the archaic nobility of a timeworn idol, ugly and powerful.

'Let her get back to health,' she says at last. 'And meanwhile let's try to decide who among our beguines might host her. Outside these walls, the world is harsh for women. We must be bound to one another.'

7

As THE HEAVY WOODEN DOOR swings shut behind him, Humbert steps back to avoid a wheelbarrow loaded with sacks of bistre-brown cloth. The small, stocky man pushing it is sweating, despite the chill wind whistling down the alley. Humbert watches him go by, struggling to roll the large wooden wheels on the uneven paving stones, then lingers a while in front of the building from which he has just been unceremoniously turned away.

It is not the first time he has been to the prison of For-l'Évêque. But on his previous visit, he was allowed into the small room where the female prisoner is being held, to hand over in person the books and letters he had brought for her. Today, the jailers are unyielding, agreeing only to pass on his presents and messages, in exchange for a few coins. Humbert has no particular desire to converse with her. His master, though, will ask him how she was, and he will have to say something in reply.

The gate that gives onto the alley of Saint-Germain-Auxerrois is imposing, surmounted by a bas-relief showing a bishop and a king kneeling face to face, on either side of the Virgin in majesty. The sun is already low on this winter's mid-afternoon but he can still make out the details of the scene: on each side of the principal figures are the coat-of-arms of France—innumerable fleurs-de-lys traversed by an upright cross—a judge in a hooded robe, accompanied by assessors and by a clerk dressed as a man of the Church. The image symbolizes the treaty made eighty years previously between the Bishop of Paris and King Philip Augustus.

Like many clerics who have studied in Paris, Humbert knows the story. Arguing that the Church should not cause blood to flow—*Ecclesia abhorret a sanguine*—the sovereign tried to thwart the bishop in his efforts to extend his legal rights ever further over the city. After a year of inquiries and protracted negotiations, the king agreed to recognize some of the bishop's privileges, but made further encroachments on his own power impossible. After the treaty, the bishop built this château of For-l'Évêque on the banks of the Seine in order to house his tribunal and his prison. And in order that blood not be spilt on Church lands, prisoners are interrogated there with finesse, if not restraint: broken, crushed and stretched, but all without the smallest drop of blood breaking the skin. Those condemned to have their ears cut off are taken well away from the château for their sentence to be carried out.

The bishop's prisons have a sinister reputation. The cells are dug deep under the château, and prisoners are left to rot there in the cold and damp, chained to the wall. Fortunately, Marguerite does not have to suffer this treatment. At the request of the Inquisitor, for some time she has been kept at the disposition of papal justice in an annexe and allowed visitors, at least until now. The prosecutor William of Paris is more concerned with the trial of the Templars than with that of an obscure beguine from Valenciennes, and so he is allowing her additional time to repent. This is a common tactic of the inquisitors: to keep those suspected of heresy in seclusion in the hope that they will come to their senses and ultimately admit their error so that a proper trial may be conducted. But it seems that in the face of Marguerite's obstinacy, the conditions of her detention are growing harsher.

Humbert turns his eyes from the looming walls of the châ-teau. It will not be long before night falls. He must return to the monastery of the Cordeliers. The Franciscans' lodgings are not far from those of the Dominicans of Port Saint-Jacques, on the other side of the Seine. He hesitates a moment over which route to take, but decides to follow the rue de Fourneaux down to the river and walk along the banks to the Pont aux Changeurs bridge.

Obstinacy, he thinks as he walks… Yes, undoubtedly this is the word that best describes her attitude, though it is a qual-ity so rarely found in womankind, creatures condemned by their constitution to weakness of character and instability. But Marguerite is bloody-minded to the point of insanity, or close to it.

And this crazy book she has written, *The Mirror of Simple Souls*! In which she allows herself to criticize priests and theologians. To talk of reaching a oneness with the Creator through love, with no need of the Church's intercession. Other mystics before her have hymned this sort of ecstatic union of hearts. Some like Hadewijch, the beguine of Antwerp, have even put their visions and raptures on paper, winning many followers. But none of them have been so radical, so critical, so inflexible as Marguerite Porete. Above all, nobody has dared confront several bishops and an inquisitor in order to defend her writings.

Whatever his old master Brother Jean de Querayn says, Humbert suspects Marguerite might deserve her fate. But who can deny the force of her faith?

The Franciscan shrugs his large shoulders, as if to rid himself of these disturbing thoughts. These visits to Paris are always a joy, but also an ordeal for his soul, so healthy and disciplined when he is close to his brothers back in Valenciennes, but which starts to quiver and twitch when in the city, like a magnet drawn to an opposing pole.

When he reaches the banks of Val-de-la-Misère, the wind blows his cape over his face. The winters are getting colder every year. Or is his body simply losing the heat of youth already? Long ago, when was studying at the Collège de la Sorbonne, he would criss-cross the city in summer and winter, his stride long, his arms pumping at his sides, ready to do battle with words or fists. He ended more than one night fast asleep on the river shore, or on the rubbish piled up in an alley near the ramparts, stupefied by an excess of wine and the caresses of prostitutes. And now here he is, shivering like an old man.

Adjusting his hood, Humbert approaches the steep, grassy riverbank. Below, the river is the colour of mud. The wind whips across the water, stirring it up into waves. Dozens of vessels manoeuvre with difficulty, fighting against the current ripping through the bottleneck in the lee of Notre-Dame Island, as they struggle to reach the narrow channel created for boat passage under the Meuniers Bridge. Fixed to the stone piles of the footbridge, a dozen waterwheels spin at great speed, lifting a wall of foam. The bargemen lean on their oars, guiding the hulls of their boats through a labyrinth of floating pontoons carrying yet more mills. Their cries mingle with each other above the river, now as jammed with traffic as the alleys of the city.

Humbert takes a deep breath of cold air. He knows now why he chose this route along the river. There is more life here than anywhere else. The Seine pulses its energy and power through Paris like the heart pumps blood through the body's veins. He misses it all so much!

He spent six years of his youth in this city into which the whole world flows. The largest city in the Occident. More than two hundred thousand souls. Bretons, Normans, Picards, Burgundians, the English… Merchants from Flanders, financiers from Tuscany, all the princes of the great courts of Europe.

Artists, and especially intellectuals. Clerics from the borders of Christendom, from Scandinavia, Hungary, Poland, the Orient. All living together in the narrow space inside the stone walls built for Philip Augustus. And he among them, breathing the heavy odours of this multiform humanity, as a young plant is nourished by manure. His mind rubbing up against other minds, his body against other bodies.

In his day the students used to quarrel a lot among themselves. They would live in different areas according to which land they hailed from, and incessantly provoked and insulted each other, taking great pride in their reputations. The Breton students were a rabble of drunken dunces. One year, they battled the Picards so violently that houses were burned and people were killed. But the University of Paris was the intellectual centre of Europe. The most brilliant scholars with the most audacious minds taught there, and even dared to criticize the theological teachings and spiritual authorities of previous centuries. They demolished certainties, contrasting faith and reason, Aristotle's philosophy and Christian dogma, the eternity of the world as the Greeks conceived it and the creation as taught in the Bible. These subversive professors avoided the condemnation of ecclesiastical authorities by making their arguments during recognized scholastic exercises like the *disputatio* and the *quodlibet*. Humbert was particularly gifted in these oratorical jousts where each scholar would debate others in front of a vast audience and expound his arguments with force and passion.

Then he had to abandon everything.

Moving away from the river, Humbert crosses a small square surrounded by gabled houses. Delicious smells waft from the ground-floor stalls whose wooden shutters are open to display roast geese and other joints of meat on platters dripping with fat. Serving boys cry out to passers-by, while at the back of the shop cooks turn heavily loaded spits. Between For-l'Évêque where he has come from and the Châtelet where he is headed—the two most terrible prisons in the city—lies the belly of Paris: Goose Place, Tripe Alley and the Great Abattoir where the carcasses of freshly slaughtered livestock hang from enormous hooks. Further on, near the riverbank, stand the fishermen's stalls, and pedlars with baskets around their necks, hawking eels, pike and perch with stiff glistening bodies, while fishwives call out the daily catch.

The cold weather has diluted the usual stench of these streets, the smell of fish mingled with the pestilential stink of the blood and rotting meat that are poured out on the street. Nothing of this has ever disgusted Humbert. And under the austere cape enveloping him, he feels his body quicken and tremble, just as avid as it once was. But as he crosses the Pont aux Changeurs, weaving in and out of the crowd on the narrow embankment running between the double row of houses and shops, the disturbing image of Marguerite comes back to him. Austere—and yet luminous. Her face was transformed when she spoke of that state of grace reached by a soul touched by faith. Has he himself ever come close to such conviction?

On the square in front of Notre-Dame cathedral, small groups linger in front of the façade, its bright colours a patch of warmth amid the grey of the fading daylight. A man's finger points to the gallery of the kings above the Portal of the Last Judgment as he explains details of the statues to a merchant in provincial garb. What happens next is no surprise: while the naïve visitor lifts his face, his helpful guide cuts his purse from his belt.

Humbert shrugs his shoulders, hesitates a moment in front of the cathedral door. But no, he must get back. Soon the streets will no longer be safe. He passes the Hotel-Dieu hospital, heading towards the Petit Pont to cross the other arm of the Seine.

His feet have often taken this route. Not far off is the alley that students used to call the Vale of Love; the vale that he himself liked to travel, humid and deep, had lain between the breasts of Marie, where he slipped his member back and forth until it squirted in her face.

8

THERE ARE DAYS when disequilibrium reigns, hours when the devil places his finger on the sinister side of the scale of souls. During these days and hours one must be particularly attentive, for then the signs multiply, less distinct perhaps, but surer guides than in moments of great clarity.

This morning, when Ysabel leaves the infirmary in search of a potion from her herbarium, she allows herself to stop for the muffled chants that drift from the portal of the chapel. She lingers for a moment, her arms dangling like logs of wood at her sides. Lifts her head to the still-grey sky. Decides to make a detour.

The inside of the chapel is dark, and even more chilly than usual. By the altar, the girls huddle together to keep warm. They are few in number. Two have kept to their beds with fever, while others are feeling hoarse. The choir sings harmoniously none-theless, but the bodies that usually sway to the slow rhythm of the antiphonies are stiffened against the cold, forming a fragile wall of dark capes, diaphanous faces peering over its top.

As her eyes become accustomed to the darkness, Ysabel can soon make out a kneeling figure on the nave side. She draws nearer and sees it is Ade. She is glad to meet her, even in the solitary contemplation of prayer.

Ysabel does not see the young woman often and she regrets this, for Ade must be intelligent and educated. She sometimes helps at the school, explaining the rudiments of reading and writing to the poorest young girls from the town and even to some of her beguine companions. For others who are better educated, she gives classes in Latin and teaches the subtleties she has learnt from the Benedictines. Occasionally, to assist Perrenelle, she composes letters to religious authorities or clerics living abroad. But most of the time, she remains at a distance, joining the community only for the daily masses and chapter meetings, to hear readings or lessons from the mistress of the Beguinage. Ysabel does not remember her ever having eaten a meal in the refectory. Of course, Ysabel's own work does not allow her to go there every day either, but still she likes sharing supper with her sisters. It is a chance to talk, to see how everyone is faring, particularly the youngest girls who are newly arrived in the common house, and to get a sense of the mood of the Beguinage, which, like any large body, must be kept in harmony.

Of Ade, she knows only that she lost her husband in the disastrous battle of Courtrai, when the knights of France, led by Robert II of Artois, found themselves driven into a sodden field by the Flemish militia, where they were thrown to the ground and slaughtered by lowly foot soldiers. And no doubt, thinks Ysabel as she comes up to the young woman, Ade has lost more than her husband. For the old beguine once had to tend to her—and saw the marks on her body.

*

Now Ade shivers and turns her face towards the newcomer, finally aware of the gaze resting on her. She offers a greeting but hesitates, gets to her feet and walks off, her footsteps ringing out on the flagstones. At the doorway, Ysabel catches up with her.

'I am sorry, Dame Ade, I did not mean to disturb you.'

'Do not worry… I was lost in my thoughts, and seeing you, I remembered my duties.'

The young woman seems even paler in the winter light. She has naturally white skin, but today this whiteness seems faded, like snow soiled by soot. Her lips are pinched with weariness. Yet she smiles and asks Ysabel how she fares.

'Fine, thank you. And yourself?'

'Well, very well.'

'It does not seem so. You look tired.'

'We all are. Winter is harsh, and my servant had to go back to her family. Her mother has fallen ill.'

Ysabel lets a silence fall. Behind the thick chapel wall, the girls' singing stops, too. There is so little sound in the Beguinage on this freezing morning, when all the sisters are huddled indoors and the birds have ceased their song, that they can hear the sounds of the city from beyond the encircling houses.

'So you have nobody to help you at home?' she resumes.

Ade smiles again, a polite smile that gives nothing away.

'I have help for the wood and the hearth, don't worry. Apart from that, the house is not so big. I can look after myself.'

Then, before Ysabel can respond:

'I must leave you now, please excuse me. This morning I received a present from my sister-in-law. A fur mantle. I must write to thank her.'

Thus abandoned, Ysabel picks up her errand where she left off. She gathers the medicines she needs, stows them in her pouch, then heads back to the infirmary, daunted by what she knows awaits her.

During the harsh winter, sickness has flourished. The dormitory is full, and the beds have had to be pushed together to make room for more straw mattresses. The patients sleep badly, disturbed by the coughing of some and the moaning of others. An atmosphere of fatigue and gloom reigns.

Pushing open the door, however, she hears not groans but cries. Two bodies are rolling on the floor, while Agnes tries timidly to separate them.

Ysabel rushes towards the brawling pair. She recognizes one of the furies by her hair, spread on the ground like a bloody cloth alongside a torn-off bonnet. The other girl is Benoite, a laundrywoman who sometimes works for the Beguinage and is being treated for stomach pains, but should have been sent home a long time ago, to judge by the energy she is displaying.

Maheut is on her back, crushed by the laundrywoman's weight, kicking and writhing frantically to get free.

In the nick of time, Ysabel seizes an arm raised to strike and pulls it back. Benoite turns her head in a fury, but as soon as she recognizes the old beguine she lets her arm fall and drops heavily to the ground at Maheut's side, while the young girl's legs continue to flail at the empty space above her.

Now she must usher off the other patients who have crowded round the spectacle on the floor, try to soothe Agnes. Then wait, without touching her, leaving her where she lies on the cold stone, dressed only in chemise and torn gown, for Maheut to grow calm.

*

'What happened here?' asks Ysabel, when she has taken Maheut back to her bed.

'She turned into a fury and threw herself on Benoite,' Agnes replies. 'I could not separate them. You saw for yourself.'

'And just before that, what happened?'

Her assistant is silent.

'Agnes!'

'She is cured now. We cannot keep her for days and days behind a curtain. The others are curious, they want to catch sight of her. I cannot always be here to watch over things!'

'What did Benoite say to her?'

'I don't know.'

Ysabel knows only too well.

'She is cured now,' Agnes repeats. 'We have to send her away.'

Ysabel knows she is right. She spoke with Perrenelle days ago, but she has been overwhelmed by the influx of sick patients and the need to care for them all. Still, she cannot suppress a huff of impatience.

Agnes lowers her head. Ashamed of herself, Ysabel lays a hand on her assistant's shoulder.

*

I am being unfair, she tells herself that evening, poking the fire in the brazier so the embers will catch again. There are all sorts of ways to be ill. Agnes merits my attention as much as the others.

She knows that her assistant's life has not been easy. Her husband was a violent spendthrift who ruined his family and then fled the kingdom to avoid paying his debts. Agnes has had no news of him for a year or more. She came to the Beguinage on the recommendation of her cousin Brother Geoffroy, a Dominican from Sens and apparently her only close relative, whom she had asked for help. She brought with her only a trunk stuffed with poor clothes, and a few dishes saved from the domestic shipwreck. Perrenelle offered her a house, which though modest gives her a more independent life than the communal lodgings. To express her gratitude, Agnes now feels obliged to labour at a task to which she is not suited.

Ysabel watches her walk away now, fleeing her own peevishness. She sits down at the bedside of old Cathau who is still dying slowly, but without the cries, gasps, flatulence, and putrid bodily excretions that often accompany the passage to death. Instead, she has the calm air of one who lies dozing in the afternoon, so tranquil that you could find peace just sitting at her bedside.

Yes, I am unjust.

The old beguine rests the poker with which she has just stirred the embers of the fire against the wall, and rubs her shoulders and arms. It has been a frantic, troublesome day. But she knows that something can be built on these troubled waters.

Disequilibrium is not disorder, her grandmother used to tell her. It is necessary for life. It impels movement.

Then, as with each of her unorthodox life lessons, Leonor went on to invent a story. A story that often said more than what it purported to illustrate.

Imagine a man sitting on a riverbank, watching the water flowing by. He feels numb, lifeless compared to the fish that glide between the rocks below, tossed on the current. Now imagine that the man decides to cross the river. With arms outstretched, delicate but bold of foot, he moves from rock to rock, gauging the support each offers him, righting himself when a rock tips beneath him. He feels his heart beating, the blood flowing to his face, pins and needles tickling his palms and his hands. It does not matter what is on the other side of the river, because while he is crossing it he is alive.

To fight imbalance, to reconcile contraries, to re-establish harmony—this is the only true mission that we can accomplish on this earth. And yet we perform it so badly. Thus thinks Ysabel, sitting at her kitchen hearth, where for once no stew is bubbling.

Yet, she told herself, it is easier to balance the humours of the body than those of the mind. In winter, roasted fish or meat to keep the body hot and dry; in summer, boiled flesh, watery wine or dandelions to keep it cool—even the simplest peasants know that. But to rekindle a glacial heart, or to temper a boiling mind...

Ysabel gets up, pokes again at the fire and adds a log. The flames sputter, flicker, then leap up suddenly in ragged waves, turning blue, before they settle down once more, purring.

She stretches out her hands to the fire, suddenly serene. One must trust in contingencies, for God is their master. The barely glimpsed solution is the best. She need only keep her wits about her.

9

A<small>DE SAYS NO</small>. Despite the respect she owes to the elder beguine, she refuses.

The old beguine sits opposite her. She is small and sturdy, her face creased with wrinkles. And those strange eyes, neither blue nor green, filled with all the shades of the sky, of the plants of her garden, of the light when it shines through a raindrop. At night her eyes must have the colour of the celestial vault, dark and pricked with pins of light like Ysabel herself, quivering with nebulae, with veils of stars suddenly obscured by the movements of clouds.

Ysabel does not know it, but Ade has often watched *her*. Ever since the day she was delirious with fever and allowed herself to be undressed. The hands of the beguine were the first to touch her since those of her husband. But instead of enflaming her body as he had, Ysabel's fingertips left behind small streams of coolness that, along with the small vial of bitter potion, had allowed Ade at last to get some rest.

They say she is kind. Perrenelle, the mistress, trusts her. But Ade is suspicious. Ysabel saw the marbled streaks on her belly but has kept her secret. Even so, the young widow does not like to feel Ysabel so close. The infirmarer is one of those carnal presences that she tries to ignore without ever being able to do so, even here among these wise and pious women.

'Your servant has left, you told me,' Ysabel goes on. 'The girl can help you. She is small but strong.'

'Again, I thank you, Dame Ysabel, but as I said before, I can look after myself. Others might need her.'

'I am speaking to *you* after giving the matter due consideration. Maheut, as I told you, has red hair. I fear that many here share the common prejudice against those of her colouring.'

Ade raises her chin. 'Who says that I do not? Is not red the colour of the devil?'

'It is not Satan who dwells in that child. But fear—and loneliness.'

'There are other places for those without a home.'

'In our own infirmary, she was beaten this morning. If she were sent somewhere else, the same would happen again, or worse.'

'If she is the source of such disorder, why do you want to keep her here at any price?'

'We will act with discretion. I will get Maheut out of the infirmary this evening, the brawl will be a perfect excuse, and bring her to your home. You live apart from the rest, and among our companions almost nobody knows her. She will cover her hair and remain indoors as much as possible. If anybody asks, you will present her as a niece who has come to keep you company and help you. By the end of winter, if we can hold our tongues, nobody will bother with her any more. Only Agnes is in on the secret and she will say nothing. She herself once came here in need of refuge, so she knows what that means.'

Ade lowers her head. Ysabel seems to have everything planned out. But she cannot let herself be overruled like that. She cannot imagine welcoming a strange woman into her house.

'Is Dame Perrenelle aware of this?'

'Of course.'

'And the prior of the Jacobins?'

'It is up to our mistress whether and when she tells him.'

Ysabel's tone has shifted. Her voice is different now, brusque.

'There are few rules in our Beguinage, as you know, Dame Ade. But one of them is essential, even if it is not written in any book: solidarity.'

'I came here to pray and retreat from the world,' objects Ade.

'In that case, you should have chosen a convent.'

'You are not being fair, Ysabel. The Beguinage has always welcomed women devoted to solitude. There are mystics among us who live in total isolation.'

Ysabel looks her full in the face, narrowing her eyes.

'Are *you* a mystic, then? Or perhaps a woman who cannot move past her mourning?'

Ade lowers her head once more; the blow has hit home.

'God loves prayer,' Ysabel adds in a softer voice, 'but I am sure that He loves charity just as much.'

*

Shortly afterward Maheut comes through the door. A shapeless silhouette under a woollen cape. She moves slowly, like a sleep-walker. Ysabel leads her towards Ade who, despite herself, holds out her hands as a sign of welcome.

'This will be only for a few weeks. Until we can find another solution,' promises Ysabel.

The newcomer shows no reaction, and Ade lets her hands fall.

'Take her to my bedroom,' she says, 'she can lie down on my servant's old bed.'

The two women's steps ring out on the stairs, then are muffled by the rug in the bedroom. A few minutes pass before Ysabel comes down again. Her face is calm.

'She is getting used to the place,' she says in a low voice. 'Do not worry about anything. When she feels comfortable, she will go to bed.'

'Will you at least tell me who she is?'

'I do not know. But perhaps she will confide in you.'

Heading for the door, she adds:

'I left you a healing draught. You can give her a mouthful tomorrow morning if you find her agitated. I will come by after Mass, and bring clothing for her. Her tunic was torn in the fight.'

*

After the visitor has gone, Ade lingers a moment longer in her kitchen, her mind troubled. How could she have let herself be thrust into such a situation? It's as if Ysabel has taken control of her will. A feeble will that has yielded to others in times past. But this girl in her house will only bring evil, she is sure of that.

When she finally goes up to her bedroom, barefoot so as not to waken the child, she finds her as Ysabel left her, sitting on the side of the bed, wrapped in her cape.

Ade sits on her own bed, gratefully feeling the softness of the quilt stuffed with goose down. She wants only to snuggle underneath it and forget herself in sleep.

She lets a few minutes go by, then says in what she hopes is a soft voice:

'Take off your clothes and go to bed. The day has been an ordeal. You should sleep—and so should I.'

Maheut lifts her head. Ade looks into an angular face with wide-set eyes. Then the girl stands up, lets her cape fall to the ground, then her chemise, and slips naked under the sheets, face turned to the wall. Ade does not see her hair, which is bound in a drab headscarf, but she glimpses a svelte body whose whiteness astonishes her, as it did Ysabel.

After praying to the Virgin Mary to watch over her sleep, Ade lies down in turn, on her right side, as is her habit, with an arm under her head. A position she has learnt will protect her against unruly dreams. But sleep does not come. The closeness of this strange girl breathing the air in her bedroom and exhaling her odour—or rather that of the acrid herbs she has been treated with—is troubling. Her presence is different from that of her servant, a peasant, somewhat heavy, somewhat unclean, but shapeless in sleep, burrowed in the bottom of her bed like a mole at the bottom of its hole.

Maheut moves in her sleep. Perceptibly. A rubbing against the rough sheet. A rustling. Ade thinks of the whiteness she glimpsed. And of her own skin, which she has not looked at for years, each morning slipping on her chemise with eyes averted. But she has not forgotten how white she is too, another kind of white, less dense and thick. The difference between milk and cream.

Sometimes her husband used to pass his tongue over her body, like a cat lapping. But when he straddled her, he was an animal with another kind of power. Tall and broad-shouldered, with thighs muscled from cavalry charges and swordfights.

The day they met, the sight of him had both stirred and frightened Ade. She was very young when she was wed. Barely fourteen. The body of a child, the breasts just swelling, narrow hips.

So slim and so white, you are a budding lily, he had sighed when he undressed her for the first time. And he handled her like a unopened flower. Holding and caressing her without penetrating her intimate places. So soft, the coat of a foal, he said. And he blew on the down of her legs to see her quiver. So supple, the skin of a lamb. And he licked her breasts until they stood up under his tongue. So secret, a chalice that quenched his thirst. And he slid his head to the hollow between her legs, into the tightness of her cunt.

Heart beating, face feverish, she let him do as he wished, at first afraid, then greedy for his touch. She began to await the evenings with increasing impatience.

And then one night the flower had blossomed. She had arched her body like a stem bending in the wind.

Now Ade sighs, stirs under the quilt. She is thirsty, but does not dare light the candle to go fetch water. Behind the shutters closed against the winter, the darkness is absolute.

Dark enough to hide us from the eyes of the devil himself, her fair husband had whispered, blowing out the rush wick on the oil lamp.

Ade shakes her head. He had taken her, softly at first, then forcefully. Night after night. In every possible manner. Even those that are forbidden. Face to face, with her sitting on him, like fornicators do. From behind, on her knees with her head on the quilt, like animals do. And also by the other orifice, as some men do with each other.

She had been hurt and yet had come in all these positions. Shame only came afterward. Was this why God had punished her?

The young woman a few paces away from her turns over suddenly. Ade is startled and, despite the cold, pushes back the quilt smothering her. She must have caught a fever. She gets up and tiptoes to the bedside table on which sits the flask Ysabel left. She grasps the neck and drinks the thick, bitter liquid straight down.

She does not know where her soul roams during her sleep, but in the early morning, she wakes to find her thighs moistened by her own wetness.

10

AFTER THAT FIRST NIGHT when Maheut came to share her bedroom, Ade has had no more shameful awakenings. But she still sleeps badly. Her slumber is filled with phantasmagorical images that seem to spring from nowhere. Dreams filled with lies. Her husband alive. Tender and loving like in the beginning. And her bedroom—where she now lives or in the château of times past?—is hung with white silk. Scarlet spots on the gauzy fabric. A child cries. A little girl, with hair like flames.

Some dreams are sent by God. Others are sent by the devil. Others still are merely caused by the body. Ade does not know which kind she is having. She sometimes wonders if old Ysabel could find a cure. But she does not dare speak to her about it.

She has seen a lot of the infirmarer since Maheut settled in her house almost two months ago. Since mid-March, the air has grown milder—and the earth softer along with it. Ysabel has been able to resume work in her garden—digging flower beds, planting rue and wild strawberries, clearing out the sage bushes, choosing sunny spots for the marjoram to prevent it from yellowing, tending the modest tufts of violets she planted to brighten her vegetable patches because their humbleness, beaded with dew, reminded her of her native countryside. But each evening, after wielding trowel and hoe, with sweat on her forehead and hands smelling of soil, she goes to visit Ade and Maheut.

Ade has made an effort to be welcoming to the young girl. But Maheut is anything but friendly in return. She answers questions in monosyllables, drags her feet over household chores; she is clumsy and useless, except for bringing in the wood and tending the fire, which she seems to do with pleasure.

She seems educated, however; she certainly knows how to read. Ade surprised her one morning in front of the lectern where she had placed some books sent by her sister-in-law. The girl was following the lines of text with her eyes. Without doubt, she could become a more discerning companion than the servant was. But most of the time, Maheut stays sitting in front of the hearth, not moving until nightfall. Then she goes out, wrapped in her cape, and stays a long time outside. Ade imagines her walking the walls of the Beguinage like a ghost, past the houses, the large communal building, the infirmary and the chapel. She does not know her any better than when she first arrived in her house, and so, for Ade, she remains a girl from outside. She sometimes hopes that one night Maheut will go through the gate of the Beguinage and not come back.

'We live together like two strangers,' she says to Ysabel. 'I am not the companion she needs. Perhaps she would be happier elsewhere.'

*

For her part, the old beguine savours the free time left to her now that the beds in the infirmary are emptying. When she can, she leaves the Beguinage at dawn to collect herbs in the marshland, on the other side of the postern. In the evening, she prepares them and sets them to dry. Her house is full of their fragrance. Sometimes, though, fatigue grips her. Perhaps it is the change in seasons as the world emerges from winter, to which her ageing body has adjusted less quickly than before. Or else the clouds that still hang over the city.

The trial of the Templars still has Paris in a fever. Yesterday, the last Saturday of March, the brothers prepared to defend their Order were finally released from their prisons and brought together in the gardens of the bishopric adjoining Notre-Dame. Despite the intimidation and the torture they had suffered, there were more than five hundred of them, so many that the pontifical commission charged with trying them could not hear them all. They were asked to select representatives: six, eight, or ten men of theirs choosing to testify for them. It is said that the Templars are growing in strength and courage again, and so the affair might be resolved. But this very day another piece of news has arrived at the Beguinage, one which worries Ysabel. It concerns one of the sisters of Valenciennes, Marguerite Porete. It seems that William of Paris, the Inquisitor General, has ordered her to be investigated. William's sudden interest in her, after what amounts to almost two years of imprisonment, has surprised the beguines. Many know her, at least by reputation; her arrest and transfer to Paris caused a huge stir at the time. Some of them, who like Marguerite hailed from Hainaut in Flanders, have even visited her in her seclusion. Ysabel is not one of them, but thanks to Perrenelle, who informs her about all the goings-on in the city, she knows a lot about the prisoner.

It is Marguerite she discusses with Ade during her daily visit.

*

As usual, Ade receives her in a comfortable upstairs room equipped with a fireplace. Near the window are a lectern and a worktable bearing a writing case. The two women sip a sage infusion, while Maheut holds herself apart. Despite the young woman's sombre mood, Ysabel notices that she has grown stronger. She has already heard from Ade that her appetite has returned. Maheut devours the dishes prepared by the servant her hostess has decided to take on for a few hours a day, having given up asking her guest for help. Her slim body has recovered its energy and vigour. Contemplating her face, licked by the soft light of the flames, Ysabel finds her almost beautiful in her peculiarity. The protruding forehead under the cloth turban, the green eyes slightly slanted. The short but thick eyelashes, astonishingly curved. The high cheekbones, the small but straight nose, the fleshy lips. Her passivity, which so exasperates Ade, does not fool the old woman. Maheut is an animal ready to leap.

'The book this woman Marguerite wrote, which got her imprisoned, have you read it?' asks Ade.

'*The Mirror of Simple Souls*… It has been banned for years.'

'They say it is a guide for the instruction of the laity.'

'From what I know, the text is complex. I am not sure that it is accessible to everybody. It offers a sort of pathway to union with God.'

'Why do they denounce it so?'

'I don't know the details. But the Bishop of Cambrai condemned it as heretical five years ago, and had it burned in the great square of Valenciennes. He forbade Marguerite to continue spreading her ideas—either orally or in writing. But she is so convinced they are right that, far from obeying him, she added several chapters to clarify her thoughts.'

'That could have been dangerous,' Ade remarks.

'The woman sought support among the most eminent clerics. She won over three of them, including a Franciscan of Valenciennes, and the venerable theologian Godefroid de Fontaines, who died last year. So she decided to send *The Mirror* to Bishop Jean of Châlons. With that she had gone too far. Marguerite was brought before two new courts, first the inquisitor of Lorraine, then the new Bishop of Cambrai. And finally she was sent to Paris.'

'They say she was insolent.'

'Insolent? I don't know. But she always refused to swear an oath or to testify. And she continued this behaviour even in front of the Inquisitor General. He punished her with a major excommunication, and for almost two years now he has been waiting for her to submit to his investigation. It seems he has lost patience.'

'Is this woman—Marguerite—in possession of her reason?'

Ysabel sighs, her eyes fixed on Maheut's profile. She is not mistaken. The girl's features are tense, attentive. While she seemed lost in her own thoughts when Ysabel arrived, ever since the conversation turned to Marguerite Porete, she has been listening.

'They also say that during the whole time of her imprisonment, she has continued to disseminate her writings,' Ade continues. 'Is she really one of us?'

Ysabel detaches her gaze from Maheut. The question deserves some thought. There are so many ways of living one's faith outside the Church. Not all beguines have the opportunity—or the desire—to join a great institution like the Paris Beguinage. Many live together in small groups, in modest houses in the hearts of cities, and go into some trade or other. Others prefer to lead a solitary existence. Some who are called 'wandering beguines' live by begging and preaching in the streets.

'I think that Marguerite taught for a while in the beguinage in Valenciennes,' she finally answers, 'but she did not live there. Not recently, in any case. She led a circle of Friends of God. She is a woman of the minor nobility. It seems she used to have a lot of support in Valenciennes and Flanders... I am afraid she has lost it.'

Ade lifts her bowl to her lips and blows on the hot infusion. She has perceived the tension in Ysabel's voice.

'Don't worry yourself unduly,' she tries to reassure her. 'No beguine has ever been condemned. If she really is one of us, she will perhaps be rebuked, but I doubt she will be severely punished.'

*

Later, when she goes out that night, Ysabel thinks again of this exchange—with irritation. Ade is so little aware of the realities of the world. She spent a great part of her childhood within a convent, then married, and, having lost her husband, later retired to a beguinage. She believes what she hears, and thinks she understands what she knows nothing about.

Of course, some self-proclaimed beguines did lead lives that hardly conform with the apostolic spirit. Some even cause scandals. Rumours coming from the towns of the Upper Rhine speak of sisters exposing themselves in public, preaching loudly in the street with much mimicry, genuflections and contortions. Some so-called beguines are actually members of heretical movements like the Waldensians or the Brethren of the Free Spirit. But whatever the case, any woman who is neither wife nor nun is suspect. Especially if she insists on preaching, usurping the privileges of the clergy. And of men.

Fortunately Louis, the sainted king, always defended the beguines. And along with him, some of the greatest scholars at the University of Paris, for whom their way of life was an example to other laity. A living sermon. The authority of these learned theologians continues to protect them well after their deaths.

Ysabel lets her hood fall back. It is still cool this evening, but the sky is totally clear. She raises her eyes to the moon, which is almost full. When it wanes again, it will be time to harvest the first medicinal herbs from her garden.

She crosses the courtyard and heads, despite the late hour, to her planting beds. The smell of turned-over earth will calm her.

A bench beckons. Seated and still, she tastes the silence of the night, the odour of soil and manure, heavy and full. Here the air seems warmer than in the courtyard.

She remembers the sermon given by Robert de Sorbon, one of King Louis's close companions, who compared the Beguinage to a field. He had given the sermon in the final years of his life, on the occasion of a festival commemorating the discovery of the relics of Saint Stephen, on 3rd August. Sometimes Perrenelle cites the sermon in chapter meetings.

Robert had offered a moral interpretation of the parable from St Matthew: the Kingdom of God is like a treasure hidden in a field. The first question in his Biblical exegesis was 'What field is this?' and he answered, 'In the field of the Beguinage, open to all winds, is found the hidden treasure of the Kingdom of Heaven. It is so well hidden that the university masters with all their powers of reason are unaware of it. For in order to find it, you have to have humility.'

When Ysabel uses her hoe, holding one hand firm on the ash shaft and the other on the handle, pushing with her foot on the blade to break through the hard crust, when she becomes one body with her tool, and through it feels the mood of the soil— then Ysabel knows that she has found this treasure.

A soft sound draws her attention. A dark silhouette has slipped into the garden. It wanders among the patches surrounded by interwoven branches. Then stops. It remains motionless for a long moment, lifts its arms, pushes back the hood and lets fall a mane of hair to its shoulders. In the white halo of the moon, the locks shine like a cascade of amber.

11

A WEEK LATER, Ade and Humbert pass by each other without knowing it. The time for them to meet has not yet come.

He is preparing to leave the city, impatient to return to his
brothers and his old master. He has spent several days in retreat
at the Cordeliers monastery, alternating slow walks along its
garden paths and long hours seated in its vast library, compared
to which the modest manuscript collection of the Valenciennes
monastery seems paltry.

The streets here are quieter than in the city centre, and greener
too. Gardens, orchards of espaliered grapevines and apple trees,
vegetable plots growing larger and larger as you approach the
walls, then through the postern gate and towards the last reaches
of the city and the surrounding plain, fields undulating with
spring wheat. The streets around the Cordeliers monastery bustle
with young men with tonsured heads and long habits. Dozens
of them, books under their arms. In large groups, or ones and
twos. Absorbed in intense discussions, sometimes rowdy debates.
The wealthier people of the area avoid them.

This left bank of the Seine is home to the 'upper city' of students, as opposed the 'lower city' of the traders on the opposite
bank past the Grand Pont. All the university buildings are here,
gathered around the Sorbonne. Here too Humbert has left many
memories here, also regrets; he misses the days when he still
believed that the energy flowing through his body like burning

lava would lift him to the summit. Instead, he often ended up in the gutter.

When he passes close by Ade in front of Notre-Dame Cathedral early that afternoon, he is returning from a second visit to For-l'Évêque. Once again, he has been turned away, but this time he was expecting it. The situation of the beguine Marguerite has changed dramatically. Prosecutor William of Paris summoned eleven theology professors and five canonists from his Dominican monastery at Port Saint-Jacques to ask them for advice on her case. Humbert admires the Inquisitor's caution, no doubt inspired by the interminable and catastrophic trial of the Templars. William was strongly reprimanded by the pope for having helped the king and his henchman Nogaret during the daring arrest of the soldier monks three years previously, and was even temporarily stripped of his powers. More circumspect this time around, he is trying to establish how it might be possible, since Marguerite refuses to testify or even take the oath, to put her on trial for heresy without exposing himself to criticism. Particularly since most of her accusers are far from Paris in the Hainaut, which belongs to the Holy Roman Emperor rather than to the King of France. What's more, Marguerite Porete's appearance and the piety of her pronouncements do not make her an easy target for accusations. Humbert does not know what the legal experts told the Inquisitor, but the inquisitorial machine has been set in motion.

In any case, Humbert will have shown himself to be loyal and conscientious by trying once again to visit a woman he does not much care for. It was the least he could do for Brother Jean, who welcomed him as a father when he first arrived at the monastery of Valenciennes. In the space of a few weeks, Humbert had lost both his parents and his little sister, barely ten years old, their lungs ravaged by the harsh winter. It was so cold that year that the Seine froze solid, before the thaw carried away houses, bridges and watermills, crushing boats against the quayside at the Port de Grève and sending them to the bottom of the river with all the goods and men onboard. Alerted to the disaster back at home by a courier, Humbert had hurried back to the Hainaut, to find only his dying mother left to embrace. The priest praying at her bedside told him she had been lying abed for days, barely able to breathe, as if she were saving her last breath to bless him.

Humbert had found the family château in poor repair and freezing cold. The kitchens were empty. His parents had hidden the gravity of their situation from him. If only he had come to visit them earlier, perhaps he might have been able to do something.

After that calamity he had broken off his studies, giving up on his master's degree. Sold the estate to pay off the debts. Finished were the subtle scholastic debates on faith and reason, the eucharist and the eternity of the world. He entered the local monastery of Valenciennes, took up the monk's habit and fastened at his belt the three buckles symbolizing the three vows of the Order: obedience, poverty, chastity.

*

While Humbert strides across the cathedral's forecourt, Ade stands motionless amidst the gawkers and market stalls, her eyes lifted to the façade of the cathedral. She is not looking, as most visitors do, at the great portal of the Last Judgement. She finds it too tortured, with a stiff Christ displaying the stigmata of his sacrifice in the tympanum, while under his feet the damned souls march towards a hell which vomits its horrors across the arches to the right. Instead she stops in front of the most discreet portal and gazes at the composition of Virgin and Child sculpted at the summit.

The stone figure is one of absolute simplicity. Mary is seated on a throne, framed by a dais, with Christ on her knees. She looks back at the viewer, her features relaxed by an imperceptible smile, as she presents her son for all to see. Under the tight folds of her garment, her legs seem to be holding those of the child, while her right hand is placed, fingers open, on Christ's belly. The left hand holds a sceptre.

Maheut stands at Ade's side. Ade does not see it, but the girl's face has come alive at last. But Maheut is not interested in the cathedral. She is watching the performance of a man and his tame monkey a few feet away. The small beast darts and cavorts, jumps onto the head of its master, rummages through his hair and his shirt, its strange face contorting like that of a child, grimacing, smiling and begging in turn. The monkey opens its mouth wide, while its master holds out and then hides an apple, draws its lips back over pointed teeth, lets off sharp cries that drown out the calls of the sellers at the food stalls, hawking the fish and waffles of the Lenten season.

Soon, Ade will buy Maheut and herself two cheese pastries, which they will eat in the street, licking sticky crumbs from their fingers. For the first time since they have met, they will delight in the same moment.

*

It was Ade who suggested to Maheut this detour across the Notre-Dame forecourt, on the way back from an already lengthy walk through the city streets. The day before, during one of her almost daily visits, Ysabel had asked Ade to carry a remedy to the wife of Sir Pierre de Crété. A burgomaster to the king and dealer in silk, he is one of the faithful patrons of the Beguinage. For years now, at the beginning of every summer, his wife has suffered from itchy rashes on her skin, that the herbalist has learnt to treat with burdock poultices. But this time, the itching has started earlier in the season. The servant who took the message to the old beguine said her mistress was also struggling to breathe.

Ysabel did not have any fresh burdock leaves but she did have some extract left. She also prepared some elfdock wine to which she added juniper berries and chamomile flowers. She was too busy to transport the remedies herself and rather than send a servant or messenger, she preferred to give them to somebody she trusted to pass on her instructions. The elfdock wine had to be taken first thing in the morning and before each meal. The burdock extract should be poured on clean linen, which should then be laid on the skin in the places where it was inflamed.

'Would you do me this service, Dame Ade? You could ask Maheut to keep you company. A walk would do her good. She needs to get her strength back.'

Ade saw Maheut's features stiffen. Was it merely at the idea of sharing a walk with her? As the days went by, the girl still seemed just as distrustful, even hostile, to the point of avoiding Ade about the house, refusing to share her readings and her prayers. The rare times that Ade had tried to find out who she was and from whence she came, she was met by stubborn silence.

Ysabel had also noticed Maheut's malaise. But she thought it was time that the girl faced the world. She was too young and too lively to remain cloistered in the walls of the Beguinage without having chosen that life.

Maheut had not dared to refuse.

*

Pierre de Crété lived on the other side of the city, in the western parish of Saint-Germain-l'Auxerrois. They left early in the morning, Ysabel's phials carefully wrapped in a linen cloth. Ade could find her way to the church by following the Seine. Although she preferred not to follow it too closely, because of the bustling workers and boatmen who thronged the banks, noisily unloading bales of wheat and hay, she could still glimpse the river between the high buildings that lined its banks. For the first time, she felt Maheut draw near, slipping her arm into hers and leaving it there, the hand tightening each time a passer-by came too close.

Thus they made their way, pressed tightly together, through streets cluttered by stalls, handcarts and sledges. Both of them wrapped in the long cloaks of grey camlet that sisters usually wear outside the Beguinage. It is never good to be a woman alone on the streets of Paris. Their long habits and modest behaviour are some protection. But in such a crowd, how can you avoid the brush of a hand, or a body rubbing up against yours?

On the outward journey, though, everything went well. When they neared the Saint-Germain church, Ade asked for directions from a shopkeeper sitting at an open window. The house of Pierre de Crété was two streets away, and easily recognizable thanks to its great carved gateway that opened onto a vast courtyard.

Welcomed by a servant, Ade and Maheut passed through several reception rooms before reaching the bedroom where the sick woman lay. The drapes had been drawn. Dame Alice was stretched out on her bed, wheezing and pale. Near the bed was a little girl dressed in a blue silk gown, small and delicate as a fawn, with thick chestnut-coloured curls.

'Oh, thank you,' she cried when she saw the two women enter. 'It's a mercy you came. Mother is suffering so.'

While Maheut withdrew into the shadow of the bay alcove, Ade took off her cloak and sat at the patient's side. Her neck and arms were badly inflamed.

'This time,' the sick woman sighed, 'it's affecting my whole body.'

'Perhaps you have eaten some food that is not agreeable to you,' suggested Ade.

'I do not see how.'

'It's the worry,' the child cut in, brows arched above eyes of the same luminous blue as her dress. 'It seems that the king is going to change the currency again. Papa will have to sell more silk!'

'Clémence, I beg you,' said her mother. 'This is not a conversation for a little girl.'

Ade gently raised the sheet and then the chemise. The red blotches extended across the woman's belly and thighs. She asked for a goblet and a clean cloth.

Maheut watched Ade delicately apply the cotton moistened with the brownish extract onto the raw skin. She was used to seeing these long, fine hands turning the pages of a book or joined in prayer—Ade prayed so much!

Clémence was also watching Ade and thinking her perfect. The pure oval face, the calm eyes, the slender, supple body, so well-cared-for... The little girl, who had grown up surrounded by disorder and had little self-discipline, wished she could be like the beguine.

All three of them remained at the bedside of Dame Alice until the bells struck the hour of none. When Ade and Maheut left, the patient was softly dozing and seemed already somewhat better. Clémence accompanied them to the door and, as they left the house, grasped Ade's hand and kissed it.

*

Perhaps it was the sight of the young girl so full of life, her tenderness towards her mother, or maybe she was just tired from fasting during Lent... but Ade felt worn out and downcast on the way home. So she suggested to Maheut that they pass by the cathedral.

So here they are on the Notre-Dame forecourt, finishing the pastries Ade has just bought, licking their fingers and exchanging, if not a smile, then at least a friendly glance. Maheut's eyes have lost their sharpness. They are cloudy now, like raw emeralds.

This must be the moment when Humbert is leaving the fore-court and passing close by them.

'We must go back now,' suggests Ade, 'it's getting late.'

The two women walk along the Notre-Dame cloister towards the rue des Marmousets. Instead of going as far as the Pont aux Changeurs, Ade, tired of the crowd and the jostling, decides to take the wooden Pont Planches de Milbray, exposed to the wind but less crowded, which will allow them to cross to the opposite bank near the Beguinage further upstream.

The man starts to follow them the moment they begin their crossing. His riding boots ring out behind them on the wooden planks suspended above the muddy waters. They do not notice him right away, with the noise of the other people on the bridge, the rushing of the river, the rumbling of the watermills further down, the grinding of wheels turning in the current, the clacking of paddles on the water. The wooden bridge carries them past the bank and over the muddy marsh fed by the winter tides, going as far as the crossroads of the rue de la Coutellerie and rue de la Vannerie. Tall houses line the street here, amplifying the noise of the man's heels ringing out on the paving stones. The sound follows the two women across the Place de Grève…

Maheut turns and glimpses the stocky, ponderous figure of a man-at-arms. She quickens her step, as the clacking of the boots behind them accelerates; Ade feels her little fingers dig into the crook of her elbow. They pass by the apse of Saint-Jean-en-Grève, then the Saint-Gervais cemetery, heading towards the rue aux Moines de Longpont. Just as they slip into an alley, the man starts to run. He overtakes the two women, gives a cry, then tears off Maheut's hood, freeing her hair from the scarf around it.

12

M AHEUT IS STILL DISTRESSED, pacing up and down the upstairs bedroom. Ade, frightened by the indecency of the man's act, is also struggling to master her disquiet.

After the assault, they stood petrified in the middle of the street while onlookers started to point their fingers and laugh. The man walked back the way he came—but not before casting Maheut a long, hard look, a sneering smile on his lips. Then they ran back to the Beguinage. Guillaumette opened the door for them, irritated at first by the frantic ringing of the bell and the hammering of the wooden clapper, then shocked at their appearance.

Stretched out on her bed now, Ade feels the beating of her heart begin to slow. She fans her face with her hands and gets to her feet. Aware of her ruffled appearance, she rearranges the veil over her hair, smoothing the wimple around her neck. Then she turns to Maheut.

'Oh, do stop stirring yourself up so. Come here, I will give you something to drink.'

But the girl keeps darting back and forth, like a bird caught in a trap.

When Ysabel arrives a few minutes later, Ade is in the kitchen. It takes only a few minutes to recount the incident to the old beguine.

'This man, did you recognize him?' Ysabel asks.

'No, I barely saw his face. A thick nose, a black beard... that's all.'

'And Maheut? Does she know him?'

'She won't say anything. Just paces up and down.'

'Perhaps he was just a drunkard who wanted some sport. It would not be the first time.'

'But Maheut's reaction is so strong. She frightens me.'

Ysabel lifts the sides of the heavy skirt she wears to work in the garden, and climbs the stairs. Standing in the bedroom doorway, she watches Maheut pacing without saying a word, then steps forward and takes her by the shoulders. The girl tries to pull away, but grows still when she recognizes the old beguine.

'Come...'

Ysabel leads Maheut to the window seat. Compels her to sit. Puts an arm around her shoulders and holds her close.

'Do you want me to give her the medicine?' whispers Ade.

Ysabel replies with a shake of her head.

Ade sits down facing the two backlit silhouettes. Both are short, but one is broad and stocky, the other slender—and trembling like a puppy.

Time passes. Inside a floorboard squeaks, the rafters creak, the fire crackles in the hearth. Outside somebody is pulling a hand-cart, its belly scraping the ground, a woman's voice calls—muffled sounds, filtering through the Beguinage wall against which the house leans. To this familiar backdrop are added both the faint sound of Ysabel's breathing, and Maheut's distressed panting.

Little by little, the girl's breathing calms. Ysabel withdraws her arm from her shoulders, takes her hands between her own and softly warms them, loosening the fingers. Something blue glints in her palm.

'The stone will not help you,' whispers Ysabel. 'Your fear will only subside for a moment. Then it will reawaken and come back stronger.'

Maheut shakes her head.

'You must speak now. Without fear or shame. Whatever happened to you, we will not judge you. But if we don't know what you are afraid of, how can we protect you?'

*

A rustling of wings on the roof. A dove begins its sweet, sad trilling.

Maheut shakes her head again, but she can no longer hold back what torments her. At first she lets fall a few hesitant words. Then finally she tells them. A muddled story, a confused complaint.

The tale is a common one: that of a girl from the minor landed nobility. So many families of this rank have seen their fortunes worsen for several decades now—Ysabel witnessed it herself in her native Burgundy. The world into which they once plunged their roots is finished; the soil in which they once prospered and grew is barren now. The nobles have lost power over their estates as the king imposed his own over the entire kingdom. The old system founded on exchanges of goods and services was swept away by a monetary economy, constantly manipulated by a sovereign in search of wealth to replenish the royal treasury. Thrown into debt by divided inheritances and the devaluations imposed by Philip the Fair, many of the nobility mortgaged their estates, while others sank to the level of the penniless peasantry.

Maheut's family did not experience quite such a decline. There was enough money for the son. He was sent to his overlord's estate to train as a knight, with all the costly equipment that goal required. There remained nothing at all as a dowry for the girl. Another lord of a nearby estate, who over the years had watched Maheut's juvenile figure mature into curves, one day caught a green glint in the girl's eyes—a glimmer that some called serpentine but in which he saw a promise. He feared neither serpent nor devil. He was ready to take the Redhead—even without any dowry.

'I didn't want anything to do with him.'

Maheut's father listened to his daughter. He thought she was too young for marriage, but did not outright reject the suitor, with whom he had a longstanding dispute over a parcel of land that the match would resolve. Instead he asked him to wait until the girl started bleeding.

'Had my father lived, he would never have permitted it!'

But her father died, his thigh and groin torn open by a wild boar sow that he had cornered without noticing that she was protecting her young. The son came back for the funeral and agreed to the marriage while Maheut was still weeping for her father.

*

She tells them of the engagement celebration at the château of Guillebert, her future husband, which she had not even attended, hiding in a cupboard instead. Of the affront to both families. Her brother's anger. Her own pain faced with this young man she did not recognize as the happy companion of her childhood, whom she had once admired almost as much as her father, but who was now betraying her.

She recounts the night when Guillebert's men came to fetch her. The manor's doors had been left open, the servants instructed to stay in their quarters. The men enter her bedchamber and bind her, drag her out of bed in her chemise and throw her on a horse, carrying her off like an animal. She struggles, falls from the horse, is put back in the saddle.

'I cried, but everyone let them carry on. Including my mother.'

After the kidnapping, Guillebert respected all the stages of the marriage ritual so that the match would not be contested. The engagement was formalized by a priest. Two days later, the marriage was celebrated in the chapel of the château, followed by a banquet with guests that, just as much as the sacraments, would seal the union of the two families.

Maheut tells of the drink she was forced to take beforehand to calm her. The priest who pretended not to hear her protests. The ring rammed onto her finger. The congratulations that followed. Guillebert's whole family is present, and her own brother, her uncles and cousins. Her severe mother-in-law orders the servants to bring food. The feast is heaped onto the long table. Venison and boar, hares, chickens, capon pâté, fishes of all sorts: roasted, stuffed, and boiled, eels swimming in sauce... She refuses to eat. Guillebert stabs his dagger into the leg of a game bird, grabs his young wife by the neck and stuffs the flesh into her mouth.

What happens after the feast, on the other hand, Maheut will not say. But her companions know without her telling. A girl's body crushed by that of her husband. The stink of the cheap wine that he slobbers on her lips. The young breasts that he crushes in his fists. The chemise lifted, the thighs pushed apart by his knees. Night after night. A whole week. Her tender flesh staked to the bed.

'How did you get away?' asks Ysabel.

'On horseback. He wanted me to accompany him on the hunt. He is a fast rider but heavy. I led him onto our land and jumped a ditch. Two ditches. He was angry. And he fell.'

Ade listens in silence. It is like a story told at bedtime, a fairy tale.

'What then?' asks Ysabel.

'He was not moving. I turned my back to the sun. Rode a whole day without stopping. Then I tied the horse to a tree. I gave my silk belt to a man passing in a carriage for him to take me along. Gave my cape and robe to another in exchange for peasant clothes. I wanted to come to Paris to hide. I needed a large city.'

Ysabel sees once more the figure crumpled at the gate of the Beguinage.

'Do you know what happened to Guillebert? Was he seriously injured?'

Maheut lowers her head.

'You are afraid they are looking for you? He or his family? The king's provosts?'

'Yes, and also my brother. I do not want to go back there.'

'That man in the street, was he of your household?'

'I don't know. That's what I thought, but I did not recognize him.'

Ade finally stirs.

'From the direction we were headed, he must have realized we were of the Beguinage. Is it not risky to keep Maheut here?'

Ysabel shakes her head. 'No strangers will come in here.'

*

That evening, while Ade lies awake, Maheut sleeps deeply. Just now, before leaving, Ysabel asked the girl a final question.

'You come from the North, from what I understand. From what region?'

'From the Hainaut.'

'So it is from there that you know this beguine Marguerite Porete, whom we were talking about the other evening. I saw your ears prick up when we mentioned her name.'

'My mother used to meet with her.'

'In Valenciennes?'

'Both in Valenciennes and at our home. Marguerite was a friend of hers…'

Maheut broke off, then added curtly: 'She was a friend of my mother's. But I did not care for her.'

13

MARCH COMES TO AN END, then the Lenten penitence. On 19th April, at the end of the mournful Holy Week, Easter is celebrated at last. At the Beguinage the young girls throw rose petals onto the floor of the refectory and place eggs dyed red on the long common table, decorated with corncobs and sunflowers. After Mass the food is served: roast lamb and pork, flans and meat pâtés, rissoles dripping with butter.

Now the workers hired to repair winter damage to the buildings have arrived. They are to restore the fireplace in the dormitory that was threatening to collapse, and repair two house roofs. The Beguinage resounds with their strong voices and noisy laughter. Perrenelle lets the men get on with it, provided that they are not vulgar or impertinent. The energy emanating from their solid bodies and sturdy arms is of the same joyous nature as that of the spring sunlight, or the clear, fluted song of the first warblers.

The master roofer and his apprentices, perched on the tiled roofs, sing as they work. Their refrains sometimes mingle with the modulations of the choir heard through the door of the chapel, which has been left open for the heat to come in. The men break off their work to listen to the girls, transfixed on the rooftops, like lookouts entranced by a siren's voice.

April also brings the gardeners and landscapers who help with the heavy work of the vegetable garden. They open up the soil, flatten it, break down the clumps with a long mallet—all under the suspicious gaze of Berthe, the beguine whose job it is to ensure that the beds of lettuce, peas and beans, chard and scallions, cabbage and broccoli, turnips and leeks that will feed the women of the Beguinage throughout the year are all planted at the right time. Once the soil has been turned over, Berthe has them mix in ashes to make it less clammy, followed by cow and donkey dung—not too deeply, she says, so that the seeds can sit in it—then puts the finishing touches to the beds with a hoe. From her own garden, Ysabel looks on joyfully as the heavy Berthe, her body as round as a barrel and encircled by a belt wrapped several times around her robe to lift it above her ankles, wields her tool with great delicacy, making the soil fine and light so the roots can stretch down into it.

May arrives. Ysabel's garden is fragrant with herbs and flowers, and she lifts her eyes towards the sky with less defiance. And then, on the twelfth of the month, as the air shimmers with springtime radiance, fifty-four Templars are taken outside Paris, near the Porte Saint-Antoine. To be burned alive there.

*

Only a few weeks ago many believed that the trial launched under pressure from Philip would turn out in the Order's favour. The four spokesmen chosen by the accused to represent them before the pontifical commission made a strong case. Particularly Peter of Bologna, who bravely refuted the absurd accusations, as well as rejecting the confessions—including his own—extracted by torture and false promises. A growing number of Templars arrived from the provinces to defend their brothers. Then Philip de Marigny, newly appointed archbishop of Sens and—not by chance—brother of the king's chamberlain, quickly convoked a provincial council. The Templars of his territory having confessed their faults but now withdrawn their admissions were declared to have relapsed. Therefore they were condemned to be executed—against the advice of the pope but with the support of the king.

*

The pyres are set side by side, their stakes pointing to heaven. Even as they mount the faggots, the men refuse to admit the crimes of which they are accused. As the straw catches fire, they cry their innocence and their terror into the faces of an uneasy crowd.

The acrid odour of their torment is carried over the Beguinage walls to the garden where Ysabel is working. A plume of black smoke fills the sky, raining down flakes of grey ash, as light and fragile as snow or as butterflies. The beguine watches them twist and twirl, then says a silent prayer as she mingles them with the soil.

Over the following days, four more brothers are led to the stake, then nine more at Senlis. Finally, the bones of Jean de Thure, the Templar treasurer who has been dead for years, are exhumed and burned.

Some say Philip allowed the burnings because he lost patience with the time-wasting manoeuvres of Pope Clement, who has once again postponed the council that was to be held in Vienne to decide on the Order's future, for more than a year this time, to October 1311. Doubtless there is some truth in that. But something else is afoot. Ysabel is not the only one to sense it.

14

'PHILIP THE FAIR TAKES HIMSELF FOR God's vicar,' murmurs Jean de Queyran.

For several days, Humbert's old master's health has been weakening. His mind is still agile but old age is catching up with his body. Humbert stays at his bedside, where his master lies propped up against a pillow covered with rough cloth. It is cool in the cell, damp air flowing in through the narrow window. Spring comes late to these northern parts.

The monastery is silent. Lunch is over, the sext prayers said. But Brother Jean does not want to doze off. Humbert anxiously contemplates his master's gaunt face, the sagging flesh, the skin clinging to bone, showing all too well what it will look like when he has been returned to dust. The eyes are moist, as those of the elderly often are, but behind the tears that cling and tremble there his gaze remains keen.

'What do you mean?' asks Humbert.

'He thinks the pope has failed to deal with the heretical order and so it is up to him to defend the true faith.'

'Don't you think he is more concerned with the Templars' gold? The kingdom's treasury is empty once more!'

'You don't look at things with sufficient perspective, Humbert. You have to back away from the landscape to appreciate its power... Please help me.'

The master tries with difficulty to sit up. Humbert slips an arm about his shoulders. Under the robe, which gives off a sweet, slightly nauseating odour, he feels the stiffness of the body, the rigid skeleton, the vertebrae seemingly welded together. Hard and brittle. The old man has almost certainly been suffering in silence for days. But Humbert knows that he will not give up the conversation.

It was by exchanges such as these that they first grew close. Jean de Querayn's erudition is a spark that the young man has used to ignite his famished mind since he exiled himself to Valenciennes. It is a lively town, certainly. All sorts of people and cultures rub shoulders here. The nobility, even. Henry of Luxembourg, Holy Roman Emperor, was born there. Countess Margaret of Hainaut used to stay there and her grandson Jean built a mansion in the town's eastern quarter. The courtly life of the town attracts clerics and the erudite. But Humbert misses the impassioned intellectual tournaments of the Sorbonne, that almost technical dissection of texts, those adventuresome lines of argument, sometimes vain, but which allowed thinking to blossom, minds to sharpen, and which had brought Humbert joys as searing as girls' caresses.

With Brother Jean, he has discovered a kind of thinking as sharp as that of his Parisian masters, and a kind of curiosity, an almost juvenile craving for knowledge, which he himself feels he has lost.

*

'The Templars are only one of the targets of this royal piety,' Jean continues. 'Philip is haunted by a fear of heresy.'

'The times require it,' Humbert replies. 'Religious orthodoxy is attacked on all sides. The Cathars, the Waldensians… Now the brothers and sisters of the Free Spirit, who reject the ideas of sin and hell and who dare to declare man equal to Christ in perfection…'

'The times, of course. But are these deviants so numerous compared to the community of good Christians? Our sovereign sees them everywhere. His obsession with evil is like a magnifying glass that distorts his sight.'

Humbert sighs. He knows what Brother Jean is thinking of.

Philip the Fair's reputation has long since spread beyond the palace walls. He is said to be cold and inflexible of temperament, severe towards himself as well as his subjects, whose moral health and purity he sees as his personal responsibility. So much so that a few years ago he issued an edict, a sumptuary law forbidding any ostentatious form of dress, stupefyingly finicky in its detail: no common merchant may have a carriage or be accompanied at night by a servant bearing a wax torch, nor may dukes or counts have more than four robes made in a year, or have more than one variety of meat or fish served in their bowl.

The king's purifying rigour has gained a keener edge since the death of his wife, Queen Jeanne, who softened her husband's austere soul with her tenderness and humanity, and the loss of his fourth son, Robert, only eleven years old. Since then, Philip has thrown himself into pilgrimages and displays of piety, as if he were trying to rival Louis, his venerated ancestor.

'No doubt you are right, Brother Jean. But we will have plenty of time to discuss this tonight or tomorrow. Now you should get some rest.' He passes his hand over his face, feeling a sudden desire to leave this dark, close cell that smells of death.

'Philip is forever coming up with new perils that supposedly pervert the order of the world. Even within the Church. Have you forgotten the affair of Bishop Guichard?'

Humbert understands that he must yield. Brother Jean has the fragile, brittle body of a fledgling, but his obstinacy is unshakeable.

'I have not forgotten.'

'In the court's gardens, in front of everyone gathered for the occasion, he was accused of having poisoned the king's wife and of trying to do the same to the princes. Of being the spawn of the devil, of having practised witchcraft and magic—and sodomy! And then there was that shameful trial of the late Pope Boniface VIII, pursued even after his death, for having denied the Trinity, the virginity of Mary, transubstantiation, the resurrection of the dead, and even accused of sodomy and witchcraft himself.'

'Philip never forgave the pope for having opposed him.'

'You still don't understand, Humbert. The king does not merely exploit people's credulity for the purposes of his political manipulations. His perverted mysticism disturbs me more than his plans to solidify his power.' The old man closes his eyes. 'My son, you must return to Paris.'

'So soon?'

'I fear for Marguerite.'

'Do you have news?'

'A missive came from the Cordeliers a few days ago. The canonists gave their judgment at the start of April. Until then, they said, Marguerite had only been suspected of heresy. But her obstinacy, rebelliousness and bravado have obliged them to move from "suspicion" to "very strong presumption". Her refusal to cooperate has been judicially turned against her and the vice is tightening. Brother Nicholas writes that a week before Palm Sunday, William of Paris summoned twenty-one masters of theology, almost the whole university, to the Mathurin Church to hear their opinion of *The Mirror of Simple Souls*.'

'And?'

'They disavowed it—or at least two of its chapters. I am not even sure that William ordered them to read the whole book. All this smacks of manipulation.'

'You worry too much, Brother Jean.'

'I don't like where all this is heading. William has moved with great skill and prudence, purporting to stay his hand until he has duly deliberated and sought the advice of experts. Now he is free to attack Marguerite directly. I fear the worst. And what's more…' Jean lowered his voice. 'There is that which she entrusted to us. I do not know what to do with it. My health is declining. Not all of us in the order are her friends.'

*

Humbert does not answer. But Jean does not need to hear him to know what he thinks. His pupil does not understand his affection for Marguerite Porete. It goes beyond the usual cordial relations between Franciscans and Beguines, based on a history of exchange and mutual support—as well as a shared apostolic ideal. There is quite another order of relationship between Marguerite and Jean.

He knew her when she was a child. Their families were close. But the difference in their ages and the girl's attitude ensured he did not know her well. Someone would introduce you to her, praising her wisdom and fine education, and then you would leave her forgotten in the corner of the room. She had no particular charm, was drably dressed, and he remembers finding her boring in those days. He regrets that now.

For behind the invisible walls she had built around herself, and through which she only granted passage to books that seemed far too taxing for her age and sex, she was in fact growing, and weaving the thread of her own story. She was a unique being, sombre yet luminous, with a will of iron and a celestial mind. He understood how special she was only much later, having lost touch with her due to his new duties as a lector at the Franciscan monastery. She wrote to invite him to her house to attend the meetings she was organizing with a circle of the Friends of God, various men and women of the minor nobility and some local merchants. Strangely enough, Jean—the elder, the educated—had the feeling of being chosen by someone more mature and learned than he. Marguerite aspired to surround herself with people capable of following her flights of intelligence. She was touching in this respect. But on the rare occasions Humbert had accompanied his old master to a meeting, he remained silent, appearing absent and even bad-tempered.

'Not all of us are her detractors either.'

As if having guessed the paths followed by his master's thoughts, Humbert resumed the conversation. 'I have heard criticism of her at the Cordeliers. She has offended many there with her scorning of the teaching of clerics. Not to mention her rejection of the ideas of penitence, fasting and even of moral precepts! She is not far from the errors of believers in the Free Spirit. She has even managed to upset the beguines of Saint Elisabeth in Ghent.'

'The Saint Elisabeth beguines are fine and wise souls—but somewhat conventional. And mostly uneducated.'

'You are harsh, my brother. They consecrate themselves to the faith as they should. Marguerite thinks the love of God means she may dispense with the law and the supervision of the Church. But love can do harm as well as good. It is born in the mind but ends up consuming the senses of the weak.'

'Although a woman…' Brother Jean smiles '…Marguerite is far from being weak. Still less ignorant. Her *Mirror* is a brilliantly argued text that many priests would be incapable of writing. I would not like to see it disappear.'

15

AFTER THE EXECUTION of the Templars, it rains for three days without stopping. Water falls from the sky in sheets, snatched this way and that by gusts of wind. The beguines huddle in the shelter of their houses, running to chapel with capes held above their heads.

On the fourth day, from her window, Ysabel sees the dawn break. The rain has stopped. A shudder of impatience seizes her. She can stay cooped up no longer. She needs fresh air to chase away the images lurking in her mind—those grey ashes floating over her garden. However light they were and however gentle her prayer, whatever the welcome offered by the soil of her plot, she cannot stop thinking of the pain, of the skin licked by flames till it swelled up and burst, of the lungs filling with the suffocating smoke that brought merciful death. The executioners sometimes use the boat hooks with which they built the pyres to pierce the hearts of the condemned at the moment the straw bursts into flame. She hopes that the Templars were granted this merciful gesture.

More than a month has passed since the incident at Notre-Dame. At first, Guillaumette, who had been taken into confidence about the danger to Maheut but not told the details, had trembled at every ring of the bell outside the gate. It was her duty to open the gate to visitors, and until then she had performed it with pride and, it must be admitted, with curiosity too. But now she was afraid of being the one to let evil into the Garden of Eden. She did not know exactly what harm this stranger was capable of doing, only that he looked like a man-at-arms. She sensed Ysabel's worry. To see her old friend shaken like this was for her as frightening as the swaying of a bridge over an abyss, or the shuddering of a wall thrown up against barbarians. Guillaumette herself had known misfortunes, about which she kept silent, out of shame. They had taught her to count more upon the strength of certain souls than upon the derisory lock to which she held the key.

The days went by. Nobody knocked at the door but visitors from whom they feared nothing. Reassured, Ysabel has resumed her plant-gathering trips to the fields to the east of the city in the early morning. The infirmary needs her presence less now. With the fine weather, the number of patients has diminished. Even the woman with the bad chest, whom they thought lost, has sufficiently recovered, thanks to various poultices and decoctions, to be able to return to her family. But there have been two deaths, all the same—the woman recovering from childbirth, who left an orphaned baby behind, and old Cathau, who died in silence at dusk one day. Towards the end she was breathing so softly that nobody noticed her sudden stillness.

*

The day the rain finally stops, as soon as she sees the first house roofs glistening in the sunlight, Ysabel puts on her cloak and takes a basket. No doubt the herbs will be too wet to be gathered this morning, but the meadows have other riches. She softly opens her door and slips into the narrow passage that looks eastward to the houses abutting the Beguinage wall. Ade's house is right at the end. Two sharp raps at the shutter are enough. There is a scraping noise from inside, then Maheut pokes her drowsy, smiling face out of the window.

'I'll be ready soon, wait for me...'

The girl hurries to pull on her chemise and robe in front of the hearth's still-glowing embers. During the night she came downstairs to sleep in the kitchen, next to the fireplace. She has been doing this more and more often; she loves the smell of the fire, the scent it leaves on her skin and hair, the crackling sound climbing all the way up the chimney to the roof, as if an animal were scratching on the tiles. She wraps herself in her eiderdown and falls asleep on the bench, listening to the house protesting against the wind, or softly purring as night closes in. This house is so silent... A tomb.

In a few minutes, Maheut is ready. Ysabel greets her with a hand on her shoulder. A candle flame is already flickering in Guillaumette's room; she hears their footsteps as they leave.

*

The two women walk quickly to the Barbette passageway. The inner city has barely awakened, the strolling sellers of milk and fresh vegetables pushing their donkeys laden with fragrant baskets from their smallholdings outside the city walls. When they reach the gate it is filled with jostling carts that have been awaiting its opening since dawn. Curses ring out as a horseman in a hurry urges his mount into the press. Ysabel and Maheut step nimbly between puddles of mud and piles of dung until their feet reach the earthen road on the other side, and they leave behind first the high crenellated walls that dominate the surrounding countryside, then the tower of the Temple of the soldier-monks.

A few hundred yards further on, the air smells different. It is no longer filled with the stench of the city, but the scent of fresh greenery. In gardens, spring lettuces push up their tender green leaves. The beguines pass two Marais gardens, of the Saint

Gervais church and the Hôtel Barbette. Before them, the fields glisten with dew.

The infirmarer glances from time to time at her companion. Maheut's face has turned pink from the brisk walk. Her cheeks are rounded now, giving a newfound grace to her fawn-like face; her lips are swollen as if stung by nibbles or kisses. A lock of hair slips from her bonnet and she blows it back off her face.

The girl certainly knows how to walk, with the quick, regular stride of those used to long hikes through the countryside, stopping now and then to watch the gallop of a horse in a meadow or to inspect the sky for a change in the weather, wordlessly sharing her contentment all the while.

'Today,' whispers Ysabel, 'I'm going to tell you a secret.'

Maheut shoots her an expectant glance.

'The first thing is to find north-northwest. You see the rising sun…'

A pale phantom is emerging from the mist.

'Don't turn your back on it, just take a step to the side and leave it on your right.' Maheut does so.

'Now, go towards that meadow up ahead and look carefully around you, under the plants, especially those that seem the greenest, and at the edge of the trees, in the moss.'

'What am I looking for?'

'Fairy rings,' laughs Ysabel, swinging her basket.

The hour of Mass has passed. Once again Ysabel will have earned Perrenelle's reproaches, and Maheut a pinched smile from Ade. But the walkers are oblivious to everything, absorbed in their quest. Maheut even more so because she does not know what mystery she is pursuing.

'There,' says Ysabel suddenly.

The girl approaches, wrinkles her nose in disappointment. Then grows curious. The great, velvety, ochre-coloured mushrooms form an almost perfect circle in the grass.

Ysabel kneels down and delicately breaks one of the short, thick mushrooms off at the stem. She turns it over, revealing the fine, tightly packed gills. Brings it to her nose, softly sniffs it. Then holds it out to Maheut who smells it in turn, more out of bravado than desire. She has always known to steer clear of these strange creatures that emerge from the earth in a single night, double in size in a day, and change colour according to the weather. Without doubt mushrooms are evil, linked to death, and, it was said, to obscene practices. You only had to know their names: Judas's Ear, Stinking Satyr, or Shameless Phallus.

But Ysabel puts the mushroom in the basket.

'Did its scent remind you of anything?' she asks.

Maheut shakes her head.

'It smells like white flour.'

'I did not notice.'

'Smell it again.'

Maheut's nostrils approach the thick, chalky cap. A wet, powdery scent, yes, perhaps flour.

'You must learn,' Ysabel insists.

'About the scents of mushrooms?'

'I see the idea amuses you.'

'Forgive me, Dame Ysabel.'

'No, don't worry. You are only acting as one your age does with a woman of mine. But I would like you to pay attention to what I am about to tell you, for I know that you are capable of understanding. What does this smell tell you? It tells you to forget what you think you know, to hush the voice in your head, all those low jokes and rumours, those foolish things people tell each other in order to seem important. In the silence that follows you will be able to hear, see and smell the nature around you. For it is richer and more subtle than you think.'

The beguine delicately picks another specimen and shows it to her in the golden light.

'Some mushrooms do people no good. They are hard to digest and can bring on bad temper, sometimes even suffocation and death. But others are delicious. This one here, for example, that grows in circles, though we know not how, and which ignorant minds associate with witches' sabbaths. The Creator has given it a smell that you did not know how to recognize but which tells us that it is good for the body and tastes good too. As good as bread. This evening, I will cook it for you. And, my girl, I swear that you will ask for more!'

16

M AHEUT IS NOT the only person invited to Ysabel's table. The old beguine came back from the marshy fields more heavily laden than she'd foreseen. As she approached the city walls, a gardener called out to her from his plot. A child with inquisitive eyes sat curled up at his feet.

'What would you say to a rabbit, ladies? Only five *deniers*.'

'And where did it come from, this rabbit?' asked Ysabel with a smile.

'I don't know where it came from, but it passed through my garden.'

'The lettuces attracted it, no doubt.'

'No doubt!' the gardener laughed.

A few minutes later, the deal done, Ysabel returned through the gates of the inner city; at the bottom of her basket was the rabbit wrapped in a cloth, probably poached on the lands belonging to the Temple or to Saint Martin's Abbey. The returning fine weather gave her the idea of putting together one of those 'spring dinners', as she used to call them in the days when she was still a wife and mother, when she would serve the first harvests of the garden, with a roast lamb or suckling pig, at a large table that brought together her son and the stewards, gardeners and ostlers of her estate. Today, as well as Maheut, Ade and Agnes would be her guests.

The simple trestle table at the Beguinage is modest compared with the long, solid oak one of her former home. The trenchers are of wood, the bowls of terra cotta. The menu will be simple, too, but delicious, opening with a dish of sliced apples, the first of the season. The rabbit has been draped with bacon, stuffed with chervil, and roasted slowly on a spit. To serve alongside it, boiled broad beans with ginger and saffron, great bowls of brown bread soup, mushrooms fried in goose fat, and a lettuce to round off the menu. Then there will be waffles, bought from a street seller near the Temple. There are two sauces on the table too: the first a cameline made from toasted bread with ground cinnamon and almonds, diluted with verjuice; the other made of fresh herbs.

Ade is already seated at the table; if she appeared worried on her arrival, she seems more relaxed now, happy to be here. Maheut has settled near the fireplace as is her habit, with the sleepy air of a well-fed animal before she has even begun to eat. Ysabel is holding a jug of wine, about to pour, when Agnes makes her entry.

*

'They have condemned her!'

The door slams.

Agnes's cheeks are marbled with purple. The others stare at her in astonishment.

'Who are you talking about?' asks Ysabel, without breaking off her pouring. But she has already guessed.

Her assistant pauses to catch her breath. She seems different from the grey, furtive woman who paces up and down the corridors of the dormitory. There is no fear in her voice, no pity. She is excited, thinks Ysabel. And something else. For some time now she has been growing more self-assured. Brother Geoffroy, the Dominican cousin who helped her gain entry to the Beguinage, has left Sens to settle in Paris. He is close to William of Paris, the Inquisitor, whom he has joined at the Jacobin monastery. Agnes has already visited her relative twice. Speaks of him whenever the occasion arises. She is rediscovering her family, her origins. Who could blame her?

I am to blame for my lack of vigilance, Ysabel tells herself. In April, the condemnation of Marguerite Porete's book was bruited about the city. Ysabel was worried at the time. But since then, the trial of the Templars, the notable presence of their fellow brothers arriving to defend the Order, and finally the unexpected and brutal execution of several dozens of them, have pushed the Valenciennes beguine from her memory. Thinking Marguerite protected by her insignificance at a time when the king was making ferocious war on the powerful order of soldier-monks—and perhaps also fooled by the lightness of the spring air, distracted by the first soft shoots of her garden and the whistling of the nightingale that had come back to make its nest in the bushes along the vegetable patch—Ysabel had let her guard down.

'This is not good news,' she sighs.

Agnes slips onto the bench beside Ade. She leans forward and washes her hands in the basin of warm water set on the table for ablutions. Her goblet is full; she takes it in her hand and rests it in her lap, eyebrows knitted above her dark eyes.

'A guilty verdict is never good news,' agrees Agnes. 'But the Inquisitor had offered her absolution in exchange for her cooperation. And yet she still refused to talk.'

'How could he condemn her if she did not admit anything?'

Agnes grows flustered. She is eager to explain—but the affair is complicated. She does not want to make a mistake or look ridiculous in front of Ysabel, still less for her words to be reported to others and come back to Geoffroy's ears. He welcomed her into his home, had her sit near his hearth. He spoke to her in confidence about the inquisitorial trial that had just been held.

She had the feeling that he wanted to warn her. Above all else, this attention had touched her.

'The canonists said they learnt everything at their first meeting in April. The fact that her book had been condemned several times but that she was obstinately teaching it despite everything. That therefore she was not only heretical, but had fallen *again* into heresy.'

'Lapse and relapse,' whispered Ysabel. 'A priest's quibbles.'

'But this woman is spreading dangerous ideas!'

Agnes's manner of speech has also changed. She does not seem to realize that by this verdict one of their own is doomed to certain death, and of the worst kind, being reduced to ashes so that at the Last Judgement she cannot be resurrected before God. Hearing her talk, Ysabel does not know if Agnes's cousin is speaking through her, putting his words in her mouth, or if she is simply becoming again what she was before her husband's transgressions and the humiliation of their ruin: a woman of the old nobility, cultivated and capable of holding her place in conversation.

Agnes adjusts her wimple and turns to Ade.

'"Love, simply Love, and do what you want." This is what she says, what she has written. So is everything permitted under the pretext of love? So we should concede to nature whatever it wants, without any reproach from our conscience?'

Ade turns pale.

'She is speaking of a spiritual love,' Ysabel interjects. 'Nature has nothing to do with that.'

*

Maheut turns her head to the fireplace in an attempt to ignore the conversation. She remembers identical words, even if they sounded different when whispered, wailed, proclaimed, sometimes sung. '*Desiring heart, loving soul, sublime love, sea of joy, lineage of the soul...*'

Her mother, transfixed in devotion alongside Marguerite, in that small chilly room where the beguine received them, and where Maheut was sometime dragged along.

Her mother, by turns radiant and tormented. Absorbed in endless prayers, neglecting her daughter, discouraged by her silent hostility and too weak to try to soften her, to the point of abandoning her on the day when Maheut really needed her the most.

In the fireplace, the fire is burning strangely. Tiny flames flicker under the log Ysabel added, to take hold of a slender branch, where they dance side by side like pointed tongues.

How old was she when it happened? Ten, or a little older. It was a day for tears and contrition. Squeezed between the folds of women's capes, she found herself before another fire, much grander than this one, which warmed the cheeks and hands of the crowd gathered around it. It must have been winter. With her head lowered, for once, Marguerite stood in the centre of the square, the majesty of the belfry built by the merchants' guild to the west bearing down on her, the great stone cross erected by the church rising to the east. A priest at her side, sent by the Bishop of Beauvais. They meant to shame her. They had chosen to reduce her book to ashes in the heart of her own town, before her faithful believers, to frighten them, but also before everyone else. The merchants from the cloth hall, their apprentices and their servants had all come out of their shops. She had endured guffaws and gobs of spit. *The Mirror* had burned—and burned well. And the thought had occurred to Maheut that they would be just as capable of throwing Marguerite herself onto the pyre.

A scraping on the floor. Ysabel sits down heavily at the table.

'Let us leave that subject and eat,' she says. 'I am only afraid of the consequences of such a condemnation, and the spreading of the news about the city—afraid for our sister beguines.'

*

For the rest of the meal they discuss calmer subjects. The supper is delicious. The rabbit is juicy and crisp, the beans delicious, the mushrooms firm, with a delicate flavour of light earth dried by the sun. Agnes eats heartily, Ade is more restrained in dipping her bread in the bowl they are sharing but seems to appreciate the meal. Only Maheut shows little appetite. Ysabel has set aside a rabbit thigh for her. She nibbles it languidly before putting it back on the platter half-eaten.

The gathering is small, but for all of them, even for Agnes, about whom she has been insufficiently curious, seeing only what her appearance suggests, Ysabel feels a troubled affection. The women surrounding her seem to know so little of life. They are so vulnerable. Of course the Beguinage is a place of shelter for them. But are they aware that their very existence is an irritation to many priests and others in the church? Do they think of their sisters outside this haven established by the saintly king, who are less protected than they are?

Only Maheut has within her what it takes to put up a fight: the energy, the courage and the youthfulness. But how much longer can she remain among them? She does not belong here, but nor has she a place in the outside world.

Tomorrow, thinks Ysabel, I will gather a bouquet of violets and carry it to the Sainte Chapelle, where the remains of our protector are buried. Louis will appreciate these fragile, modest flowers.

When the meal is over and Ysabel is busying herself to prepare an infusion, Maheut suddenly jumps to her feet. Clapping her hand to her mouth, she stumbles over the bench, pushes open the door and rushes out into the courtyard. The three others hear her retch and vomit while the water boils on the fire.

17

ADE BLAMES THE MUSHROOMS. She was wary of them and only ate a few mouthfuls.

Ysabel, however, doubts this diagnosis. She ate a large bowl without suffering any ill effects. Nor did Agnes turn up her nose at the dish. Whereas Maheut barely touched it, which surprised Ysabel.

The girl has vomited again this morning. In the basin in Ade's hands, Ysabel can see no remains of food, digested or not. Only a sort of phlegmy mucus. Ade stands in the light from the window as the old beguine examines the yellowish liquid, rolling it around the edges of the basin. Maheut is still in bed.

'Do you think it is serious?'

'I do not know yet,' says Ysabel. 'I must examine her. How do you feel yourself?'

Ade shakes her head. 'Fine.'

'You look pale.'

'It's nothing. I slept very little.'

'Is something worrying you?'

Ade hesitates. 'No, it was probably the excitement of our evening. A richer dinner than usual. Nothing important.' Then she adds, 'My brother wants me to remarry.'

Ade herself is surprised by the confession. She had no intention of broaching the subject. Perhaps the words escaped her lips because of the gift received yesterday from her sister-in-law.

More books. In the accompanying letter, Héloise hopes they will keep her company in her solitude. She regrets not having seen her in so long.

Ade hardly knows the young woman, having met her only on the occasion of her marriage to her brother, for which Ade briefly left the Beguinage. She can barely picture her face. Round cheeks, a small nose, long hair, fair without being truly blonde. She must have blue eyes. She seemed a likeable and gentle woman. Ade suspects her brother takes advantage of his wife's sweetness in order to dominate her.

'He suggested a new match a few months ago. He awaits my answer.'

'What do you think about it all?'

Ade regrets having confided in her. But it is difficult not to answer now.

'I scarcely want to.'

'You are still young.'

'My age does not matter.'

'It does matter. You can have children. Start a family. I lost a husband of whom I was deeply fond. But despite everything I remarried. Life was different with my second husband. But I had no regrets.'

'You made your choice; allow me to make mine. I did my duty. I was married against my will, in order to satisfy my parents. Then I began to love my husband. Now, I only want to be left in peace.'

Ade's tone is brusque. She's just like an ocean wave, thinks Ysabel: it rolls in to shore, and up to your feet. Then it falls back, until it's further away than it was a minute before.

*

Sitting by the fireplace where she has lit a blaze to chase away the damp air in the house, Ysabel gazes at Maheut with a heavy heart. The girl has taken off her chemise, and like that day—it seems so long ago already—when Ysabel saw her wounded body for the first time and bathed it, she is standing naked, her arms at her sides. The purple marks on her torso and thighs have disappeared. Her thighs and shoulders still tremble. But her haunches are heavier, her breasts hang on her chest and their aureoles have spread and darkened as if drawn in ink.

'When did you stop bleeding, my dear?'

'I don't know. I never bled regularly.'

Ysabel rinses her hands in the bowl in the sink, dries them, and warms them before the fireplace. Then she goes over to Maheut and presses them against her belly. Closes her eyes and wonders what she should feel. Her grandmother knew. She could sense the presence of a baby from the first weeks merely by putting her palms on women's bodies. But this was not a gift Leonor handed down to her. Ysabel has to trust her eyes. And even if it is hard to accept, she understands what they tell her. There are only so many ways to say it.

'You are pregnant, my dear.'

'No,' says Maheut.

'More than four months gone, according to what you told us.'

'No,' repeats Maheut.

18

W ITH HER EAR glued to the bedroom door, Maheut hears them. Though they speak softly, she can make out the words, and understands what awaits her.

All those prayers, those hours on her knees, those books. Ade is just like her mother. The same calm voice, the same hypocrisy. The kind that makes you bury your head in a pillow so as not to hear the cries of your child.

'She must be sent back home,' says Ade.

Ysabel does not answer. Maheut hears only her footsteps on the floorboards. She is dressed only in her chemise. She stands shivering, holding her breath, not daring to move lest the boards creak and they hear her.

Four months. That is nothing. She has seen a cow calve prematurely: a parcel of blood and flesh. Her belly is still flat. How can what it carries have a human form? Ysabel knows about herbs. Surely some of them could help her. The servants used to talk of it when she was a child. They laughed to see her blush. One insolent maid, who was later dismissed, quipped: If there were no herbs, this house would be full to the rafters with the bawling of your father's bastards!

'She is carrying her husband's child. She must raise it in his family,' insists Ade.

'He took Maheut against her will,' says Ysabel at last.

'There was a marriage. It was her duty to satisfy him.'

'How can you say such a thing, Dame Ade?' Ysabel's tone is brusque. 'It was a forced marriage. In secret. She had no choice. The Church is opposed to this kind of union, even if our provincial squires have a hard time accepting it. In God's eyes, mutual consent is the basis of the union of man and woman. It is a mystery as deep as that of the incarnation.'

'Her brother gave his word. She owed him obedience. You heard her as well as I did, it was an alliance between two rival families. She was a peace token; this union was more important than her. Maheut acted selfishly and rashly.'

'No peace, no harmony can be born from a couple at war.'

'It is our role to be peacemakers. Our temperament is made for it. To soften souls, to soothe conflicts. If she had only shown her husband humility and obedience he would surely have treated her well in return. He must have cared for her.'

'He showed it in a strange way.'

There is a rustling sound, then more footsteps, but lighter and more nervous. Ade is pacing the room now. Maheut feels the wooden door grow hot under her ear, tremble at her avid listening. For a while the two women are silent.

'The heart's vein runs through the finger that wears the wedding ring,' Ysabel says in a calmer tone. 'The ring must not be forced onto the hand. No love, no solidarity can be born from violence… I do not understand your attitude, Ade. This agitation, this anger you are showing.'

The other woman does not answer. Her feet continue to pound the floor, just as the blood pounds in Maheut's temples. Then all of a sudden Ade stops, and cries out in a strange voice:

'She is expecting a baby! Even prostitutes know that a baby can only be conceived if one feels pleasure!'

Maheut lets herself slide down the door. She does not hear Ysabel's answer.

Somewhere in the distance, like a sound heard under water, there is a creaking of floorboards, the slam of the door. Then nothing.

She is cold, she is thirsty, yet she still does not dare move. She feels as abandoned as when she arrived in Paris. Those first two nights when, frightened and famished, she slept outdoors, in the ruins of a pitiful hovel, covered with some rags found among the debris to protect herself from the cold—and from men on the prowl. The second night one of them came close. She smelt him—he stank of urine and vomit—but he did not see her. In the morning, she asked a woman the way to the Beguinage. It was the only place in the capital she had heard about. From her mother, of all people—how ironic! Will she now have to flee from here, too?

She knows what awaits outside for a pregnant girl with no husband. She will not let herself become one.

19

'I AM COUNTING ON YOU to take care of her,' Ysabel snapped, as she left without a backward glance.

This old woman who thinks she knows everything and knows nothing! She looks at you so smugly, her own heart at peace, and thinks she has the right to judge you.

Ade broods over her anger. There is no peace in her heart—it flees from her. She hoped to find it here at the Beguinage. It was all she hoped for. That feeling lost since childhood, when she had flowed through life like a spring stream, smoothly wending its way across the land. Her body and soul perfectly in tune.

Then they brought this redhead into her home, who only had to open her thighs to conceive a baby—and who now wants to get rid of it. Ysabel had asked her where her anger came from. Not from Maheut. No, she was just a crude, vulgar instrument. A stone fallen into the stream, a little heavier than the others, which raises a cloud of mud from the bottom.

Ade joins both hands and presses them to her chin. A gesture like prayer, but only a gesture.

*

At first there had been smiles, encouraging, then pitying. Sympathetic glances. Whispering behind her back. Her husband's eyes. Worried, but still tender. Then after months, and the new year had passed, less and less so. Angry, hard and distant.

She had prayed, made offerings to Mary who bore Jesus; to Saint Anne, her mother, who after suffering twenty years of infertility was told by an angel of the birth of a daughter; to Saint Cunegonde, who although she had made a vow of chastity with her husband Emperor Henri, concocted miraculous potions to help women to conceive.

She had taken aromatic baths, spread oozing black tinctures on her belly, and done other things too that she would never admit. She went to the Lady's Spring and left an offering of a piece of bread and a faggot of wood before bathing naked, the cold water making her skin bristle. Confided her problems to a healer woman, on whose advice, fighting hard not to vomit, she had eaten a sheep's womb just before giving herself to her husband.

Soon there was nothing left of the attentive man of the early days of their union. Then their couplings had been vigorous but she had taken pleasure from them. He no longer used any of those caresses that brought her to orgasm. Now he barely put his hands on her skin, just lay heavily on top of her, lifted her chemise and forced himself into her, thrusting at her angrily before spewing into her and falling onto his back. She did not move, just closed her thighs to keep his semen in, and prayed.

They did not talk about it, nor about the obscene practices for which they were perhaps now paying the price.

The months went by. He visited her every evening, except when she was menstruating, then he left her room. The rest of the time she no longer saw him except at the banquets to which he invited his allies and neighbours. Her mother-in-law glaring at her across the table. Ade was afraid they were thinking of repudiating her. The shame of being sent away by her husband, of going back to her family.

Then after many months, the bloody stain, the humiliation that sullied her thighs, did not appear. She waited one moon, then two. Her breasts were tender, deliciously swollen. She asked for someone to call the healer woman, who advised her to eat fruits and honey, and said she would give birth to a boy.

Peace came back for a while.

*

Her husband had given her a gold ring, set with a fine ruby; her mother-in-law a pouch containing a birthing charm that she had tied to her thigh the whole time she was carrying her own son. 'It contains a parchment relating the deliverance of Marguerite of Antioch. It will protect you, like it protected me, against a sudden death.' Swallowed by a dragon, Marguerite had come out unharmed by piercing the beast's spine with her cross. My own baby, Ade had thought to herself, will need no violence to come into the daylight. When the time comes, I will make myself wide open and he will slide out without suffering. He will be born with pink, fresh skin.

She put her hands on her belly and caressed it. Sang so the little one would not be afraid in the dark. Sometimes he was so calm that she was afraid he was bored, so she took him for a walk in the gardens and told him the names of flowers. Other times, he would kick and wriggle about, so that she laughed, and her husband did too, impatient to hold this vigorous heir in his arms.

He lay with her every night now, waiting until she fell asleep before he drifted off.

The conjugal chamber hung with white. Fennel poultices applied to the back and thighs of the young girl who is preparing to expel a new life from her narrow hips. A great fire and the basin to bathe the newborn. Ewers full of warm water and piles of clean linen. Wine for the midwives.

But the baby does not want to be born.

It turns, goes back up deep inside her. She screams, her entrails torn.

They call the healer and the priest. The man pushes a tube into her, trying in vain to baptize the baby's head while it still lives. The woman pulls, hard.

Ade faints. It is a girl. She never saw it.

20

'LEAVE THAT. You will only make yourself sick and empty your bowels. Sit with me so we can talk a little.'

Ysabel creeps silently into the workshop and watches the thief from the doorway. Maheut jumps in fright, then puts the flask in her hand back on the shelf. It was a stupid thing to do, but better than doing nothing. She would have thrown herself down the stairs if that had been dangerous only for the baby. She cannot remain in this crippled state. Just as her father taught her when they practised archery together, she slowly, determinedly gathers her strength.

'I do not want this baby.'

'The question is not what *you* want or don't want. You have no choice.'

'You could help me.'

'Not in the way you want.'

'It can be done. When the woman was taken against her will, it can be done. The Church forgives.'

'The baby is already living. It has a soul. It would be a mortal sin to kill it. You know that.'

'Satan put it in my belly!'

'Listen to me, Maheut. Carefully. I have helped you up to now and I will do so again. But I will not harm the little one you are carrying.'

'It does not exist, it is nothing!'

'Yes, it is. One day, he will walk up and down the earth and shake his hair in the wind like you do. In your belly, he feels your anger and bitterness. How do you think he will be born? How do you think he will grow up? From now on, you are his mother, whatever you say. You are responsible for his well-being—as your mother was for yours. She betrayed you, and you are about to do the same.'

Silence.

'Remember what I taught you the other day in the marshes. About those mushrooms that you distrusted. Your child, if you want it, will have the scent of fresh flour...'

*

Ysabel thinks back on these last words as she walks through the frippers' quarter an hour later to reach rue Troussevache. It is not the smell of life but that of death that fills this neighbourhood. There is a lingering stench of rotting meat not only from the Great Abattoir but also from animals gutted in the streets surrounding the covered market. There are some strangely sweet scents in the air too, and she knows where they come from. They hang over the rue Neuve-Saint-Merri as she walks along it, wafted on a light northerly breeze from the nearby Holy Innocents Cemetery. In this wasteland, enclosed in walls built by King Philip Augustus, are buried most of the parishioners of the Seine's right bank, but also the dead from the Hôtel-Dieu hospital, victims of epidemics, nameless corpses from the morgue and drowned bodies from the Seine. The poor are tossed into pits on top of each other, wrapped in a simple shroud, and the pits are constantly being reopened and stirred until they become full. Since they do not all belong to the same institution, occasionally several pits can be open at the same time. Not long ago the contents of one of them had to be turned over.

Ysabel knows what is said about the soil in that place. That it has the power to dissolve flesh and bone. But so many dead have been piled up in the cemetery now that the ground has risen into a hillock. No doubt pigs and stray dogs come at night, despite the wall, to root among the cadavers. Even in death, the poor cannot rest in peace.

Fortunately there is plenty in the narrow street with which to distract oneself. It has changed so much these last ten years! As has this whole quarter. To the north and south of the cemetery, from the shadow of the Abbey of Saint-Magloire all the way to the other side of the city walls at Saint-Martin and Saint-Denis, the food shops and wool workshops that used to dominate the streets have given way to a new and more refined trade. At first there were just a few single-storey shops, then workshops equipped with winders, warpers, spinning and bobbin wheels from Italy. Soon different voices could be heard in the streets—the sing-song accents of merchants from Lucca, Genoa, Venice and Florence who brought their bundles of raw skeins or precious fabrics. There, where calloused hands had once cut meat from carcasses or carded rough wool, agile fingers were working with the most precious of fibres, the soft, shiny thread of the silkworm from China.

The silk quarter has spread despite the stench from the cemetery. Perhaps that is some consolation to the dead...

In any case, women have found welcome opportunity there. They have arrived in large numbers from other areas of the city and the provinces, attracted by the promise of a well-paid trade that is considered respectable for their sex. Among them are many beguines who have chosen not to live in an enclosed community but who stay close to one another nonetheless.

Women are everywhere to be seen in these well-paved alleyways, still shining from the water sloshed out each morning.

Leaning in doorways to watch over their stalls, busy in their shops, chatting and calling to each other from their selling windows, their faces more open and their bodies more free here than elsewhere.

Ysabel blesses them with a smile, even if her step is heavier than usual. The woman she is visiting on rue Troussevache has a stall that cannot be missed, one of the biggest and best provisioned. Jeanne du Faut is not content with selling garments bought from others. She employs her own weavers, embroiderers and makers of silk headdresses from whom she commissions trimmings, ribbons, headscarves, pouches, gloves and belts. Some women work in the neighbouring houses; others she has installed in her home. She also has a workshop not far off for spinners whom she supplies with raw material, and also owns many properties that she rents out to other merchants.

Ysabel has not seen her old friend for weeks and feels suddenly impatient. Jeanne is precious to her. The silk merchant has seen sides to her that nobody else knows.

The circumstances of their meeting, more than twenty years ago, fostered a closeness between them. The day Ysabel passed through the Beguinage door for the first time, Jeanne du Faut did so too. Two new arrivals, both recently widowed—an immediate connection. And for the first few months they lived together, until another house in the Beguinage became free.

Jeanne was ten years younger than Ysabel—no longer a child, but not yet finished with flights of fancy and laughter. And they did laugh—a lot! They shared a bed, and, sometimes in the darkness of their bedroom, confidences about their respective husbands, and about the pleasure they had given them. Jeanne, whose husband had given her very little, had learnt how to satisfy herself alone. After all, as she joked one of those nights when neither woman could find sleep, her confessor saw no problem in this and even appreciated that she had told him about a sin that he considered merely venal. An unsatisfied woman had to expel her seed in order to take comfort, he lectured. If not, her excessive humidity might lead to adultery!

She showed Ysabel how to do it, putting her fingers and once even her tongue between her thighs—and laughed at her astonishment.

But in the end Jeanne grew bored in the Beguinage. Her father, dead for several years, had been a cloth merchant. She was used to seeing foreign merchants at their home, artisans from Flanders or England.

'You could work alongside your brother,' Ysabel had suggested, 'and continue to live among us.'

Jeanne had shaken her head. She had acquired a taste for not depending on anyone.

'Silk is the future,' she had replied. 'Look around you. People spend so much money in this city. The courtiers and prelates. The merchants, financiers and aldermen too. Especially them—they want their wealth to be seen! They need garments that shimmer and shine, collars in serge and capes in brocade!'

She was laughing, but she had thought her plan through seriously. The silk trade was dominated by women, making it one of the rare guilds in which they could act without being the wife, sister, or widow of a master.

Not depending on anyone.

Jeanne's house has a double gable. She bought the building next door a few years ago and expanded into it. From the first floor, two rounded bay windows framed by foliage jut out over the street, sheltering the ground floor and the shop front from bad weather. A girl sits on a chair by the door. Ysabel recognizes Juliotte, whom Jeanne du Faut found in the street two winters ago. The little girl answers her smile with a tilt of her head. She is a mute. But her eyes are lively and intelligent.

'With such a guardian, the ablest of thieves could not steal even a ribbon!'

Jeanne appears at the window.

'What do you think?' She lifts a piece of brocade into the light.

Ysabel enters the shop, goes to her friend with hands outstretched. Jeanne has grown even heavier. Her breasts and hips are squeezed into a severe gown, but one spun from the finest wool. 'Opulent' is the word that describes her best.

Ysabel's eyes have not had time to adjust to the half-light when Jeanne hands her the brocade. A thick offcut, embroidered with velvet.

'Beautiful, isn't it?'

'Very beautiful.'

'A dealer from Lucca brought it to me. He is offering to become my supplier. His products are expensive, but I know a few gentlemen ready to pay even more for cloth of this quality. He told me his workers were trained by the best weavers in Constantinople.'

A smile.

'A handsome man, too.'

In the shop the piles of offcuts are arranged on trestles. At the back, a woman is examining a piece of cloth and shaking her head. Béatrice la Grande, Jeanne's faithful assistant for years.

'What is it, Béatrice?' asks Jeanne. 'You seem dissatisfied.'

'This cloth from Basile lacks finesse. I have mentioned it to her several times now. I wonder if she is really using the silk we send her, or replacing it with another of lesser quality.'

Jeanne nods. 'Leave that now. I will check the work and deal with it myself.' Then, turning to Ysabel: 'Come, my dear, let's chat a while. As well as his brocade, the merchant left me some candied fruit that I want to taste.'

*

On her way back to the Beguinage later that morning, the taste of sugar still on her tongue, Ysabel steps more lightly. Jeanne du Faut has agreed to accept Maheut into her home. Did she ever really doubt it?

21

O VER THE FOLLOWING WEEKS, Maheut's departure is prepared. To those who ask, Ade explains that the young girl must go back to her family. Ysabel tells Agnes that the girl is leaving—but without revealing the cause of her departure. As for Maheut, she does not leave the house, even at night. She feels more soiled than after her wedding night. A worm in the fruit. She hopes her body will expel it, but feeds herself anyway, because she promised Ysabel she would. Ade was present for the vow, and Ysabel charged her once more with watching over the girl until her departure. Ade did not answer, and speaks even less than usual now. Maheut sometimes wonders if she too is waiting for the worm to fall from the fruit.

The girl is to move to rue Troussevache on the first Monday in June, in the morning. Two of the embroiderers are set to leave Jeanne du Faut's home that day, to live together in rue Quincampoix; one of them wants to open her own workshop. Jeanne encouraged her and offered her five hundred *livres* to set the business up.

'She was a good and faithful partner,' she told Ysabel. 'It is only right that she should take off on her own.'

Such is the solidarity in the silk quarter.

So two beds will be free, not a bedroom as such but a corner that can be made ready for Maheut and her coming baby.

It is all planned out.

And then things get complicated.

On the evening of 29th May during the group reading in the chapterhouse, Mistress Perrenelle la Chanevacière collapses. Ysabel rushes to her side and lifts her head. Her face is disfigured by a frightful rictus. She puts her cheek to the mistress's mouth and feels a weak breath on her skin, so she loosens the older woman's clothes, pulls open her robe and vigorously rubs her chest. Perrenelle comes to, but the rictus remains. The left side of her body is unmoving, from the shoulder to the leg. Ysabel spends the following days at her bedside, pouring sips of broth and medicine between her taut lips, washing her body, removing her stools. Perrenelle no longer resembles an ancient idol, but one of the madwomen carved into church capitals. Grimacing and horrible. Eyes overflowing with distress.

Then the first Sunday after Ascension and before Pentecost, the Beguinage, already put to the test by its mistress's ordeal, learns the chilling news. Three weeks after having been declared a relapsed heretic at the monastery of the Jacobins, Marguerite Porete has been led to the Place de Grève to hear the inquisitor officially pronounce her guilty. Present are the bishop of the city to represent the authority of justice, the provost of Paris acting as bailiff, a Dominican chosen by his order for the inquisition, and a master of theology. After declaring Marguerite guilty of falling into heresy once and then falling again, William the Inquisitor reminds his audience that her book is heretical and erroneous. He adds that it should be 'exterminated and burned' before demanding that any person possessing a copy give it up, on pain of excommunication, to himself or to the prior of the Dominicans of Paris before the next Feast of Saints Peter and Paul.

After this verdict William proclaims two more. Also guilty is Guiard de Cressonessart, a priest claiming to be the Angel of

Philadelphia sent by God to reinvigorate believers in Christ, who is condemned for having supported Marguerite and for having, like her, stayed silent and refusing to take an oath. The third is a converted Jew who returned to his faith 'like a dog to its vomit' and who spat on images of the Holy Virgin to show his contempt. All three are delivered to the secular arm of justice and led to the Châtelet prison.

The next morning, Marguerite is led once more to the Place de Grève to be burned alive. Only the Jew is brought with her. Guiard de Cressonessart recanted out of fear of the flames. He gave up the leather belt he wore around his body to mortify it and which he had previously refused to take off. His punishment has been commuted to perpetual imprisonment, which simply means a slower death.

*

It is on this Monday of Marguerite's torment that Maheut is supposed to leave the Beguinage. Ade has prepared a bundle of clothing into which she has slipped two chemises and a nearly new robe she no longer wears. She can barely control her impatience. Maheut sits next to the now-extinct fire and waits, arms around her belly. She is pale, but her rounded cheeks, swollen lips, the new curve of her breasts and hips, all give her a provocative air of health.

Ysabel, who is to lead the girl to her new home, is late and Ade is worried. Then one of the serving girls knocks at her door. Perrenelle is in a very bad way. The old beguine refuses to leave her side. She fears she may die at any moment. Ade must accompany Maheut.

The young woman sighs and puts on her cloak. Both women leave by the gate, heads down, walking slowly, under the intrigued gaze of Guillaumette.

In the rue du Figuier the air is cool and blustery. Gusts of wind from the river rush down the street. The two women hold their hoods in place with one hand as they walk. The Place de Grève is not on their way, yet they find themselves heading there. Ade will later say that they went on Maheut's insistence. The girl knew Marguerite, had heard the news of her condemnation, desired to see her before she died. Ade yielded out of compassion towards the condemned woman, whose last moments she wanted to accompany with her prayers. How much did their decision owe to curiosity on the part of Ade, or to bitterness on that of Maheut? Ysabel would never know.

The two women join the rue de la Tixeranderie about halfway along, but then instead of turning to the right to rue de la Verrerie and Saint-Merri, they let themselves be pushed leftwards by the crowd, towards Mouton alley and the great square on the banks of the Seine, where an unmissable spectacle is about to take place.

Meanwhile Humbert is crossing the Pont aux Changeurs. He covers his mouth and nose with his cloak before ducking down the narrow alley of the tannery, which stinks of tawed hides. He is frightened and does not know why. Maybe the speed with which everything has happened. He has not had time to get used to the news. He arrived in Paris three days ago, quickly learnt of the condemnation of Marguerite, news which had not yet reached Valenciennes, and here he is already on the way to witness her burning. How will he tell his old master about this? At first all Humbert's compassion was for Jacques. But now, hearing the noise of the crowd, imagining the pyre being built up, the woman tied to the stake, the flesh roasting in the flames, his thoughts are with her. Perhaps that is where the fear comes from.

Ade, Maheut and Humbert reach the square just as a silence spreads through the crowd. The street sellers and conjurors cease their harangues, the apprentices their scuffles, the rowdies their ribaldry. Marguerite has begun to climb the pyre. The women approach from the north and the man from the south, weaving in and out of the crowd. Ade tries to hold Maheut back by her sleeve, but she is determined to get close to the victim. Humbert glimpses her hooded silhouette before turning his gaze to Marguerite.

The chroniclers will recount that in her last moments the woman gave many noble and pious signs of penitence, which filled the hearts of numerous witnesses with holy compassion and brought them to tears. But at this instant, Humbert sees her as he has always known her to be. Absent. Lost in the secret that resides in her.

The provost places a copy of *The Mirror of Simple Souls* near her feet, no doubt the one that William of Paris submitted to the theologians six weeks previously. The hulls of boats tied up at the port knock against the quay. The wind is rising. The girl in the dark pilgrim's cape is standing close to the pyre. Suddenly she lets her hood drop, freeing her flame-coloured hair. The onlookers around her back away, murmuring. Her companion has already pulled the hood back over her head and is tugging her away by the hand. For a fraction of a second, Humbert glimpses her face. A lily bowed on a fragile neck.

As the Franciscan turns away, head down, shameful of fleeing but eager to be as far away as possible when the wood catches fire, a nagging question distracts him from the funereal scene at the centre of the square. What is Maheut the Redhead doing in this place—and in the clothing of a beguine?

Part Two

November 1311 to November 1312

In everything a Beguine says,
Listen only to good
Whatever happens in her life
It is religious.
Her word is prophecy;
If she laughs, it is amiability;
If she weeps, it is devotion;
If she sleeps, she is ravished;
If she dreams, it is a vision;
If she lies, think nothing of it.

If the Beguine marries,
That is her conversion:
Since her vows, her profession
Are not for life.
Now she weeps and then she prays,
And then she will take a husband:
Now she is Martha, now she is Mary;
Now she is chaste, now she marries.
But do not speak ill of her.
The king will not tolerate it.

About the Beguines
RUTEBEUF (1245–1285)

1

T HE CHILD SITS on the floor, near the window. A thread of saliva flows down her chin from her open lips. She raises her head, then her left hand, open as if to grasp the shadow of the bird that is ruffling its feathers on the gable. Her eyes are wide open, her breath suspended.

The eyes are the only thing she has inherited from her mother. Well-spaced, pulled slightly towards the temples. Green, speckled with bronze and gold. Other than that she has the round face and chubby cheeks of a very young child whose features have yet to show themselves. As for the hair, there is nothing red about it, except for the occasional glint, just now for example as the sun pours its light into the room as well as the bird's shadow. In the main it is a chestnut brown that is getting darker as she grows. Perhaps she will end up black-haired like her father.

The little girl must have managed to get out of the bed where Maheut makes her sleep, not liking to feel the child's skin against her own during the night. And she is calm, the young woman tells herself, drawing up her shivering legs under the bedsheet. She does not bother me at every turn. On the other side of the attic, Juliotte moans and nestles against Ameline, the embroiderer with whom she shares a bed. The room is freezing; autumn has already returned: so fragrant, so full of life in the woods where Maheut used to gallop, so sad in this great city where the outdoors offers only the cold, the gloom and the mire.

Fortunately, despite the child, the days are lighter here than when she lived in Ade's home. More joyful. There are four girls living in the silk-house now, along with Thomasse, the serving girl who sleeps in a cupboard next to Jeanne du Faut's bedroom. But every morning they are joined by the embroiderers and Béatrice la Grande, who is responsible for the shop. A lot of work is done in this house, there is laughter and song too.

Jeanne du Faut is demanding but she is also just. Generous. There is something else about her too, which Maheut cannot put her finger on. She sometimes reminds her of the cat that her father's manager acquired to get rid of the rats and mice in the barn. A swift, sure animal. Bounding hither and thither one minute, the next curling up into a ball, a look of dreamy contentment on its face. Likewise, sometimes Jeanne snuggles up in front of her hearth, gathering her generous body about her, her round arms, opulent hips and thighs like two great columns under her skirts. She buries her head between her shoulders, and wraps herself in her flesh, a radiant, unmoving mass.

Her house is as efficient and lively as she is, but moves to deeper, hidden currents, unspoken desires, pleasures partaken. Try as she might to keep herself apart and ignore the chattering of the other women, Maheut can sense the atmosphere and her body responds to it despite herself, feeling forgotten shivers of excitement once again.

Juliotte moans again. Maheut sees her tousled head emerge from the bed. The mute girl opens an eye, squints in the daylight, and then sees the baby. Right away she is on her feet, dressed only in her chemise, runs barefoot across the floorboards to scoop up the almost naked child in her arms and carry her to back to the warmth, with her, under the eiderdown.

A grunt of reproach.

Maheut smiles. She fears nothing from Juliotte. She sees no

real judgment in her eyes. If she could speak, her words would be honey. But she no longer has a tongue.

Nobody knows what happened to her. Ameline says that it was torn out, that she looked in Juliotte's mouth while she was sleeping and that there was nothing at the back but a nub of shrivelled meat. But Ameline is a teller of tall tales. What is certain is that Dame Jeanne found Juliotte—a name she gave her, since nobody knows what she was baptized—on her doorstep one morning, famished and half dead with cold, and that Jeanne took her in. Maheut carries a memory of a similar experience in her own body.

Juliotte's silence has made her a friend. Maheut finds her maybe even more astonishing than Jeanne du Faut. The little girl has no words, but does have lively eyes, a fine ear, and agile hands. She keeps watch over the stall like nobody else—and everybody in the neighbourhood knows this. Thieves have spread the word, and the little bell she rings at the least incident to alert the women around the shop is talked of even in their taverns near the ramparts. But that is not her only job. Juliotte takes care of everything. She spreads the floor with fragrant herbs in summer and winter. When the weather is dry, she airs their sheets and blankets in the sun to chase away the lice, and when it is damp she dries by the fire the wicks of tallow lamps. She coats the inside of pots with honey to catch flies, makes cheese tartlets fried with monkshood powder to poison the rats and mice in the cellar. Revives stale wine by dipping elderflower and cardamom into it. Removes stains from her companions' robes with a mixture of animal urine and ox gall and gets spots out of pieces of silk with verjuice, without them losing their colour.

But what she really prefers is helping in the kitchen. She cannot taste the dishes with her mouth, so she does it with her nose, standing with eyes closed above the pot.

Nobody knows where she got her expertise. Juliotte observes, copies, invents. Asks for nothing, and gives willingly. Has treated Maheut like a sister since her arrival. She was there the day of the birth, heating the water and assisting Ysabel, who had been called the day before when the labour pains began. During all those hours that Maheut struggled, screaming and sweaty, to expel the stranger from her belly, Juliotte mopped her forehead with a cloth, massaged her arms, legs and thighs, slipped bitter, soothing potions between her lips. Maheut knows that she can count on her to take care of the little one.

The mute, the redhead and the bastard—more or less. What a brilliant team!

In the bed, hidden under the eiderdown, the child laughs and Juliotte along with her. Squeaks and gurgling. From downstairs, the creaking of the shop window being folded back.

It is high time they got up. Jeanne du Faut has allowed her girls to be a little lazy this morning. The previous two days, with an important order to prepare and guests in the house, they had worked more than their usual hours. But as the day dawns, not only is the shop opening but the embroiderers will be arriving soon. There is also the merchant from Lucca, whom the mistress is expecting to visit and Maheut is curious to meet. She loves the accent of the Italians, their booming voices, their grand gestures, the sweets they offer to every girl. Sometimes she amuses herself by repeating in her head the strange, sing-song words they exchange when she watches them open their coffers and untie their bundles.

The mistress, who presented Maheut to her household and acquaintances as a distant, recently widowed relative of Ysabel's, has given up on turning her into an embroiderer. The girl dulls and tangles the shiny thread, muddling stitches with her short, thick fingers, more like those of a young lad. Now she is employed in the shop to assist Béatrice la Grande, who manages the work ordered from outside the shop, distributing the outgoing skeins and examining the incoming sewing. Meanwhile, Maheut sorts and stores, pulling out the swatches that the workers need and the articles that clients want. She must also keep the shop clean.

'The stall is like a frame,' Jeanne always says. 'It tells you the value of what is presented within it.'

*

Maheut pulls on her robe, washes her face and hands in cold water, wraps her hair down to the roots in a large square of cloth, quickly darkens her eyebrows by passing a finger rubbed with charcoal over them. She slips down the ladder to the floor below where the mistress has her bedroom and living room, and the embroiderers their workshop, for whom Jeanne has left a bay window open onto the street so they can profit from the daylight. From there, a wooden staircase, whose spiral steps hang from a single timber carved from the trunk of a beech tree, descends to the shop. The shutter is already raised and the sounds and smells of the streets pour through, the ringing of steps on the paving stones, the clatter of hooves, the cries of the rival street sellers.

Up in the attic, Juliotte strokes the hair of the suddenly silent infant, and plants a kiss on the little, open hand that reaches once more towards the window.

2

YSABEL SHIFTS ON HER SEAT. On her right she glimpses the face of Jeanne la Bricharde. The mistress has assumed that distant air with which she habitually rebuffs those who irritate her.

From the pulpit, the reedy-voiced young priest pursues his sermonizing.

'Good brides of Christ,' he intones, 'should live totally cloistered. Those who are not cloistered should consecrate themselves entirely to Him to prove that they are worthy of His love.'

The hair around his tonsured scalp is losing its finely coiffed appearance. A lock slides down his temple. His face is long, as dry and knotty as his body—already a dead tree at his age—but it is sweating like that of a plump, florid man under the effort of his haranguing.

To begin with, he was merely boring, studiously unrolling the *sermo modernus*, dissecting Biblical quotations and *exempla ad infinitum*, recounting at length and with relish the ascetic life of the blessed beguine Marie d'Oignies, who despite her marriage had retreated to a hermitage, and in return had received mystical visions and ecstasies. Now that he is approaching his conclusion, he is becoming downright unpleasant—and judging from La Bricharde's expression, thinks Ysabel, I am not the only one to reckon so.

Since she entered the Beguinage, Ysabel has had the opportunity to hear dozens of sermons in the little chapel. Many theological discussions, commentaries and lectures too. The beguines are fond of these sermons and the new mistress, elected after La Perrenelle's death, particularly so. Unlike Dame Chanevacière, Dame Bricharde is an educated woman, who reads and writes Latin perfectly. From a wealthy family linked to the court—her father and her brother were in the service of the king's bankers, her aunt Isabelle de Tremblay supplied fine garments to the royal household—she received the best sort of education, thanks to tutors who were richly rewarded for initiating her into the subtleties of thought. She regularly invites members of the University to speak in the chapel—this one is from the Sorbonne—as well as Dominicans, Franciscans and even secular priests. Many clerics actually request invitations, since the beguines are seen as a desirable audience for those who wish to practise the art of sermonizing.

It must be said that there was never so much preaching in Paris as in these last decades, nor so many learning how to preach. The changing times transformed towns into great hives of activity, busy with the gathering and storing of goods and arms, attracting new people by the promise of work. The religious authorities suddenly found themselves powerless faced with the influx of poor labourers: the paupers who work on the cobblestones, haul goods at the ports, toil in workshops and taverns—the porters in the covered markets, the apprentice butchers and tanners, and the brothel wenches. These urban drifters are unsettled and elusive, quite different from the old serfs and peasants who had been tied to feudal lands and subject to their lord and their priest from birth to death. How to struggle against this tide? Hamstrung by its decorum, and a language that is alien to most of the faithful, the Church let itself be overtaken by the growing number of laymen who had begun to sermonize in the streets, haranguing crowds in the vulgar French tongue, sometimes professing heretical ideas. The Church had decided to react by training tougher preachers of its own.

Ysabel smiles. All those young people who have flocked to the capital to be instructed by the great masters! Determined to gain a perfect understanding of the Bible so as to correct the theological errors of 'non-authorized' preachers, they train themselves in Latin, of course, but also in the speech of the people. They are given manuals to support and guide them, exhorted to use epi-sodes from the lives of the saints and martyrs in their preaching, but also to include amusing anecdotes and personal stories...

I am being too severe, sighs the old beguine. But this clumsy, pompous man in the pulpit exasperates her. He drones on in the same tone, incapable of alternating gravity and frivolity, of using pauses, of playing with rhythms and rhymes. Ysabel tries to concentrate her attention on the greasy dangling lock that is brushing against his ear. He feels it tickling, tries with a hesitant hand to smooth it into place, but it immediately slips back. Even this comical gesture does not succeed in lightening his ponderous speech.

'When Christ decides to address uncloistered women per-sonally, he demands their total devotion. This the beguines must remember. They must chase distraction from their lives.'

The priest wags a condescending finger. La Bricharde does not react. Her body is as strained as her face.

Does this dead tree realize that the very founder of his school came to preach in this chapel long ago? wonders Ysabel. He was a theologian with a different talent, and different words too.

At the time, Robert de Sorbon had defended their sisters so well! The little library at the Beguinage holds a copy of each of the sermons he gave there. Unlike other clerics such as Ranulph de la Houblonnière, who under the robust vaults of this same chapel expressed his worry that the beguine's habit might serve to hide behaviour contrary to religion, Robert had cited them as a model. *Benignea* was what he called them—'beneficent ones', making their name synonymous with goodness and humility, and their Order with love.

'Wherever you go,' this cleric now goes on, 'whether you are listening to a sermon in Church, or outside the walls in public, you ought to do everything necessary to honour your divine love, and yearn for your next moment of solitude, so that you may commune with Him, for it is in solitude that Christ reveals His secrets. Do you believe that even if you spend your day in town, the Spirit of God will still descend on you? Certainly not! But He will do so if you kneel before an altar with an image of the Cross or of the Virgin Mary, or if you prostrate yourself on the ground beside your bed.'

Ysabel sighs. She knows what sentiments are behind this lecture. Ever since beguines began to appear in the heart of large cities, where they stood out as unaccompanied women, the sisters had been dogged by suspicions of scandal. Mocked, suspected of hypocrisy, accused of changing their status at their convenience. The old woman has not forgotten the cruel ballad *About the Beguines* by the late troubadour Rutebeuf, which some still sing: 'Now she is Martha, now she is Mary / Now she is chaste, now she marries.' The Franciscan Gilbert de Tournai complained that the beguines' way of life meant one never knew whether they should be called laywomen or nuns.

On the eve of the Second Council in Lyon, for which the pope had ordered bishops to prepare memoranda about abuses in their dioceses which needed to be reformed, Gilbert had written a report accusing the beguines of idleness, and worse still, of producing erroneous translations of the Bible into the common tongue that they then read out in public. More than the freedom of their status, he criticized the freedom of their thought. During the same Council, a bishop had declared them guilty of a dual refusal of obedience, to priest and to husband. The man now before them is surely the bishop's intellectual heir.

The cleric mops his brow with his sleeve and looks out at the audience of women, seemingly in expectation. What does he expect in return for such a speech? Ysabel cannot say. With a few exceptions, she does not know what effect his words might have had on her companions. Agnes, whose austerity seems even more strengthened by her contact with her cousin Geoffroy, is no doubt delighted with it. And perhaps Ade recognizes herself in this ideal of solitude advocated by the ecclesiastic. But what would her friend Jeanne du Faut think of it? She who, in the preacher's words, spends all her time 'in town' and actually lives there, who does pray but works even more, who is devoted to Christ but also to her shop and to the women she employs there. More than once Ysabel has suspected Jeanne of using her status as beguine to maintain the freedom to which she clings. But don't all beguines do the same, in one way or another? Who could reproach her for it?

Jeanne offers work to her companions, and sometimes lodging too. She protects them, without the help of the walls that protect the great Beguinage, with no royal support or money from rich donors—all thanks to her own wealth and energy. Those who live outside the precinct have been left exposed since the death of Marguerite Porete, their behaviour and manner of dress increasingly scrutinized. Despite this, the silk shop owner continues to shelter Maheut and her child.

*

Ysabel bows her head. Her thoughts slip their moorings. In the half-light of the chapel nobody can read the expressions on her face, so she is free to follow the meanderings of her mind. She smiles. Sighs.

She misses the baby girl. Her tender cheeks, her dreamy look. Gentle and endearing. But she is growing like a plant without roots beside a mother who does not see her, leaving it up to others to feed and care for her. But how could it be otherwise? Between those two there has been only violence, from conception to birth.

So young and so narrow-hipped. It is a sin to impregnate girls of that age.

The baby's shoulders had got stuck. Jeanne du Faut hesitated to call the midwife. There were too many rumours about the beguines—frightful stories of illegitimate babes whose necks they were said to break, or whom they drowned at birth.

Until then, Ysabel had attended only one childbirth, that of a serving girl in her last husband's household. The midwife was too late; the baby had started coming out, accompanied by surges of liquid, even as the girl stood working in the kitchen. Everything had been easy. The little boy had slid out like a fish pulled from the river.

Whereas Maheut had been shrieking for hours.

Ysabel had peeled down the top of her robe and tied it about her waist. Her upper body now covered only by her chemise, she washed her arms and hands with soap, before drying them with a clean cloth, as her grandmother had done. Then—just as she is doing now, in this chapel filled with the sourness of an unmanly priest—she closed her eyes. She put her hands on Maheut's belly, slipped her fingers into the distended birth canal, let herself be guided by them, cupped the tiny head in her palms, stopped herself from forcing its passage despite Maheut's screams, instead thrust her hands even deeper into the flesh, humours and blood, turned the tiny body around, and then guided it out by the rhythm of the young mother's desperate pushes, while Jeanne du Faut, with the help of Juliotte, held the girl still, encouraged her, mopped the sweat from her face and readied clean linen and blankets for the newborn.

Leonor. That is her name. The same as Ysabel's grandmother. A priest who was a friend of the household came to baptize the newborn girl. She was perfect, but so small, and fragile of breath. Ysabel offered herself as the first godmother, and asked that Ade be the second, in case she could not fulfil the role for as long as necessary. Ade had come with Ysabel to the birth, but only stood stiffly against the wall, as white and useless as a spectre.

Now Ysabel feels a touch on her arm. La Bricharde puts her hand in the crook of her elbow. The old beguine opens her eyes. She is often tired these days, as several people have remarked. No doubt they are worried about her, but it is merely old age claiming its due, and, what is more peculiar, gradually blurring the boundaries of time, allowing images of the past to surface in the present. It only takes a word, a burst of light, or the outline of a face for the ghosts to appear. As if they have not been left far behind, but instead are all around her, invisible but ready to show themselves at the slightest opportunity.

A rustling, the friction of robes. The choir is assembling and beginning the communion song. The upward spiral of the familiar modulations erases the sermon's coarse echoes.

I have too much to do today, thinks Ysabel again, but tomorrow I will visit the little girl.

*

An hour later, when the beguine has again returned to her herbalist's workroom, the young Sorbonne cleric crosses the courtyard of the Beguinage, wrapped in his cloak, without having obtained from La Bricharde the invitation to dinner that he was doubtless hoping for. If he is of bilious humour, it does not show on his face, which is tense with the same fierce expression he wore during his sermon. As he approaches the main gate, someone bangs the door-knocker on the street. Guillaumette pulls aside the door leaf, and steps aside. The preacher takes advantage of this moment to dart through the doorway, slipping past the towering, dark-clad figure of the man who enters as he leaves.

3

H E IS TALL, with long legs and broad shoulders. A sallow face, shaved this morning but with the beard already darkening the chin. A haughty eye. High cheekbones over hollow cheeks. He walks with big strides, like a man used to the countryside. As he does so his cape flies up, lifting the robe underneath. The knots in the cord that draw it tight around his slender backside bouncing against his groin.

A knight in the habit of a Franciscan.

La Bricharde looks him up and down. Charmed by his appearance, but wary all the same. He doesn't want to sit down, drinks off the cup of wine she offers him in one draught. Engages in the game of conversation with reluctant amiability. Seems both hurried and uneasy.

'I have never met Jean de Querayn, but I know him by reputation. How is he?' Jeanne's tone has changed slightly. Become more brusque. The man seems to notice it. He lets out a sigh, smiles. Then at last he sits in the vacant chair opposite the mistress.

'Brother Jean has a tired heart. For weeks now he has barely left his bed.'

'I am sorry to hear that. Can he still pursue his work?'

'He has plunged back into the New Testament. I think he finds new sources of reflection there.'

La Bricharde inclines her head. 'Like all of us... He is very kind to have sent you to bring his greetings.'

'I had to come to Paris for the affairs of my community. He thought I should meet the new mistress of the Beguinage.'

'Will you be in the capital long?'

'A few weeks. My master is worried about not being able to supervise my training due to his health. He wants me to complete it among the Franciscan masters. The prior of our monastery has agreed to this idea.'

'No doubt he thinks you will make a good preacher. The Franciscans need those. It is an honour for you.'

'Brother Jean also thought that I might draw some benefit from my visit here. He is persuaded...' Humbert punctuates his words with a light smile. 'He thinks—like his great inspiration Jacques de Vitry—that one cannot become a talented preacher without following the example of the beguines.'

The mistress nods. 'We have not taken vows, but we do follow a path close to that of the mendicant brothers. I am told your master frequented the beguinage in Valenciennes.'

'He liked to go there.'

'I am also told he knew the beguine who was burned in the Place de Grève last spring. A woman of your town...'

'...Marguerite Porete. Yes, he knew her.'

'Were they friends?' La Bricharde asks.

'I would not say that.'

'Was he interested in her writings?'

'Yes, he has read them.'

'And you?'

Sitting motionless in his chair now, Humbert tries to understand what she is getting at.

'I have read them,' he finally replies. 'Excuse me if I am impertinent, but why these questions?'

'We follow what happens in the world. I know that Jean de Querayn experienced some difficulties on account of the support he gave this beguine.'

So that's it. La Bricharde is well-informed. The old master's troubles have received little publicity. The Beauvais inquisitor had summoned him, but Brother Jean was too weak to go. The prior undertook the trip in his place and obtained a pardon for him on condition that he stop writing and not make himself heard outside the monastery.

'He is an old man. He no longer has much to fear,' she went on. 'Our companions are more exposed to danger. The condemnation of Marguerite has affected us all.'

'I was not present when the Inquisitor publicly pronounced the sentence. But I was told he never explicitly called her a beguine, precisely so as not to cast opprobrium on you all. He knows that the king protects your institution.'

'Philip protects this Beguinage out of devotion to his ancestor, Louis the Saint. But for how much longer?'

'You should not worry yourself... As for me, I am not here to preach Marguerite's ideas, if that is what you fear. I have read *The Mirror of Simple Souls*. But unlike my master, I do not adhere to her thought. Once again, I have simply come to greet you in his name. And also, as I said just now, to look for a young girl from our country who has donned the habit of a Paris beguine, whose family are eager for news of her.'

'I understand you, my brother. So let us drop the subject.'

La Bricharde rises and gathers her robe around her. She is a woman elegant in her austerity. She must be fifty years old, but her face is smooth under the veil and wimple that frame it. A little haughty.

'Just remind me of the name of this young girl before we begin our tour.'

'Maheut the Redhead.'

The mistress frowns. 'I do not recognize the name.'

'She may have only passed through your house. Her brother

is worried; he has not received a letter from her for months, and her mother is not well.'

'Dame Ysabel may be able to help you. She is among the eldest in our community, and she knows many of our sisters in the city.'

*

Humbert has never set foot in a beguinage other than the one in Valenciennes. La Bricharde notices his surprise at the simple beauty of the buildings as he follows behind her. She shows him in turn the vast communal hall panelled in oak where chapter meetings are held, the chapel, modest but with a chancel decorated by floral carvings and illuminated by candles, and even the vegetable garden with its enormous marrows and neat rows of leeks.

All here is orderly and clean. Were it not for the houses bordering the inner courtyard he might think himself in a monastery. Yet life here seems less constrained. Two women pass by, chatting, baskets on their arms, heads wrapped in simple white cloths; another woman, wearing a fur-trimmed cape, steps through the doorway of a fine dwelling with two floors; the gate opens and closes several times for figures in a hurry to pass in and out. Now that Mass is finished, the beguines attend to their activities.

In offering him such a comprehensive tour, La Bricharde, he understands, is not merely trying to show him how well-looked-after the place is. No doubt there are petty squabbles and sinful thoughts here, as there are elsewhere. But there is something different in the air. An atmosphere of industrious harmony. The beguines of Valenciennes, poor souls bound by their dreary rules, are far from having reached such perfection. He understands all the better the vigilance with which the mistress protects her domain. Informed as she appears to be, she must be anxiously following the news. Particularly that coming from Vienne.

Not much is filtering out of the Council organized by the pope in the city on the banks of the Rhone after months of postponements. The main subject is the Templar Order, whose dissolution King Philip the Fair is demanding—it is said that at the end of October hundreds of brothers surrounded the town, declaring themselves ready to refute the accusations, and that more and more prelates are lending them support. But alongside that central question, other matters must also be addressed. Pope Clement V hopes to launch a new Crusade to liberate Jerusalem. Other prelates are demanding a reform of the Church. In their provinces, the bishops have been gathering lists of grievances— from abuses of power and wealth to overweening arrogance, from simony to debauchery, absenteeism to ignorance. The list is long. The status of the beguines is one of the issues to be discussed.

Since the condemnation for heresy of Marguerite Porete, all the old complaints about these women have been revived. But now it seems their critics' suspicions, their worries about the freedoms accorded to the pious laywomen, have evolved into actual accusations. The prelates of the Germanic lands, where beguines are particularly numerous, have always been most anxious to pull them back into line. Nobody has forgotten that seven years ago, in Metz, a beguine was accused of false prophecies. Her feet were put to the flames before she was thrown into prison. In Colmar and Basel, other beguines were accused of heresy. The bishops in the East, who had been trying for years to subject isolated women to the authority of parish priests, were now strengthening their control over beguinages, subjecting the opinions of candidates for admission to strict interrogation before they could be allowed to enter. Their strong influence within the Council made some fear the worst.

'They talk of a sect! They use the same word for these saintly women as for heretics!'

Humbert cannot forget the way Brother Jean behaved when they last spoke. The old man had still not recovered from the death of Marguerite. On his return from Paris, he made Humbert recount again and again what he had seen on the Place de Grève. By dint of repetition, faced with this tearful old man, who in his shock seemed pathetic to Humbert for the first time—an unsettling feeling—the younger man's tale gradually slid from actual memory towards hagiography. Standing tall in her white tunic, dignified and serene—this is the image Jean has of his friend. The violence of this world has spared the old man; he does not know the smell of burning flesh.

With the passage of time, his pain has faded, but his obsession with the devotion of Marguerite and her peers seems stronger than ever. This disturbs Humbert, who sees in his master the same obstinacy that led Marguerite to the stake. Was the threat of a trial not enough for him? Humbert remembers having reacted a little sourly to his criticism of the Germanic bishops.

'One cannot accept everything in the name of a faith that claims to be directly inspired by Christ,' Humbert replied. 'You have heard the rumours from the East of young girls wandering the streets causing scandal. Others accosting passers-by with their noisy chanting and begging for alms.'

The old man gave him a disappointed look. 'Yes, that is what is said. Also that they mix with men as perverted as they are—the *beghards*. That they copulate and preach in caverns! Nothing but vile lies! These clerics simply cannot accept that there are cultivated minds among the beguines, and that they write and preach. After all, that is where the clerics' power lies! Marguerite was not executed for perversion. Never forget that. She is the first woman to be burned for a book.'

*

An icy wind hits Humbert in the face. At his side, La Bricharde has stopped. He notices her watching him closely, before he pulls himself together and carries on his way. They stand before the door of a big, long building, near the chapel. This must be the infirmary.

Walking through the common ward, where the sickbeds are set out in rows, close enough to allow for some intimacy between the patients, he notes that the infirmary is just as well-cared-for as the other buildings of the beguinage. It does not stink of misery as such places usually do; there is even an agreeable scent in the air… A mixture of burning bark and herbs. A dozen patients lie under white sheets and woollen blankets. Some raise their heads upon seeing the Franciscan pass by. One extends a hand to him, but he pretends not to see it. Further down, a woman is sitting at the foot of a bed. She turns at the sound of their steps, then rises heavily, coming to meet them with a smile.

This must be the beguine that La Bricharde mentioned. A sturdy old woman with the thick skin of those who spend their lives in the open air. Her robe gives off a strange smell as she approaches, a mixture of sage and camphor. For an instant Humbert feels he is falling back into himself, slipping away, as he sometimes feels when he is sinking into sleep. For the first time in years, he has just thought of his mother.

Ysabel for her part admires his imposing figure, surprised at the habit that seems so ill-suited to him.

'Dame Ysabel,' says La Bricharde, 'I present Brother Humbert, who has come to visit us from Valenciennes.'

Another beguine is hovering behind the old lady. Humbert has not noticed her until now. An ungrateful face and needy air.

'And this is Dame Agnes, who assists Dame Ysabel.'

'Your infirmary is very well maintained,' declares Humbert.

'Thank you. So far this autumn has been more clement than the last. We have few patients.'

Ysabel turns to the bed at whose foot she is lingering. 'Only Margot is truly unwell. Her mother brought us this poor girl two days ago, but she waited too long. I fear she will not survive the night.'

A slight figure is barely visible beneath the bedsheet.

'What is she suffering from?'

'It is her heart. I have known her since she was a child, she was always fragile. She needed rest, but her parents still have four little children at home. They sent her out to work as a wool carder.'

La Bricharde turns expectantly to Humbert, but he remains silent.

'Dame Ysabel,' she says, 'Brother Humbert has asked me if we have among us a young girl from Valenciennes.'

Ysabel raises her eyebrows. 'Valenciennes? I don't think so. There is Tiphaine, but you mentioned a *young* girl, and she has not been one for a long time.'

'She would be about seventeen,' Humbert puts in. 'Red hair.'

Ysabel only smiles more broadly. 'Red hair?' A pause, then she pouts.

'No, truly, I think not… Would you care to continue your visit of the infirmary?'

*

A few minutes later, La Bricharde and the Franciscan are back in the courtyard. Humbert gave only a cursory glance to the infirmary's steam bath. He has the disagreeable feeling that he is being mocked. The old woman seemed sincere. But that look she gave him, with those eyes that took everything in while giving nothing away… And the reaction of that other one behind her, a jolt of surprise… He has had enough of traipsing through every room and corridor in this place, he wants only to turn around and go back to the Cordeliers.

The mistress pretends not to notice his silence. She heads for a modest-looking house near the chapel and pushes open the door. Resigned, Humbert follows her up a narrow staircase and into a large, airy room, blinking in the late-morning sunlight that filters in through a large east-facing window. In front of the window, silhouetted against the light, a woman sits at a reading desk on which a thick book lies open. Opposite her a dozen little girls sit crowded on benches, bent over psalters they are sharing. An older girl sits apart, drawing letters with a metal stylus on a wax tablet.

'Who can recite to me the letters that we learnt yesterday?'

The class has just begun. One of the little girls looks over her shoulder, distracted by the visitors' footsteps.

The woman, whose features Humbert cannot see, dips her head in greeting, then calls out firmly to the curious pupil.

'Maria, I am listening.'

But the little one has recognized La Bricharde, accompanied by a man in a Franciscan habit. She is stunned into silence.

'Pardon us for interrupting you, Dame Ade,' announces the mistress. 'I am showing this brother from Valenciennes around our buildings, and I could not miss out the school.'

Humbert advances to meet the woman at the reading desk, and suddenly stops, struck by her features. She is beautiful, of a beauty he would never have expected to find in a beguinage. A high forehead, a delicate mouth, a perfectly oval face, now bending to greet him above a broad white collar. A lily.

And it was to that flower that he compared her once before. For he has already seen her—such splendour is not forgotten. And he remembers exactly where.

'I am trying to teach them to read in the way I was taught,' says the young woman with an apologetic smile. The voice is soft but not melodious. 'Three or four letters a day, the last day of the week being reserved for the complete recitation of the alphabet.'

'Learning letters as God created the world,' comments Humbert.

'Yes. But not all of my girls know how to concentrate on their task.'

'You must have patience, Dame Ade, as the Lord does with us,' interjects Jeanne. Ade inclines her head.

Gracious and cold, thinks Humbert. A lily, yes, a noble flower, even if he prefers those of the field. He approaches the desk.

'Will you permit me to look at your book? It seems well made.'

Ade takes a step back. The volume is made of thick pages of vellum stitched with leather sinews and lined in blue satin. The psalms are divided in the usual manner, into eight groups according to the hours of the Offices and the days of the week. Each introductory text is ornamented with a miniature illustration representing a scene of the Old or New Testament: David playing a psaltery, the miraculous Virgin, the Virgin and Child. A veritable treasure.

'Does this come from the library of the Beguinage?'

'No,' whispers the young woman. 'It is a gift from my sister-in-law. My brother's young bride.'

She is blushing, embarrassed by the man's proximity. But Humbert does not move away; on the contrary, he moves a little closer.

'It is magnificent. Do you know where it was made?'

'In Champagne.'

'Is that where your family lives?'

'It is, yes.'

The girl drawing her letters has broken off from her task and is watching them intently. Humbert feels her gaze on him. Ade does too, no doubt, and hurriedly introduces her. 'This is

Clémence de Crété. She joined the Beguinage this spring for the sake of her education.'

Clémence makes a curtsy, but Humbert barely responds. He is concentrating on Ade's voice.

Her accent proves the truth of her words. She does come from Champagne, not from the Hainaut. But he is certain that she is the woman he saw on the Place de Grève on the day of Marguerite's execution, pulling the Redhead away by the arm.

4

A s HUMBERT DEPARTS the rue des Beguines, he leaves a number of worried souls behind him.

The mistress racks her brains as to the true purpose of the Franciscan's visit. She scarcely believes the explanation he gave. That he came to bring greetings from the old Valenciennes scholar whom she has never had the occasion to meet. As for his search for the lost redhead in the habit of a beguine, she does not know what to think. The man is intelligent. Difficult to read. Did he have another mission—one he was less keen to reveal?

Meanwhile Agnes is overcome with surprise and indignation. She clearly heard Ysabel proffer a falsehood. To a monk's face! Without batting an eyelid! Should she speak to the mistress? To Geoffroy? But what would she say? Maheut left the Beguinage more than a year ago and Agnes does not know where she is. Ysabel told her only that she had found another community to welcome her, far from Paris.

Perhaps it is better to keep quiet. Ysabel's condition has undeniably declined these last few months. More and more often, Agnes finds her asleep at a patient's bedside. There is also the exaggerated concern she shows for some patients. One evening, while the sick were sleeping and all the sisters had retired to their quarters—and she herself was making sure everything was in order before going back to her room—she saw Ysabel slip into the dormitory and, by the light of an oil-lamp, smear with ointment the sex of a girl who had been brought in half-dead, her belly torn by the assaults of men. A prostitute.

Her cousin Geoffroy thinks the care the beguines show the sick and the dead is dangerous, bringing as it does very young girls into perilous proximity with the flesh. Now that they know each other better, he has expressed his concern about the excessive freedom left in the mistress's hands by the Jacobin prior on more than one occasion, even suggesting to Agnes that she should retire to another less permissive community. There are some in Paris, like the Haudriettes or the good women of Sainte-Avoye, where she might be accepted despite her having been married. But Agnes has other plans. Even so, she promises him she will be vigilant.

Clémence is worried, too, though she could not say why. That man, so tall, with such broad shoulders. The way he approached Ade, like a tree casting its shadow over a meadow. Ade, whom she would so like as a friend. When she first saw her, Ade was applying a cloth soaked with burdock to her mother's inflamed skin. At the time Clémence had understood only Ade's gentleness. Never would she have imagined that her heart's path would be so fraught with difficulty.

Ysabel, who should have been the most troubled of them all, has simply returned to the patient Margot, whose breath is slowly fading. Neither the father nor mother of the child has been to visit her since her arrival in the infirmary. The beguine understands why and forgives them. But it is her duty to be here. As for the lie she told the Franciscan, God will pardon her.

The visitor seemed to her far from benevolent. There was something black and weighty about him whose source she did not know, but she sensed its power. There was no question of letting him near Maheut and her child. In any case, she reassures herself, fluffing up the pillow under her patient's head, there is little chance of his finding her where she is now living in hiding.

And once he has accomplished the duties of his monastery, he will return to Valenciennes.

In fact Ysabel is mistaken, but her thoughts are elsewhere now. Her eyes are on the hollow face, her hands on the icy forehead, she breathes softly to accompany the dying girl, to guide her, to free her lungs, her struggling heart—and the soul lodged therein.

Meanwhile in her own room, kneeling at the foot of her bed, Ade prays.

*

It is of her that Humbert is daydreaming as he strides up the rue de la Verrerie. The Franciscan has decided not to go directly back to the Cordeliers. The day is getting on and he still has much to do. Upon leaving the Beguinage he stopped to buy a hot pie from a strolling vendor, ate it while contemplating the river, then continued on his way, his mouth still salivating from the fatty meat and pastry.

As he walks, he wonders if the young woman recognized him. Probably not. That day on the Place de Grève he merely caught a glimpse of her face when she turned to pull Maheut away from the pyre. She was focused solely on her companion, fearing that her flamboyant unveiling would draw attention.

What could a woman of her quality be doing in such a place and in such company? This is what he still does not understand. He judged Ade at a single glance today. And what he saw did not fit with the circumstances of their first encounter.

On his right, the façade of the Saint-Merri church is bathed in the rays of the setting sun. Shouldering his way through the crowd of customers drawn by hawkers' cries to the meat pudding stalls around the church, Humbert stops a moment outside the entrance. He needs to consider his next move. His mind is as heavy as his body, his thoughts confused. This is what happens when you are obliged to follow several paths at the same time. If only he could have at least found the girl! But it was naïve of him to imagine that she might hide in the Royal Beguinage itself. Did she pass through it? Her presence at the execution with Ade that day and the old infirmarer's ambiguous attitude both suggest that she did. But she must now be more discreetly hidden. He will have to knock on the doors of the dozens of beguinages in the city, without even being sure that the girl he is hunting is still in Paris.

Hands crossed over his stomach, head bowed, Humbert resembles a man at prayer, except for his feet tapping anxiously on the paving stones. Through the woollen hood, he feels the sun warm the nape of his neck. He swings on his haunches as he learnt to do in the course of long hours spent praying standing up; stretches his back, feeling the suppleness of his body, sensing the muscles rolling over the bones. Breathes deeply. It will be useless to give way to frustration. After all, he has only himself to blame.

When he told Brother Jean about Maheut upon his return from Paris, that he had seen her in the Place de Grève dressed in a beguine's habit, the old Franciscan was as surprised as he'd been. He knew the Redhead's mother, whom he had met thanks to Marguerite, and now acted as her spiritual guide. When her daughter had fled, casting dishonour on her family, the woman came to ask him for help. But why had Humbert accepted this mission in addition to the other absurd and dangerous one his master had given him?

'If our family had money, we would have made you a knight, my son,' his mother had once said, planting a thorn in his heart. 'There would not have been a nobler vassal in the service of his lord. Nobody more courageous, more faithful and devoted.'

Devoted he certainly is. But his lord is merely a stubborn, foolhardy old monk.

*

The smell of hanging tripe, rivulets of blackish blood in the gutter. The afternoon is drawing to a close and soon the sellers in the covered market will be packing up their wares. A frenzy spreads from stall to stall as hawkers make their final pitches and the day's last bargains are struck. Humbert now knows where he must go.

At the mouth of rue Pirouette stands the tower of the great pillory. A chilling sight, a bell tower with empty window frames behind which a gigantic horizontal wheel is visible. The Franciscan is relieved that no poor soul is tied upon it today. A man has leant his cart against the structure and is unloading two carcasses covered with glistening flies.

He walks north, reaching the city ramparts amid a bustle of horse-drawn carts hurrying to leave the city, and those trying to enter before the gates close, then he passes through the walls near the Hotel d'Artois. The street continues on the other side of the gate, wider but disgustingly dirty, lined by crumbling shacks and many taverns. The men who slip furtively through their doors with their heads down do not come merely to drink the sour wine that is served there. Anything can be bought around here. You can find accomplices for a theft, fences for stolen goods, thugs for hire, little girls at a good price—even boys, too.

A boy sitting on a doorstep follows him with his eyes. Humbert stops, considers asking for directions and then thinks better of it. It is better to follow the landmarks inscribed in his memory. He continues on his way. The packet he carries under his robe, next to the skin, strikes his flank and weighs down every one of his steps.

5

T HE GIRL WITH THE WEAK HEART dies at the hour of compline. So absorbed was Ysabel in keeping her company that she has not noticed the time passing. The Beguinage closes its gates at nightfall—'by the time you cannot tell a Tournoi coin from a Parisian one', as the rule says. It is too late now to go to Maheut and warn her that a man is seeking her. She will do so tomorrow.

In the Silk House nobody senses the danger lurking. Maheut lies awake that night for other reasons. Earlier in the evening, Thomasse, the serving girl, left the closet where she usually sleeps to be near her mistress, and came up to the girls' bedroom under the eaves. This happens sometimes when Dame du Faut has guests for supper and they linger at the table. The little girl hurries into the attic and slips into the common bed, next to Ameline. The two of them whisper and giggle loud enough for Maheut to hear, until Juliotte silences them with a menacing growl.

Now Maheut is the only one awake in the room. She wonders what to think of Ameline's gossip. This is not the first time that she has heard about such things. But Ameline is stupid. Incredible that such a trivial girl is capable of such delicate embroidery. Bent over her work near the bay window, fingers pricking the needle through and drawing the thread, she appears almost graceful. But when she opens her mouth, that illusion vanishes.

Maheut rolls onto her back, burying herself in the quilt up to her chin. She is usually indifferent to the tittle-tattle among the girls in the house, but tonight she is feverish. In her cot, Leonor seems oblivious to her mother's agitation. She sleeps in a total silence it is sometimes frightening to witness. Without any of the grunts, snoring, tongue-clicking or tiny cries that are usual for a baby. When Maheut puts her to bed, Leonor lays her arms by her side, looks up at her and then closes her eyes. That is all.

Ameline, she ruminates, acts like of one of those animals in rut that her father's estate manager used to calm by throwing buckets of water over them. Whenever a man comes around, she trembles and blushes. And the clumsy questions she asked Maheut when she arrived, about her experience as a wife. If only she knew…

Maheut shifts to her side, curled up in a ball with her thighs tight together. But this is just a habit, or rather a frightened reflex of her body. She has forgotten Guillebert's smell, though it lurked long in her nostrils like a reptile at the bottom of its burrow. The memory of rough hands on her skin and the tearing in her gut still remain, but these are now distant sensations. The fear has died down, as well as the anger, leaving behind another feeling she cannot define.

A laugh rises from the room downstairs. Maheut recognizes it as Jeanne du Faut's. It is immediately followed by another, softer laugh that she knows well: that of Marie Osanne, the other silk merchant in rue Troussevache. Her business is the only one to rival Jeanne du Faut's. For years the women have had shops side by side. Neighbours and competitors, Maheut thought when she first settled in the Silk House. Friends, she soon realized. Nothing strange about that. Both were beguines. Yet, Maheut tells herself, there is something more between them than a shared outlook and profession. Those looks they exchange, those frequent visits they pay each other so late at night…

Maheut knows what Ameline says about this. She is only repeating the usual rumours—as if they needed to be spread further. Women living together, without a man's supervision… A murky situation in which sensuality can easily flourish and lead to illicit relations. They are like idiotic sheep that howl with the wolves!

Maheut's fever is growing worse, but actually it is she herself who is feeding it. Tormented by some demon, the young woman cannot prevent herself from imagining the brunette with her ample curves and the slim blonde rolling around together in a bed sheltered by curtains from indiscreet eyes, each shoving her fingers into the cunt of the other, like Maheut did to herself as a child, before learning that this rapture was a sin.

Her nipples hurt; her belly is throbbing. She turns over again and again. Opens her eyes without knowing if she has slept or not. The shadows under the rafters are already lightening, and soon it will be morning. My God, she wonders, am I becoming like Ameline, my flesh as weak as the stupidest of beasts in the farmyard? Ysabel would know what was happening. She would surely tell her: do not worry, for it is not torment but pleasure. And the old beguine would be happy, since such torments would mean that Maheut was starting to heal.

6

THE OLD BEGUINE has not slept either. She stayed next to the dead girl until prime. Her death was gentle, she tells La Bricharde, who has come to pray over the child's body. The image of the Franciscan left her mind during the hours of her deathbed vigil, which she spent, as is right and proper, remembering moments shared with the departed. The day the girl was first brought to her, when she was two and her parents were frightened by her fainting fits that their neighbours thought came from the devil. The regular visits after that. When she was older, Margot would come alone, not saying much but liking to linger in the kitchen, watching the herbalist prepare her elixirs. As well as her medicine, she always received a bowl of broth and a thick slice of bread to dip into it.

Dawn is breaking when Ysabel finally leaves the infirmary, entrusting the corpse to the expert hands of her assistants. But before heading to the Silk House, she goes to the postern set in the city wall to the rear of the Beguinage.

The sisters rarely take this passageway. It leads to the Saint Paul quarter, a labyrinth of alleys overpopulated with fullers, barrel-makers, plasterers, porters and other labourers who toil at the port. It takes the beguine some time to find the dwelling at the end of a muddy blind alley. Built from rubble and planks, crammed between two similar shacks, it is tiny, the interior sooty and as dark and stinking as a dungheap. The father has already left to look for work, and the mother too. A little girl comes down the ladder, barefoot, with a baby in her arms. She receives the news of her sister's death with resignation, promising to pass on the news. Ysabel tells herself that the Beguinage will have to take responsibility for the cost of the funeral. This will not be the first time.

After having performed this task, and only then, does Ysabel let the dark shadow of the Franciscan return to her mind, and the urgent needs of the living take priority over her duty to the dead.

*

A few moments later, Ade is at her side as she heads towards rue Troussevache. The young woman seems to take her role as godmother seriously, and accompanies Ysabel to the Silk House whenever she can. But this morning she has other motives than the instruction of her godchild. Ysabel has told her of Humbert's search. She takes the old beguine's arm; at the pressure of her hand, Ysabel realizes Ade must be worrying about the Franciscan too. Is he truly linked to Maheut's family as he claims? Before warning the impulsive Redhead, she wonders if she ought to consult Jeanne.

As she follows Ade into the shop, however, Ysabel realizes that the conversation will have to wait; though the shopkeeper is at her counter on the ground floor, there is a man with her.

'Ade and Ysabel, what a surprise!'

Jeanne is fresh-faced, smiling. She embraces the younger of the visitors and takes the other by the hand. 'Come, let me introduce Master Giacomo! Master Giacomo, my friend Dame Ysabel.'

The man bows. He is not tall, but well-built, his clothing made of fine fabric that emphasizes his powerful frame, the well-fitted doublet, the waist clasped by a heavy belt ornamented with enamel. Olive skin and black hair.

'He sells me those brocades I showed you.'

'Dame du Faut is a demanding customer, but she knows the quality of things.' He speaks a careful and melodious French typical of Italian merchants. His voice is serious and low, coming from the back of his throat.

'I think I can guess that you are the merchant from Lucca whom Jeanne often talks about.'

He merely smiles.

'Master Giacomo has decided to remain in Paris for a few months,' says Jeanne. 'He is lodging nearby with his cousin in Buffeterie street.'

The street of the Lombards, thinks Ysabel. That is what people call the Italian bankers. No doubt Giacomo's cousin is one of them. Jeanne is astute. It is always good to find allies among the lenders, although their situation is less prosperous now than it was when two among them, Biche and Mouche, were feeding the king's treasury. With the war in Flanders, the kingdom's finances are going from bad to worse, and amid the monetary crisis financiers are now viewed with suspicion. But once again the Jews have been the prime scapegoats. Five years ago, King Philip the Fair, like his ancestor Saint Louis and Philip Augustus before him, ordered the Jews to be expelled from the kingdom. The expulsion was of unprecedented scope: tens of thousands of men and women were arrested across the land, their goods confiscated and sold, their titles of credit appropriated by royal agents. The king redoubled his calls for expulsion, accusing the 'god-killers' of fraudulent extortions and frightful crimes 'that cannot be named'.

But everyone in the kingdom needs loans, the merchants and nobles of course, but also the small artisans and peasants, who are increasingly burdened with taxes. The Lombards are the only lenders left, and they are charging even more exorbitant rates of interest than ever. Meanwhile the king is up to his usual tricks, on the one hand striking coins containing less and less silver, blackish coins known as '*bourgeois*', and on the other hand minting gold '*agnels*', so rare as to be almost unobtainable, which are stamped with a paschal lamb bearing a long-shafted cross in the manner of Saint Louis, in order to reassure people of the stability and honesty of the currency.

All this will end badly, thinks Ysabel. But meanwhile commerce continues. Giacomo is the living proof.

'Northern embroideries and tapestries are much sought after in my country,' explains the merchant. 'I am looking for new suppliers who can satisfy my Italian clients. Dame du Faut knows everyone here, and she has promised to help me.'

The man looks Ysabel in the eyes. He has singular pupils, ringed with a deep blue, the sparkling gaze of a connoisseur. The mistress of the house seems to have lost herself in those eyes. Maheut, too, who is standing close by, her face alive with the haunting beauty that comes across it sometimes despite the headdress wrapped about her forehead.

'Look at these marvels that Giacomo has brought me,' Jeanne says.

'Marvels, it is true,' replies Ysabel.

On the counter, the silk fabric secretly gleams. The warp and background weft are entirely of gold thread. The floral design mingles buds of lilies and roses with leaves of watercress in an exquisite colour palette that plays on the dominant shades of saffron and burgundy. The old beguine lingers over the material, enjoying this congenial moment. She tells herself there will always be time after the merchant has gone to discuss the Franciscan.

Unnoticed by her, while everyone else is captivated by the visitor, Ade slips out of the room and up the stairs to the floor above.

*

The child is in the embroidery workshop, sitting on the wood floor, her legs spread out in front of her, palms resting on the ground to keep her balance. She is looking at Ameline, so Ade sees only her back.

She takes a step forward. Leonor straightens, gently raising her right hand and cocking her head like an animal that hears a noise. Ade moves forward again, very softly, holding up her robe so it will not rustle. The little hand flutters, like a feather blown by the breeze, the head tenderly bends towards the shoulder.

A few seconds later, when Juliotte slips her head around the door, this is the scene she sees: the child and her godmother sitting in the window frame, holding a silk ribbon at either end, playing at making it ripple in the light.

Two weeks of waiting, for this… Discouraged, Humbert examines the last sheet of parchment. The ruling is imprecise, the tracing of the letters irregular, the punctuation haphazard. This is the crude work of a beginner—but the most serious flaw is that skimming a few paragraphs is all it takes to discover the weakness of the Latin translation. The abbreviations are legion and often faulty, there are words missing, and the result is difficult to read. The man sitting opposite him in the tiny attic where he lives, sleeps and works—so badly—keeps his head down, pouting.

I never should have trusted him with this task, thinks Humbert. How could I have been so unwise? Bernard is a mere shadow of his former self. The other evening, seeing him again for the first time in so many years, Humbert was so happy to find him in the same neighbourhood as he'd left him years before, that he could ignore the evidence of his decline. The thin body, bony hands, sparse hair—all of which Humbert wanted to ascribe merely to the fatigue caused by hours spent at a desk in this poorly lit room.

Yet what other choice did he have? He could not approach the booksellers in the Saint-Séverin quarter or near Notre-Dame. It was too risky. They were all affiliated with the University, reproducing and circulating only texts connected to their studies. He still has acquaintances among them, though, if not friends.

When he studied at the Sorbonne, like many penniless young men in the faculties of arts or grant-holders getting by frugally in the poorer colleges, he had sweated blood copying out one book after another, all to earn enough to buy some second-hand books for his own studies from those who furnished him with copying work.

That was how he met Bernard, one of the most skilled and learned scribes. He had quit the University, tired of the sterile debates he heard there. All that endless quibbling about the Eucharist, he mocked. Which do you think it is: a Christianization of bread or the other way around? Above all, Bernard was keen to take advantage of his youth. Humbert had loved his rebellious spirit, far from those doubts and pretensions which he himself indulged in too often. He followed Bernard into taverns too, some of them on the aptly named Cock-Tugger street, where Bernard indulged his habits, not far from where he eventually settled when his family learnt of his deviance and cut off his allowance.

'Youth passes… and I am passing away!'

Just for a moment, in the bitter laugh that follows the quip, Humbert sees his companion of days gone by.

'What happened to you?'

'Wine and girls. They sapped all my strength. You should see what I have between my legs these days! A maggot that wriggles no more.'

Bernard lifts his sleeves, revealing arms covered with coppery spots. 'And then there is this. I even have them on my skull, lumps full of liquid. When they burst, a scar remains, and the hair does not grow back. Sometimes I think they are nibbling at my brain.'

'Are you being taken care of?'

'I consulted a doctor of my acquaintance. He has seen such marks before, on soldiers coming back from the Holy Land… The *Holy* Land, can you imagine…' Again that little laugh. 'He does not know what it is. Nobody knows anything. Apart from that it ends badly.'

Bernard shrugs his bony shoulders.

'Listen… I wasted your time and I pray you will forgive me. But I needed the money too much. That book, though! What intelligence! What daring! I never thought you would expose yourself to danger for this kind of writing.'

'I am doing this for a friend.'

'A *friend*? You barely had any when we used to know each other. I would have liked to help you, but as you see…'

Silence. Bernard wipes his sticky eyes with the back of his sleeve.

'You need more than a copyist. A clerk would be better. A learned one. To transcribe this into Latin. Why don't you do it yourself? You were gifted, I remember.'

Humbert prefers not to answer. The other man sighs, lets his head fall onto his hollow chest, an emaciated scavenger. The Franciscan grabs the manuscript from the desk, wraps it in a leather cover.

'You must pay me.' Bernard has not raised his head. His chin on his chest, his eyes on his belly, he mumbles to himself.

'What did you say?'

'You must pay me. I worked on it, after all… And I used good parchment.'

Humbert silences him with a raised hand. The parchment is not new. It has been scraped clean, and badly so, the old letters visible beneath Bernard's scrawlings. But he cannot bear to see the man like this. So he takes a few coins from the purse Brother Jean gave him, lays them on the table and quickly leaves the room, stuffing the palimpsest along with Marguerite's book into the bag where he has kept it hidden since his departure from Valenciennes.

*

What should he do? Who to ask now? Bernard is right. He needs an educated copyist for this work. But he has been out of touch with the circle he knew at the University for too long. He would not know where to look, whom to trust. He is aware of what he risks if he is denounced.

Ironically, Marguerite, for whom he is putting himself in danger, is an obstacle to the task he must perform: since her execution, there is more suspicion in the air than ever. Not only of the beguines—even the Franciscans are threatened.

The relationship of the mendicant order with the secular clergy has always been strained. Jealously protecting their prerogatives, the priests constantly reproach the minor orders for diverting revenue and souls from the Church. The beguines are one of the targets of their ire. Because of their shared apostolic ideal, the beguines have enabled the Franciscans to increase their own influence among the laity. Priests accuse the friars of administering certain sacraments and of encouraging people to choose to be buried in their own cemeteries, thereby diverting donations and burial rights from the parish. Worse, some of them have begun to insinuate that such closeness between beguines and friars must be concealing sinful relationships.

Royal favour has long protected both groups. But at any moment these unclassifiable women, neither wives nor nuns, neither wholly contemplative nor wholly active in civic life, these women who are neither fish nor fowl, might compromise the Franciscan Order. And now the condemnation of Marguerite Porete, followed by the investigation of the status of beguines at the Council of Vienne, has loosed slanderous tongues.

That is why my master preferred me not to translate the book myself.

Yes, this is what he ought to have told Bernard. But is it the truth?

Humbert steps out into the narrow alley outside his old friend's building. He treads carefully. Days of icy rain have transformed the ground into a slippery cesspool. The filthy weather and gloomy light are oppressive, just like the feeling of guilt that he cannot shake.

When Brother Jean pulled the manuscript from under his straw mattress, Humbert did not even let him speak. He protested, got to his feet, and would have left if he were not faced by an old scrawny man, now so weak he could not leave his bed and had to be wiped clean like a baby. His mind is also fading. More and more often, he seems to be absent, as if lost deep within himself, or somewhere else, in a place that Humbert cannot imagine, no longer wanting to communicate with the outside world.

However, Brother Jean had not forgotten his plan. He possessed perhaps the only existing copy of *The Mirror of Simple Souls.* Marguerite had written it in the common tongue so it would be accessible to everybody, but this dialect was only comprehensible in northern France, where it was banned. The text was in danger of disappearing for good. But if it were translated into Latin, it might be sent to more welcoming regions, to communities more receptive to its message, who would conserve and transmit the book.

'It is too soon, Brother Jean. It is dangerous.'

'It is not too soon, and you know it. Little time remains for me to accomplish my promise.'

'Why such obstinacy? The Inquisitor has threatened anybody possessing or circulating *The Mirror.* You know what that means. The danger we are running.'

'You do not understand, I know. But I beg you to do this for me. You will be the legs I no longer have, the eyes I lack.

I cannot force you. Accept this task only if you think you owe it to me.'

And, of course, Humbert thought that he owed it to him.

*

In Cock-Tugger street, a girl leaning in the doorway of her hovel calls out to him. She is still young, almost a child, her breasts tight against the red dress whose open laces show off her skin. But the excitement he felt a few days ago, at being back in the place where he spent his ardent youth, has disappeared. He is no longer the man he was in those days, other than in dreams.

I must think, Humbert tells himself when he reaches the noisy artery that the Grande rue Saint-Denis traces across the city. There must be other clerks who would accept the work. Paris is a belly that digests everything—even a heretical manuscript. Perhaps he should go back to Bernard. Despite the depths he has fallen to, he must still have some contacts in the world of copyists. He might give him guidance in exchange for a few more coins. But not now. The thought of going back to that attic makes his body recoil.

Better for him to concentrate on Brother Jean's other request. It is less important, but if Humbert could bring him back that satisfaction at least! He has not put much energy into it. Since his failure at the Royal Beguinage, he has continued to look for the Redhead, though with little enthusiasm and less success. He visited the small beguinage near the Cordelier monastery where he knows the mistress. She was not able to help but promised to ask around. He has also knocked on the doors of the other smaller and less organized beguinages scattered throughout the city. In vain. But that still leaves all the informal communities, 'good women' who share houses or live on the same street and support each other. Until now, preferring to spend his time receiving instruction from the Franciscans, he has been content with waiting for one or another of his contacts to come forward.

Despite the late hour, goaded by the unpleasant feeling of his impotence, at the Saint-Denis gate Humbert takes a dark alley that runs along the city walls to meet rue Quincampoix and the textile district. Why not? There are many beguines among the weavers, drapers and haberdashers here. He discreetly scrutinizes everyone he passes in the street, stops at counters, pretending to be interested in the exhibited goods while glancing surreptitiously into the shops behind. He ducks down the rue Aubry-le-Boucher but comes up against the Innocentes cemetery, so turns around and retraces his steps, starting to have doubts about his search. How to find a woman in this dark anthill where the shadows throng and mingle so confusingly?

Night falls. The sellers' cries grow more insistent. They will be closing their shutters soon. Humbert soldiers on amid the din, shouldering through the press of people hurrying to make their purchases before going home. He crosses the rue Saint-Martin once more, loses his bearings, and then reaches rue Troussevache.

Is it God or the devil guiding his steps? He does not yet know it, but this time chance is smiling on him.

8

JUST AS THE FRANCISCAN arrives in the quarter of Jeanne du Faut's shop, the bells of Notre-Dame start to ring for vespers. This is the signal for the spinners to put down their spindles and the embroiderers their needles. On Saturdays and the eves of feast days they finish work earlier than on ordinary days, which in winter see them still labouring as night falls. All the silk workshops crammed in on both sides of the well-maintained road close their shutters. But in Jeanne du Faut's house, all is not running according to the normal schedule. The mistress is furious. In the back of her shop, a fat girl stands gawping helplessly back at her, while Beatrice la Grande brandishes a silk swatch, the object of their quarrel.

'This is not the thread I gave you!'

'But it is. The very same.'

Maheut is keeping her distance, but she knows what the argument is about. This is not the first time that Beatrice has questioned the quality of the work brought back by Basile, the spinner from Rue de la Four. And the cloth brought back this evening, when it is too dark to check it except by oil lamp, seems particularly suspect.

It's a well-known trick. A silk dealer supplies raw silk thread to a spinner, so she can weave it into cloth for a fee. But the spinner then pawns the thread and buys some more, of lesser quality, to work with, hoping that the substitution will not be noticed.

Jeanne du Faut takes the swatch from Beatrice's hand, feels it, rubs it between her fingers, rolls it between her palms, like when you knead dough into a ball before flattening it out with the rolling pin. Then she holds it out to Juliotte, who has just come out of the kitchen, curious as to the reason for the delay in closing the shop. The mute girl takes the cloth between her fingertips but quickly gives it back, shaking her head. She does not want to get involved.

'This silk is not so fine or supple,' says Jeanne du Faut angrily.

'I assure you it is the same.'

'How can you claim to be a beguine and lie like that? You shame every one of us!'

Juliotte recoils. She does not like arguments, as Maheut has already noticed. When the girls in the house bicker, she usually turns her back on them. But if Dame du Faut raises her voice, she seems terrified, as if she were being torn away from all the small tasks that bring harmony to life, and cast into chaos.

Now Juliotte is beyond hope. She does not dare go back to the kitchen to prepare their evening meal, nor go up to the workshop, where she would in any case have to take care of Leonor, whom the embroiderers often forget in her corner because she is so quiet. So instead Juliotte goes to the unattended sales window and begins to gather up the merchandise exhibited there, starting with the small pieces, fearing that a thief might take advantage of the darkness to run off with them—alms purses, belts, gloves, and all kinds of embroidered accessories, trimmings and ribbons studded with pearls.

Maheut watches Juliotte for a moment then tears herself away from the spectacle of Jeanne and Basile's argument to help her. Without thinking anything of it, Maheut steps outside to bring in the swatches of lesser quality displayed at the edges of the stall.

*

Maheut has not set foot outside since the day Ysabel came to warn them that a man was looking for her. On Jeanne's orders, she has kept to the back of the shop, even when the merchant of Lucca appears, whom she knows now and with whom she has begun to exchange a few words, marvelling to see him slip between French and Italian like a bow slipping over the strings of a viol. She has remained prudently withdrawn.

She has guessed who the Franciscan Ysabel told them about must be. One of those preachers close to the beguines for whose sake her mother had turned her back on the world—and on her child. But time has passed since Ysabel's warning. Two weeks, broken up only by household tasks. Giacomo came back, bringing with him some elaborately embroidered borders known as orphreys, purchased from a dealer in Flanders. Maheut left the shadows then, eager to see these splendours that any silk apprentice—as he had called her—should know: braids of multicoloured silk, chequered like a chessboard, embroidered with gold thread and studded with cabochons, pearls and sapphires, so heavy that they can be sewn only onto the collars of ceremonial robes. Maheut admired them, certainly, but they did not provoke in her the emotion she could see in Jeanne's eyes. And so the merchant put one of the orphreys in her hands, and it is as if he had given her the reins of a horse.

Nobody could reproach a young girl, whatever her past, for wanting to forget it, to enjoy the slim pleasures of the present. The Franciscan was still somewhere in the back of her mind, but soon she rarely thought of him, only feeling the prick of her worries, as we all do, when lying in bed, drifting towards the vague world of dreams. There is just one question that nags at her: how did her mother learn that she now wears the habit of a beguine, and what does she think of it? Perhaps she tells herself that her daughter, now reformed and following in her own footsteps, will be more docile in future. What a joke!

*

So it is without a second thought that Maheut leaves the shop that Saturday, a little after the start of vespers.

Inside, Jeanne du Faut is threatening Basile. 'Do you want me to summon the guild officers so that they can expel you?'

Maheut's hair is bound tighter than ever in its concealing scarf. But Humbert is very close. His eyes, flitting between the last few women in the street outside the shops, is first drawn to the strong body under the austere robe in which the girl is dressed. Then to the lively motion with which she sweeps up the swatches from the stall. In the gathering darkness, her pale, exposed hands stand out more than they would in the light of day. Maheut turns her head at last, feeling the weight of his gaze upon her. He recognizes her then, and in the same instant she suddenly recalls the tall figure she used to see, always in the background but ever-present, when Marguerite Porete and Jean de Querayn visited her mother in their château.

9

AGNES IS NOT AS SEVERE as people say, thinks Clémence. The reclining girl closes her eyes as the beguine gently massages her face and neck with a fragrant oil. Despite her discomfort, Clémence surrenders to the rhythmic pressure that relaxes and warms her muscles. She slept badly last night. And this morning the migraine gripped her head again. Each day it gets worse.

'This should do you good,' says Agnes softly. 'Oil of borage, mixed with aloe juice and essence of lavender.' She does not say what else she added to the remedy, which she learnt from Ysabel: finely ground flowers of mallow and sage. Perhaps the herbalist would not approve of this addition, but, since she sometimes uses the flowers in her own poultices to relieve headaches, Agnes does not see how they can do any harm. And Clémence seems better already.

'You are simply tired. I think you ought to rest today.'

The girl twitches, as if about to make a gesture of refusal, but then lies still. Agnes knows her well and has understood what is bothering her.

*

The two women have been living together for more than six months now. Since Clémence was too young to live alone in one of the Beguinage's houses—according to the institution's rules but also to her parents' wishes—she slept in the dormitory in the common house at first, along with the girls of her own age. She was happy there to begin with, the youthful atmosphere reminding her of the games and laughter of childhood. But after a while she began to feel that among all the sisters in the Beguinage, she and her dormitory companions were a rather undistinguished flock.

Between attendance at daily masses, religious instruction delivered by the mistress, and the household tasks she was supposed to perform, and which others used to do *for her*, like taking care of her laundry and her bed, the little girl had ended up feeling bored. She rarely had the opportunity to join the older beguines and share their conversations, and she was not used to such impediments. As for Ade, whose perfection had brought her to this place like a wren drawn to the sun, Clémence was barely able to approach her. During her first Latin class, Ade did in fact recognize her as the daughter of the Crété woman whom she had cared for a year earlier, and greeted her courteously. But that was all.

So when Agnes asked Clémence to move into her new, more comfortable house, where she dwells thanks to her allowance from her Dominican cousin, the girl agreed right away. What Agnes expects from their living together is another story. But this change has not brought Clémence the satisfaction she was hoping for, despite the fact that Ade is closer now, living in the house opposite.

'I do not know how to explain it to you, Dame Agnes. I thought I was going to learn how to become an accomplished woman here. But instead I feel I am constantly showing myself to be stupid and muddleheaded.'

'Why do you say that?'

'You saw it yourself yesterday, during the supper that Dame Ysabel had the goodness to invite me and you to attend. I was chattering away like a crazy magpie.'

'Oh don't worry, Ysabel is used to chatter. She has even been known to indulge in it herself.'

Clémence does not hear her. She is deep in thought.

'But Dame Ade was irritated… She seems dissatisfied with me. She constantly corrects me in class.'

'She only wants to help you improve.'

'She seems so cold.'

'It is her nature. It is said she never got over the death of her husband, and since then she has avoided being touched by any sentiment other than the love of Christ. Which is admirable. She is not close to anybody here.'

Agnes reaches for the phial containing her preparation. The oil is a lovely golden yellow, but the crushed flowers are beginning to form a deposit at the bottom. She coats her hands in the oil and resumes massaging Clémence's forehead and temples with patient circular movements.

'You ought to visit your mother. That would do you good.'

'Would you accompany me?'

'Of course. But you could also invite Dame Ade. It would allow her to see you in the world that is familiar to you and where, I am sure, you are more at ease than you are here.'

'What a good idea! I might show her my father's books. I am sure she would like them. He has a whole library of them, and some are very precious.'

Clémence breaks off, then carries on in a grave tone.

'She reads so much. I would dearly love to know Latin as well as she does! I am sure that she could help me. But she treats me like just one student among all the others.'

'Books are not everything, Clémence.'

'I don't know. Sometimes, looking at her, it seems to me that they do hold a secret.'

*

While the little girl sleeps, Agnes goes down to her kitchen. The room is smaller than Ysabel's workshop but the adjoining cellar can hold many supplies. This is Agnes's domain. She believes in keeping herself to herself—and bizarrely even *from* herself. She sometimes wonders if the art of making powders and ointments counts as witchcraft. But she has long given up hoping, as poor Clémence still does, for change to come into her life simply because she desires it.

The dumbstruck admiration the child has for Ade! Like everyone here, she has been conquered by the woman's cold beauty, by her apparent piety and erudition, and by the way she holds herself at a distance from all the other beguines—all except for Ysabel, for whom she makes a great exception. When Agnes thinks that in all these years she has never been invited into Ade's home—despite her own timid hints, of which she is ashamed now.

Mourning is a fine excuse, but it is pride that devours Ade's soul. And contempt. It is easy to live as you wish when you are the widow of a knight who died for the king's glory. In that, Ysabel and Ade recognize what they have in common; they belong to the same caste.

The infirmarer talks endlessly of solidarity, of charity. But she will never let her assistant forget the dishonour that stained her household. The support of Geoffroy hardly seems to impress her, despite his growing power among the Dominicans thanks to his closeness to the Inquisitor. When Agnes suggested that she take over some infirmary responsibilities, Ysabel did not refuse. She now gives her a little more latitude, but in reality has not handed over any important decision-making.

Agnes pushes open the cellar door. By chance it is not humid. The smell of camphor and herbs fills the kitchen. The earthy, invigorating scent helps her recover. The science of plants is a power. She sees it at work every day in the indulgence with which everyone here treats the infirmarer, despite her advancing age that makes her slower and less effective. And this power, for now at least, is all that Agnes can claim.

10

M AHEUT HAS NOT PASSED through the Beguinage gate
since the day when, pregnant, she left for the Silk House,
guided by Ade. For her part, Dame du Faut has not come to visit
for a long while either. She has few friends there, apart from
Ysabel. These days she devotes all her energy to the small circle
that has grown up around her business.

When the two women present themselves at the gate,
Guillaumette does not recognize them. Her eyesight has grown
weak. It happened slowly: a sort of fog has slipped between herself
and the people around her, blurring their faces. From a distance
she can only recognize her companions by their gaits and their
voices. Her mother suffered from the same malady. She knows
what is coming. So does Ysabel, who has given up treating her.

When the visitors come closer and she can finally make out
their faces, the concierge recognizes only Jeanne du Faut. How
could she imagine that the figure hidden under a cape at her side
is none other than the flame-haired pauper taken in from outside
her gate the year before? Caught up in the surprise of seeing the
cloth merchant and the pleasure of welcoming her, Guillaumette
only gives the other woman a cursory greeting. Then she sends
her young girl assistant to look for Ysabel, who must have gone
back to the infirmary after Sunday Mass.

The old beguine's door is never bolted. But Jeanne prefers to
wait outside despite the light drizzle dampening her cape. The

smell of mud mingles with the mineral scent of rain falling on stone. The Seine is swollen from all the storms of recent weeks, and its waters are lapping over its grassy banks. Jeanne has not forgotten those winters she lived here when the river would overflow right up to the Beguinage courtyard, seeping under the doors of the houses, filling cellars and wells with dirty, muddy water. The Beguinage was built near the banks of the Seine, in a bend of the river that was once marshland. But the site has its advantages. Although the Beguinage stands on the ecclesiastical lands of the Benedictine Abbey of Tiron, the city walls at its back have long sheltered it from the authority of the church and nobility, leaving it solely under royal oversight. King Louis chose the spot for this reason—to ensure that the institution had total independence, both financial and religious. Not only was it exempt from certain taxes, the women who lived within its walls were also free to confide their pastoral care to whichever confessors or priests they chose.

'Our benefactor thought of everything, except giving us good brooms,' Ysabel would say with a laugh, as the two of them, the hems of their robes tucked up into their belts, their shoes soaking wet, tried to push back the muddy puddles seeping into the kitchen despite the cloths jammed under the door.

Despite her worries, Jeanne feels her heart softened by these memories. She spent some fine times here, in this peaceful place, free of everyday concerns and secure in the goodwill of most if not all of her companions. She got over the death of her husband and grew used to the idea of being a widow. But she also tasted an unexpected and exhilarating nectar.

In this Beguinage, within this community of unfettered women, there was a freedom that she had never known before. The duties of a wife, to ensure the orderly running of a perfect home; the debt of love and obedience—the two sentiments were often confused—she owed first to her father and then her husband… These had been constraints that she could no longer bear. Until then she had only ever had authority over her own household. The Beguinage had given her a desire for more.

But she has never regretted leaving. She found in the silk trade a focus for her energy and an outlet for her initiative. Today she is a key figure in this cosmopolitan industry that is breathing new life into the kingdom's cities, producing and selling, importing new techniques. She rubs shoulders with the nobility and the most important people in the city, even in the kingdom. Countess Mahaut of Artois makes a point of summoning Jeanne to her residence whenever she is in Paris, for the silk merchant to display her most precious articles. She receives orders from the court of Flanders. She is an officer of her guild, and recently joined the most eminent cloth merchants in Paris in the confraternity of Saint-Sépulcre, which has several chapels inside the church on the avenue Saint-Denis, where it has decked out the clergy in sumptuous liturgical vestments.

Is it committing the sin of pride to take pleasure in these achievements? Is it vanity to want to protect a position that enables her to support dozens of less well-off women?

Jeanne wraps herself in her cloak. Her worries take hold of her once more. Her gaze slips away from the neat rows of houses lining the courtyard, their outlines now blurred by the fine rain. At her side, she feels Maheut's body, stiffened by cold and by lack of sleep.

'Let us take shelter inside,' she sighs. The girl pushes open the door. Soon the smells of the outdoors are replaced by the scent of woodsmoke and bitter herbs, awakening in both of them a comforting sense of security.

Ysabel arrives soon afterwards. When she comes into the kitchen and sees them sitting there, the colour drains from her face.

'Leonor?'

Jeanne understands her friend's anxiety and rushes to reassure her.

'She is well, do not worry.'

'Seeing you both…'

Ysabel breaks off and drops onto the bench near the chimney. Her robe and face are wet. It seems she rushed back to the house without taking the time to put on her cloak. Her dishevelled hair sticks out from under her headdress. She seems to have neglected herself as she often does, but neither Jeanne nor Maheut, unlike Agnes, would call her old. She looks at them with a questioning air, then gets up and goes towards her cellar.

'First, a drink to restore our spirits. Then you can tell me what brings you here.'

It takes Jeanne very little time to recount the story, so reluctant is she to go into details. She does not know which feeling holds sway inside her. Anger, fear or disgust.

'So he is still in Paris,' sighs Ysabel, putting three goblets of mead on the table.

'I did not think he would stay on so long…' Turning to Maheut, she asks, 'What does he want, exactly?'

The girl does not answer. In a few hours she has gone from incredulity to despondency. She has spent the whole night reproaching herself. Why did she leave the shop? And why at that very moment? Once more, she sees the imposing figure advance towards her and call her by her name: 'Maheut the Redhead!' She backed away, the swatches pressed to her chest, her eyes fixed on those of the man she had just recognized—two black holes under the shadow of the hood—and stumbled over the shop doorstep, just as a small hand gripped her elbow—it was Juliotte, who placed herself in front of Maheut before backing away in turn.

Jeanne continues: 'When I saw the Franciscan enter the shop, I was shocked at first. It is rare for monks to visit us. I thought that he must be looking for someone he knew. And indeed that was the case.'

'Do you know who is living with you?' he asked, jerking his chin at Maheut. He did not speak loudly, but the tone was unambiguous.

'He spoke more harshly than when he came to the Beguinage,' added Jeanne. 'He denounced Maheut as a fugitive and said she was responsible for her mother's poor health.'

Cut to the quick, Maheut finds her voice again. 'Guillebert is threatening to take his anger out on my family. My brother promised he would find me, and he is tired of waiting.'

'I do not understand why a Franciscan is mixed up in an affair more suitable for a provost,' Ysabel remarks.

'Brother Humbert is close to Jean de Querayn, my mother's confessor. She asked him to help her. And he set his disciple on my trail.' Her tone is bitter. 'A fine idea of charity!'

'If I were you, I would be less impertinent,' Jeanne du Faut cuts in. 'Men may be about to fight each other because of your behaviour.'

Silence falls in the room. Outside the rain strikes the paving stones in the courtyard.

'He gave us two days to reflect,' resumes Jeanne in a more measured tone. 'He is returning to Valenciennes to celebrate the Festival of the Nativity and suggests he take Maheut along with him.'

'And if not...'

'If not, he will denounce the girl—and me along with her.'

Jeanne does not say any more, but Ysabel is aware of the risks her friend is running. What would people say if they found out the cloth merchant Jeanne du Faut of rue Troussevache was sheltering a false widow and a child stolen from its father in her house? Her position and connections would not protect her for long. Some envious souls would be only too happy to drag her through the mud—this woman whose success has left them in the shadows. And others would be happier still to find a new reason to denounce the beguine community.

I put her in this situation and I must get her out of it, thinks the old beguine. But how? If La Chanevacière were still alive, Ysabel would not hesitate to ask for her advice. The old mistress would surely have played on her relations with the Franciscans to win them a little time. But La Bricharde has neither the understanding nor the practical intelligence of her predecessor. She is happier with books.

The visitors sitting opposite her are waiting for her to speak. Ysabel knows the glazed look in Maheut's eyes well. A viper ready to strike. Jeanne merely seems overwhelmed. Then Ysabel breaks the silence without knowing quite where her words are leading.

'When did you say the Franciscan would come back?'

'In two days.'

'Very well. When he arrives, send him to me.'

Maheut leans over the wooden trestle. 'What are you going to say to him?'

'Don't worry. I will not let him take you away. You and Leonor.'

When the two women leave the house a few minutes later, Ysabel is already reproaching herself for this hasty promise. Brother Humbert, as she knew at first sight, is not a man to let himself be outmanoeuvred.

11

A DE REMEMBERS THE EXACT INSTANT when her heart toppled. The baby was barely a day old. The night before, Ade had witnessed its birth, terrified. As the child's first wails rang out in the stuffy room and Maheut's cries of pain began to abate, they held out the little bundle of linen to her. She couldn't take it.

And then they had celebrated the baptism, an intimate ceremony at Saint-Eustache. After the ablution and invocation of the Trinity, Ysabel had presented the baby girl to her for the second time. Leonor had been calm throughout the ceremony, even at the touch of the ice-cold water. Ade held out her hands uncertainly, the child allowed itself to be taken in her arms, she tipped back the little head. And then, for a long moment, baby Leonor gazed up into her godmother's eyes.

The look in her eyes was not vague or confused, like that of a being just awakened to life; on the contrary, there was unmistakeable recognition in her eyes, and absolute trust. The look of a newborn at its mother. Only then, when she had been welcomed into the Church and the world—with all its many creatures and mysteries—did Leonor allowed her eyelids to close.

Of course, Ade had struggled against her instinct. It was an illusion, a siren's song. This baby girl was Maheut's. Her own baby had long ago left the world of the living. She was with the angels now. As Ade had lain recovering from the ordeal of the birth, her mother-in-law had reassured her that she had done all that was necessary. She had taken the tiny body, which the priest had not managed to baptize before its last breath, into her arms, and followed the healer woman to the sanctuary on the edge of the village. There she had placed it on the cold stone of the altar, lit candles around it and prayed for hours.

'Her skin suddenly turned pink,' she told Ade when, after days of fever, she was able to listen. 'The priest baptized her then, before she died again. We called her Marie in thanks to the mother of our crucified Lord.'

For the first time since she had known her, her mother-in-law looked at Ade with compassion.

Now her daughter has a name and a sepulchre in the family chapel. She dances with the elect in heaven. She is not one of the sad souls wandering in Limbo, where the priests say that unbaptized little ones go. Sheltered from the torments of hell but unable to taste the happiness of paradise, blind because deprived of beatific vision, orphans for all eternity because after their own deaths their parents will never find them in this in-between of the beyond.

Leonor has grown, her face and body becoming firmer and more defined, like clay under the potter's fingers. Pale, with the creamy whiteness of her mother. Discreet splashes of red freckles on the inside of her thighs. But the confidence of her gaze remains. At only a few weeks old, when Ade entered the room where she was sleeping, the little girl would turn her head in her direction even before she spoke. She also has that particular way of lifting her hands towards Ade, palms upward, fingers twirling, moving gracefully through space—as if they were objects, independent of her body, at which she marvels. One day she put her index finger on Ade's cheek and it was as if she had blessed her.

Ade will never let anybody take her away.

*

'Sit down, Ade. Rest and gather your strength. We will need it.'

Ade stops pacing and sits on the bench near the hearth. Ysabel has put another log on the fire. It was raining when Jeanne and Maheut came here two days ago too. The man who has caused them so much torment will arrive under the same hostile sky.

The old beguine casts a worried glance at her friend, but she seems calmer. Perhaps it is a good thing that Ade insisted on being present. Who knows what might come of it? Ysabel pulls a few springs of fennel and anise from the bunch intended for the infirmary, throws them in the fire, sits at Ade's side. And so they wait, listening to the dry herbs crackle in the flames.

The three strokes of midday sound as Humbert knocks on the door. He enters along with the rain, which has soaked his cloak. If he is surprised to see Ade he does not show it. He barely looks around. Just stays standing by the door, a puddle growing at his feet.

'Sit down so we can talk more easily,' suggests Ysabel. 'And take off that cloak before you catch cold.'

The man takes off his cloak and holds it out to the beguine, who hangs it near the fire. He sits at the table, but he refuses the drink she offers. Ade gets up from the bench to come close to Ysabel. Now both of them are sitting opposite Humbert.

The Franciscan's eyes are gleaming, with dark circles under them. Tired, or feverish perhaps, Ysabel thinks. His face seems more angular than last time. The aquiline nose, the high cheek-bones. The odour of damp wool that he brings with him is mixed with another smell, that of sweat.

He lets a minute go by, then strikes.

'As you know, Dame Ysabel, since you suggested it yourself, I have come to you because I was sent here by Jeanne du Faut. She claims you are responsible for Maheut.'

'I took her in and cared for her. Yes, I am responsible for her.'

'So you should be happy that I propose to take her back to her family.'

'What does her husband say about it?'

'Her husband has been waiting for her a long time.'

'But in what state of mind?'

'Let us say that he is ready, if she makes a sincere apology, to pardon her bad conduct. Especially now that he is a father. If the child is indeed his.'

His lips stretch into a thin smile, but then freeze.

'You forget yourself!' Ysabel snaps. 'I am not sure that Jean de Querayn would appreciate that remark. Remember you are speaking about a young woman of good family.'

Humbert leans back on the bench. He has begun with a faux pas. He came to claim a right and now finds himself reprimanded like a child. It is this place, this stifling room in which every nook is crammed with jars, flasks and bunches of strong-smelling herbs. This old woman, with her strange eyes that do not stop at the surface of your being but scratch down below it. He is also embarrassed by Ade's presence. She has remained silent during this exchange, sitting upright with hands pressed on the table. He can feel their tension through the wood.

The Franciscan tries again.

'Dame Ysabel, pardon my impudence, but I did not come to discuss the child's parentage, as you know. Maheut hardly has a choice. She should go back to her husband's home. He is readying an army to attack her family's lands.'

'A private war? You know the king has forbidden them.'

'That means nothing to our provincial nobles. They follow their own law. One based on their honour.'

'The honour of abducting a young girl to force her into marriage?'

'She should not have refused the role her brother chose for her.'

'The consent of the spouses is the foundation of marriage.'

'The parents' consent is worth that of the daughter. And it does not matter now. The marriage was consummated and a child is the proof. It is indissoluble.'

*

Ade follows the conversation in a sort of daze, with the strange feeling that it has happened once before. But at the time it was she, not Humbert, who was quarrelling with Ysabel. She feels useless, without the strength to fight this disagreeable man, even to defend Leonor. What kind of blood runs in her veins? God must have known about her lack of courage. This is why He took Marie away from her.

She pales at this thought. Humbert notices the change and is troubled by it. He too is exhausted. He has been wandering the streets for days searching for a copyist suggested by Bernard, visiting low taverns and filthy hovels. But his old friend's directions were worth no more than his work. Yesterday, Humbert got lost in the labyrinth of paupers' shacks beyond the Saint-Denis gate. After walking up endless blind alleys, by the time he made it back to the city gates they were closed. In the end he had to share a straw mattress with a couple of dirty, sickly day labourers from Burgundy in a freezing inn on the city's outskirts.

'Abduction is just as forbidden as private wars,' Ysabel goes on. 'Whatever the nobility of your province may think. You may tell Guillebert that, if necessary, we will bring the affair before the king's court.'

To hell with Guillebert, thinks Humbert. With his wife gone, the fat swine is busy impregnating the servants on his estate. So why does he need a Franciscan to defend his interests for him? Not to mention Maheut's brother, who couldn't even manage to flush her out! Yet here Humbert is, sweating his own blood for these nobles who have neither the courage nor the ability to be worthy of the name.

Ysabel sees the determination flagging in the eyes of her adversary. He is like a soldier, still wielding his weapon although his spirit quit the field of battle long ago. His forehead is damp, the hollows of his eyes deeper than when he arrived.

She rises and, without asking if Humbert wants one, brings him a goblet of wine. He empties it in one gulp, a faraway look in his eyes. He is thinking about Brother Jean. Of the hand he took in his own when he left to go back to the capital. Bony, and so light. He left with a heavy heart, torn between irritation at the old man and the fear of never seeing him again. Now he is dreading going back and telling him of his double failure. For he senses that this woman is not about to yield. What can he do? Denounce a beguine of the Royal Beguinage? Brother Jean would reproach him more for that than for returning without the Redhead. No, the only way to make her bend is to threaten Jeanne du Faut.

The alcohol starts to have its effect. Warmth spreads through his body, frozen since yesterday, from his throat down to his stomach. Across the table from him, Ade's hands are clasped in a gesture of prayer. Why does she seem so affected? It is hard to imagine she feels any deep affection for Maheut. The pale hands unclasp and come to rest on the tabletop, trembling slightly. He remembers how gracefully they turned the illuminated pages of the psalter on the day he saw her teaching. And with what assuredness, in the moment he left the room with La Bricharde, she had taken the stylus from a pupil's hand to correct a word on her wax tablet.

Ysabel is still talking, reciting her litany. But Humbert is no longer listening. An idea germinates in his mind. He lets it grow, refines it. Yes, he knows what must be done.

12

CURSES, THEY SAY, like exorcisms or healing charms, work by repetition. The words start to have an effect when you speak them over and over again. Ysabel's grandmother, when making use of her powers as a healer, used to repeatedly list each part of the sickly body that must be protected, even going into further detail if needed. The head, and its forehead, its eyes, its eyebrows, its lips, its chin… she would whisper as she applied a poultice to treat a migraine. Nine sister glands, eight sister glands, seven sister glands… she sang to accompany a concoction served to a bilious patient, chanting a decreasing series of numbers to weaken the illness to the point of eradicating it.

No doubt, the old beguine tells herself as the year draws to an end, somebody has used an incantation of the same kind to weaken and dismember the great body of ecclesiastics gathered in council at Vienne. One hundred and fourteen major and minor prelates and all sorts of emissaries assembled on the first day of October 1311 in the great church of the city in Provence. On 7th December, Cardinal Albano died in Lucca. On the 9th day of the same month, Cardinal Suizy died in turn. Then the bishops of Tusculum and Sabine fell seriously ill. A rumour is spreading through Paris: a prophet has predicted that ten cardinals will die before Easter, not counting, he added, 'one that I dare not name', no doubt meaning the pope, who is also suffering from a sickness in his stomach. Everyone is agreed: more than at the bishops and pontiff, the curse is aimed at Philip the Fair, who forced the pope to convoke this assembly. And those behind the witchcraft must surely be the Templars.

In the Great Beguinage, news of the Council arrives bit by bit. The mistress, kept up to date by the Dominican prior whose couriers are almost as fast as the king's, remains discreet, even with respect to the wise women on her own council. So Ysabel has reluctantly resorted to asking Agnes, who is informed of the latest goings-on by Geoffroy, for news. Her assistant deplores the obstacles that are delaying Philip's plans. But each new delay is a source of comfort to the infirmarer.

This was the only concession she has obtained from Humbert: that he wait until the Council has concluded, and with it this perilous time for the Beguinage, before acting.

*

December is coming to an end, and with it the novena before Noel, nine days of fasting and prayer. While in the countryside the peasants sacrifice pigs and finish threshing the grain stored in sheaves, the beguines prepare for the happiest event in the holy year. The dormitory and houses are decorated with holly and armfuls of greenery; the women set aside their old clothing and don new garments; the Nativity Mass is celebrated in the dead of night, followed by a copious torchlit feast, enlivened by songs and a little dancing too.

January passes. In Vienne, the affair still drags on in speeches. It seems that a growing number of prelates are showing support for the Templar Order. Almost all the bishops, apart from those of France, who are subject to the will of the king unless they wish to risk his anger, have declared in a secret vote that the Templars have the right to a new trial and new defenders. It is said everyone in the city is complaining. Chosen by the pope because it was secure and well-fortified, the town of Vienne lacks the means to host such an influx of cardinals, bishops, abbots, foreign delegations, secretaries, servants… The cathedral where the plenary meetings are held is not even finished. The attendees are crammed in, bored and cold. No matter, they will have to put up with a long winter there.

Ysabel is reassured. With so many divergent interests involved, who can say how long the Council will go on? It could last for months more. But suddenly everything starts to move faster. From far away, the hunter king has long spied, manoeuvred, and threatened. Now, step by step he is moving southward: first Gien and Cluny, and then Mâcon. A month later, he is laying ambush in Lyon. The kill cannot be long in coming. After having sent his advisors ahead of him as emissaries, including the redoubtable Guillaume de Nogaret, Philip enters Vienne on 20th March, accompanied by his two brothers, his three sons, delegates from the kingdom's religious orders, a full retinue of nobles and the powerful, and dozens of soldiers. From the city's narrow streets to the naves of its churches, its sharply sloping roofs to its dark encircling walls and as far as the icy slopes of the hills beyond to which it clings—everywhere resounds to the clatter of hooves and the cries of men.

*

Is it a sign? The very day that Philip the Fair orders the gates of the city opened to him as master—or else the next day at dawn, nobody can say—without any warning, La Bricharde dies in her sleep. Her old servant discovers her, hands crossed and face calm, she will say, like a recumbent statue, as if she were already received into the Lord's kingdom. The chapel bell, which was not able to accompany the mistress's death throes, announces her death in the early morning, its sad tolling drawing sleepers from their beds.

Less than two years after the death of La Chanevacière, the beguines are back in the familiar rhythm of the funeral. The Beguinage moves at a different pace from the outside world now. Their hoods thrown back, each carrying a tall candle, like the ghosts of a procession from another time, the women accompany the deceased along the merchants' embankment, across the Place de Grève, then the Pont aux Changeurs bridge, past the shadow of the Sainte-Chapelle and the Petit Châtelet, and then up rue Saint-Jacques to reach the Jacobin church.

Jeanne la Bricharde is buried according to her last wishes, in front of the organ in the nave, alongside Agnes d'Orchies, one of the first mistresses of the Beguinage, who was appointed by Louis IX himself. On her tombstone, Agnes is depicted with joined hands, her face marked by age, surrounded by the silhouettes of six beguines bearing psalters. The flagstone prepared for Jeanne in the sculptors' workshop will render the same homage to her piety and learning by showing her armed with a rosary and a book, trampling on a baleful dragon.

By the time the Beguinage comes back to life, it is all over. On 3rd April 1311, Vienne Cathedral holds a general session that assembles all the participants in the Council, with Philip the Fair seated at the pontiff's right, with his brother Charles and his barons at his side. The Templar Order is dissolved and a Crusade promised for the coming year. But decisions concerning the moral reform of the Church have been mostly postponed. And no decree concerning the beguines has been published.

*

For Ysabel and Ade now begins the time of waiting. Every day, they expect to receive the announcement of Humbert's return. Ade tries to calm her anguish by visiting her goddaughter at the Silk House. Maheut, informed of the bargain they have made, does not even thank her. Ade sometimes wonders if she is aware of the sacrifice she has consented to, to the danger to which she is exposed. But the Redhead has doubtless understood something else too: Ade is taking this risk only for Leonor.

Meanwhile Ysabel can't stop thinking back to the moment when the tables were turned. The humiliation remains crushing. She was so sure of having defeated the Franciscan! She struck down his arguments with increasing assurance, expecting him to yield at any moment. And then he broke his silence with that odious blackmail.

'Ade is not a copyist,' Ysabel protested.

'Could you do it?' Humbert asked, turning to the young woman. She acquiesced with a nod of her head.

'Very well. The bargain is made.'

To let Maheut leave was to lose Leonor. Worse, it would mean abandoning a girl to whom Ysabel had promised her protection. The Franciscan was right. The confrontation was over; he had won. He would say nothing about the Redhead, but as soon as the Council concluded, he would bring them Marguerite's manuscript. And Ade would translate it.

*

The days flow by and the letter does not come. Ysabel finds peace in her garden, watching the movements of the heavens: the sun that climbs and shines before sinking once more, draws the plants from the earth before letting it sleep; the air—now dry, now humid; the whirl of winds blowing from the four corners of the earth, aqueous or darkly brooding, now aery, now hard like the tendon of an ankle; the phases of the moon, mother of all weather, that waxes and wanes, and along with it the blood in the bodies of living creatures as well as their other humours, milk and bone marrow.

The cycle begins again. The quivering down of the spring has already yielded to summer's vigour. Ysabel plants her feet in the soil of her herb garden and hoes the fragrant earth. The borage is in flower. Amid the thick, wrinkled leaves, the star-shaped petals shine with a strange blue that draws the eye like the glimmer of a glow-worm.

Humbert does not come.

The ageing leaves of autumn begin to tremble. The first cold snaps numb the city.

Still Humbert does not come.

Part Three

May 1313 to May 1315

'In this time, the beguines no longer sang, no longer read.'

Memoriale historiarum
JEAN DE SAINT-VICTOR

1

T HIS MAY MORNING, Ade wakes filled with joy; for some time
now, it has taken only a ray of sunlight, the trill of a bird.
Ysabel would tell her that it is because of the spring. The sweetness of the air, the sheets and eiderdowns hung to air from the
windows, the fresh herbs scattered on the floors. But in fact the
source of her happiness is more personal. A week ago, Leonor,
whose name (so justly chosen) means 'to soften', gave her a present.

Ade sees the little girl every week. Leonor will soon be three
years old. The young woman expected Maheut to slowly bond
with her child, to eventually see how special she was, and for
Leonor's sake she hoped it would happen. But it didn't. The
Redhead spends her days in the shop where she acts as Béatrice
la Grande's assistant, even helping with sales, and leaves the
care of her child to others. So Ade's back-and-forth between the
Beguinage and the Silk House continues.

Leonor still does not speak and does not grow—or at least
only very slowly. Her thin face is filled by big eyes of the same
colour as Maheut's—green, but a moist, almost liquid green, like
seaweed under water that takes on tints of azure blue or barky
brown in the shifting sunlight. Leonor moves clumsily too, and
spends most of the time sitting on the workshop floor. All her
grace and dexterity seem concentrated in her hands, which she
still waves about, making them dance in the air, telling stories
with them that her tongue refuses to speak.

Ysabel prepares stimulating broths for her, with nutmeg and iris roots. She has entrusted Juliotte with a phial of invigorating oil infused with sage and fennel flowers. After each of her baths in the little tub next to the kitchen chimney, the mute girl massages the child's arms and legs. They are delicate under her fingers, the muscles tender, yet they do not feel sluggish to Juliotte, but rather full of energy.

Sometimes, Juliotte wonders if she could be responsible for Leonor's silence. Memories she thought she had forgotten sometimes resurface. She has not always been mute; she spoke until the age of ten, but her speech limped along like a cripple. She could not master her tongue and stammered as if she were drunk or mad, mispronouncing words so badly they sounded like gibberish. The parish priest tried to correct this affliction by stuffing her mouth with burning pebbles. As he blessed her, she spat them out, but it was only because of the pain—O God, what pain! She had meant no ill by it. She never spoke a word after that. The priest fell ill with a swollen throat, and some said that the mute girl had bewitched him. She was turned out of the village.

Recently Juliotte has been trying to make funny sounds with her lips and breath, hoping that Leonor will copy her. She rubs the child's mouth with salt gum and honey, but this remedy has no more power than the others. For Leonor is not sick. She simply needs someone to support her in her growth, just as a plant needs a stake to climb up.

*

A week ago Ade came by with a rag doll bought from a shop in a nearby street. The doll had poor clothes, a badly cut dress of washed-out fabric, but its main charm was its head of woollen hair, drawn up into a bun and concealed under a veil.

As usual, Leonor turned around when Ade entered the room. As usual, Ade sat at the window ledge with the child opposite her. Usually, after they had finished playing with the silk ribbons or the little tin tea set given by Ysabel, Ade would read the child prayers and the Sunday litany and show her the symbols of the apostles—taking care of her religious education as a godmother should. But this time, she held out the gift wrapped in a piece of cloth. The little girl unwrapped it, set the rag doll on her knees and turned it upside down to watch the dangling woollen hair go blond in the soft light coming through the oilcloth window blind. Turning the doll upright once more, she put a finger on its rag cheek and gazed at her young godmother. And then she said:

'Ade.'

*

When Clémence de Crété comes to the door, the young woman is still smiling over the memory of that little word, barely murmured but perfectly pronounced by the child.

For their outing together, Clémence has pulled out of her trunk a kirtle with stripes embroidered in gold thread and a cape of vibrant blue. A doubt crosses her mind when she sees her friend so sensibly attired in a cloak of light wool, but she sweeps it away by catching Ade under the arm and pulling her along. Ade lets Clémence lead her, happy to be stretching her legs with a companion who seems so in tune with the mood of the season and of the city.

She is fond of the girl. Clémence is everything Ade never was when she was younger. Full of life. Childlike despite her sixteen years. Affectionate, too, with such naturalness that it is difficult to resist her. At first Ade was exasperated by her slow, muddled mind, but her pupil is making a real effort to learn. A few months ago, the girl offered to help Ade teach the youngest girls how to read, and proved very patient at helping them decipher the letters. In exchange, Ade gives her private lessons in her room, where Clémence comes to practise Latin and learn how to write with quill and ink. It is a rude test for the girl's patience, hours of work only to trace a few clumsy lines, her tense hand clutching the quill, the ink leaking onto her skin. But she does not give up. Her mother, who regularly visits her at the Beguinage and sometimes attends her lessons, is astonished to see her so improved.

'You have transformed her,' she tells Ade gratefully.

And in fact it is Dame Alice they are to visit this morning. Ade, who has not been back to the Hôtel Crété for a long time, is happy to be going there now, on account of the house as much as the hostess. The two companions pass the Châtelet fortress and come to the Saint-Germain l'Auxerrois tower. They are following the same route Ade took three years before with Maheut. But of course the young widow is not thinking of that. She has almost forgotten the oddly matched and reticent couple she and Maheut were at the time, how the bustle and spectacle of the crowded streets, and even the terrible fear when the man tore off Maheut's hood, distracted them from the distance between them for a while. So much has happened since then.

*

'What a pleasure! Here you are at last!' Dame Alice is like her daughter: petite and vivacious, with the same curves, although hers have grown heavier. She welcomes the visitors with open arms, folds them in a lengthy embrace. 'Come, come. I have prepared a surprise for you!'

Sir de Crété is away on business; no doubt that is why they were invited. Clémence's father gave in to his daughter's whim in allowing her to join the Beguinage, but now he feels she has stayed too long and it is time for her to enter into society. Their reunions increasingly turn into confrontations. But he is not expected back for several weeks, explains Dame Alice.

'It has all got very complicated,' she murmurs as she leads them through vast ceremonial halls to the room where their meal awaits them. 'Business is no longer going so well.'

Once again, Ade is astonished at the magnificence of the residence. The reception rooms are decorated with refinement, each of them like a display case, a concentration of the taste and cultural knowledge of their hosts. The walls of the first room are covered with pictures and precepts painted in vivid colours; the second is full of musical instruments: harps, viols, gitterns, psalterions. The following room is dedicated to games of draughts and chess. Next the three women cross a study where huge armoires hold dozens of volumes with covers in ivory and metal. Jars diffuse the soft, piquant fragrances of spices through the air.

'Oh, Mother!' Clémence exclaims rapturously as Alice, instead of leading them to her living room, guides them to the back of the last hall, towards a little spiral staircase whose narrow steps climb up to the top floor. The room where the meal is laid out is extraordinary. Never has Ade seen anything like it: large and square, hung with tapestries, the walls on all four sides pierced by vast bay windows that look out over the golden pinnacles of the mansion itself, and the roofs of the city beyond, the bell tower of the Saint-Germain church, the keep of the Louvre with its walls and towers, and finally, the wide, dark river, whose arms unite at the point of the Ile de la Cité to glide into the heavy waves of the surrounding plain.

The meal, already spread on the table, is generous and varied enough to feed many more guests than the three of them. Roast capon, pike *en galantine*, dace poached in *verjus*, cheese tarts, flan and rissoles. A banquet. The air filled with heady scents. Ade is suddenly hungry. Clémence dips her lips in a goblet of honeyed wine before handing it to her, followed by a morsel of fowl. Their hands meet above the trencher. Ade's head is spinning, so unaccustomed is she to such feasts. She surrenders herself to indulgence, her blood and appetite invigorated by the succulence of the dishes, by Clémence's tender friendship, and by the flood of light pouring through the windows. She has not seen the sky this close since she came to Paris, and now she realizes how she has missed it.

At the end of the meal, Dame Alice leads Clémence and Ade back down the stairs from the room in the sky down to the first, and then the ground floor. She takes them out of a small door in the side of the town house and across the courtyard where a peacock swaggers to an outbuilding. Inside is a huge steam room split into two. The first is equipped with a hearth and a floor on top of pillars where one can recline and sweat; in the second is a large tub that some serving girls have just finished filling with hot water as the three women enter.

'Somewhat different from our baths at the Beguinage!' exclaims Clémence as she lets her clothes fall to the ground. While a serving girl gathers them up, Alice and Ade undress in turn and slip into the bathwater that has been heated to the perfect temperature and perfumed with herbs and petals. For the next hour, the women take turns scrubbing each other's backs and washing each other's hair. Clémence massages her friend's blond locks, heavy and fragrant with myrtle and rosewater.

*

'What a beautiful day,' the girl says, hugging Ade as they make their way home.

A beautiful day, indeed, thinks Ade. Made of sweetness from dawn to the dusk that is already announcing itself in the elongated shadows of the gables and chimneys. And because she is happy, her body relaxed and purified by the bath, she suggests to Clémence that they pass by Notre-Dame on the way back to the Beguinage.

On the forecourt, the crowd is larger and noisier than usual. Excited, Clémence pinches Ade's arm through her mantle and pulls her along.

'Look! The pillory!'

A platform has been erected in front of the church. A man is exposed there, his head and arms protruding through the pillory's wooden frame. His face cannot be seen, but on his skull gleams the clerical tonsure. A sign hanging below declares his sin: *Fornicator*. Men and women alike pelt him with refuse, mud and insults. Ade's heart tightens; she thinks of the shame and terror the poor monk must feel. She crosses herself and is about to leave when her eyes meet another pair of eyes that are fixed on her. A few steps from the pillory, wearing the same tonsure as the condemned monk, stands the man she thought she would never see again.

Just as they did three years previously, Ade and Humbert's paths cross on the cathedral forecourt.

2

JEANNE DU FAUT OBSERVES Maheut and does not know what to think. The girl—who is no longer actually a girl—still lean as a stripling, with a new grace in her hips and bust, does nothing wrong. She is putting into practice all they have taught her. At this very moment she is unrolling an embroidered orphrey commissioned from Ameline in front of a customer. The man picks up the piece, rubs it between his hands, feels the subtlety and regularity of the work. 'Perfect,' he murmurs.

The orphrey is indeed luxurious: emblazoned with gold and silk thread but supple and light. Ameline might be the stupidest of the workers, but her fingers work marvels.

Perhaps Maheut is standing a bit too close to the buyer, Dame du Faut thinks, and perhaps they are passing the orphrey back and forth too much. But she herself appreciates the greedy pleasure of handling beautiful material, whether soft or coarse, smooth or rough. And of course, Giacomo knows where he is, in a house of beguines, which is not the right place to ply his charm. If he is looking for a mistress, there must be no lack of women who would let themselves be captured by his blue eyes, his fine appearance... or the money that swells his purse. Maheut, with her simple serge robe and white headdress, is surely not the kind to appeal to the Italian.

The man has returned to the Silk House after a long absence. He had gone back to his country after the Lombard Affair at the end of 1311. The previous seizure of Jewish assets had not sufficed, and so when the king found himself once again short of money, he attacked the Italian bankers, whom he accused of manipulating the exchange rates and despoiling the French with their usury. Giacomo's cousin had not waited for the threats to become any clearer. Instead he had left Paris, fearing further confiscations to add to those he had already suffered twice in the preceding years. Giacomo had followed him.

Now they are both back at last. Once again King Philip has compromised. The country needs us too much, Giacomo joked when he first reappeared a few weeks before. Jeanne knows that the Lombards have been obliged to pay a fine, but obviously it was worth it. As long as people are buying, there must be others to sell... and still others to lend the necessary money! the merchant from Lucca added.

Giacomo's thick hair is shot through with grey now. Jeanne has no idea how old he is, but he is no longer a young man. She is surprised he is not married, but then again perhaps he is. He has never spoken of it. He can be secretive, for all his gregariousness. All she has been able to glean, from a few careless words, is that his family's wealth was recently won. Beneath his courteous manners she sometimes glimpses the freedom of tone and style of those who are emancipated from the constraints of any caste. That said, he is always considerate of everyone. But lately Maheut seems to draw his attention the most.

No, decides Jeanne, brushing away her doubts, this is no illusion: they are standing too close to each other. They are talking now. Giacomo speaks a few words in his language and Maheut tries to repeat them. Her voice, usually so sharp and fast, is trying out a more measured rhythm. Then she bursts out laughing, and the Italian laughs along with her.

The embroiderers upstairs break into laughter at the same moment, accompanied by the child's excited cries. Jeanne sighs, and then smiles despite herself. The household will be hard to manage in the coming days. It has grown as feverish as the city around it. King Edward II and Isabella of England, daughter of Philip the Fair, arrived at the gates of Paris yesterday. They had set off from Dover with an assembly of nobles, including the dukes of Pembroke and Richmond, and a retinue more than two hundred strong, to pay a visit to the sovereign who, in this month of June 1313, is due to dub as knights his eldest as well as his two younger brothers.

For more than a week, acrobats and jugglers and other performers have been flocking to the city. Boats unload piles of barrels and baskets wriggling with fish onto the quaysides. Butchers slaughter animals as fast as they can; channels of fresh blood flow over the pavements near Les Halles. On rue Sainte-Geneviève, at the foot of the abbey, they slit so many stomachs that despite the slope the street becomes clogged with all the foul liquids that spew forth. And while the ogreish city prepares to feast, the young girls of the Silk House are busy cutting and sewing offcuts of cloth for the trade fair that will take place one week after Pentecost, and for which they are preparing a *tableau vivant* showing the Virgin and Child surrounded by angels.

Suddenly Jeanne senses a presence close to her. It is Juliotte, Leonor in her arms. The child is playing with a tulle crown braided around a metallic headband. She presents it to the silk merchant. 'Thank you, Leonor,' says Jeanne, smiling as she takes it.

The child does not say anything. But Jeanne knows that she spoke her first word a few days ago—her godmother's name. The girls in the workshop speak of it as a miracle. Perhaps it would be best, thinks the mistress, admiring the crown under the little girl's watchful gaze, for her to leave this house where her mother takes so little care of her and move to the Beguinage. She would receive a better education there—and probably more affection. But while Jeanne considers this plan, another idea, more suitable to the moment, germinates in her mind.

She places the crown on Leonor's dark curls. Juliotte, who understands everything, gives her the child. Maheut is still absorbed in her exchange with Giacomo and oblivious to her child's presence. She picks up the orphrey and carefully rolls it in order to wrap it up as she has been taught. Jeanne takes a step towards her, then another. Giacomo is the first to react. He raises his head, sees the little crowned girl, and exclaims:

'Bellissima!'

Maheut is frozen, her face expressionless.

'Yes, she is beautiful, isn't she?' says Jeanne. 'Her mother's eyes…'

The Italian does not answer, merely smiles. Then Maheut lifts her head, holds out her hands for the child, clutches her tightly to her chest, making her breasts stand out under her robe, and plants her green gaze in the Italian's blue eyes.

'*Bellissima!*' Giacomo says again.

From the street comes a rising clamour. 'They are here, they are here!'

'Come,' he says, grabbing Maheut and Jeanne du Faut by their hands. 'Come!' he calls out again, in the direction of the kitchen and the back of the shop, and up at the workshop windows.

The street is flooded with a crowd that pulls them irresistibly along. Weavers, embroiderers, silk merchants and other curious onlookers all move in a wave towards the rue Saint-Denis just as the royal procession arrives.

Maheut is still holding Giacomo's hand and does not let it go, despite the crush and the child that weighs in her arms. But then her headdress comes loose. She feels a lock of hair falling over her forehead and frees herself from the Italian's grasp to tuck it away. But Giacomo turns around and lifts Leonor onto his shoulders, without letting Maheut hide her red hair, as bright as the banners hanging from the windows, as festive as the torches waved by the spectators, as joyous as the cries that swell and burst from the bedecked gates in the city wall. The pair stride onward through the crowd.

Out of breath, furious and worried, Jeanne loses them from sight.

3

O N SATURDAY 2ND JUNE, after an impressive procession that sees three kings—Philip of France, Edward of
England and Louis of Navarre—with their families and retinues
cross Paris to reach Notre-Dame in an orgy of extravagant
costumes and flaming torches brandished in broad daylight,
a banquet is laid on for the guests on the Ile de la Cité in the
sovereign's newly reconstructed palace.

The next day is Pentecost and the whole assembly gathers
in the cathedral. Louis of Navarre, Count of Champagne and
Brie, his brothers Philip and Charles, as well as Hugues, Duke
of Burgundy, Guy, Count of Blois, and many more of the kingdom's nobles process down the huge nave to be girded with the
ceremonial sword.

The following days are filled with festivities. Each sovereign
and every noble hosts some kind of spectacle or entertainment.
Philip the Fair puts on a private dinner for ladies, presided over
by his daughter and daughter-in-law, in a salon of the Louvre.
Edward II, lodged with all the other English guests at the Saint-
Germain abbey, has tents put up on the far side of the three-
towered church, where minstrels from all over Europe play the
most fashionable songs while capons and jewelled goblets of
spiced wine are served by valets on horseback. Then it is the turn
of Louis d'Evreux, the king's brother, who has a wooden bridge
built between the Ile de la Cité and the Ile Notre-Dame in order

to give a banquet at the foot of the canons' enclosure, where Parisians often come to relax and enjoy the cool riverside air.

On the morning of 9th June, torches are lit across the city. Ordinary Parisians are invited to participate in the merriment. They dance, feast, and drink until dawn, while imbibing—oh, marvel!—wine flowing from a fountain. This is a day that will be remembered: Isabelle of England, after her husband and her father, takes up the cross and promises to accompany King Edward to the Holy Land.

But Ade knows nothing and hears nothing of all these celebrations. While the embroiderers and silk workers of rue Troussevache, the saddlers and bridlers of rue Saint-Denis, the weavers of the Temple, the second-hand clothes dealers of Saint-Innocent parish, the harness makers of Saint-Merri, the archers of Saint-Ladre gate and the money-changers of the Grand and Petit-Pont set up their *tableaux vivants* from the Bible, depictions of Wild Men or scenes from the tales of Reynard the Fox, Ade sits in her room at her writing desk, translating a manuscript by the flame of her lamp. She barely raises her head from her work, even when a storm breaks out in the late afternoon, sending flashes of lightning tearing through the sky above the darkened stone city.

She turns the pages, reading aloud, because to read such a text in one's head does not seem enough. Little by little, she begins to hear Marguerite's voice emerge amid the modulations and rhythms of her own, captivating and pulling her onward.

And yet Ade only entered into this book reluctantly. Despite its name, *The Mirror*, like other mystical treatises, is not meant to show readers a reflection of themselves. Instead it presents an ideal image of perfection, so that the reader may attempt to draw nearer to it. But how can one trust a book that is condemned for heresy?

The opening words put her off, like a barely opened door slamming shut. A pretentious warning:

> *You who would read this book*
> *If you indeed wish to grasp it,*
> *Think about what you say,*
> *For it is very difficult to comprehend,*
> *Humility, who is the keeper of treasury of*
> *knowledge*
> *And the mother of the other Virtues*
> *Must overtake you.*

… is followed by this impudence:

> *Theologians and other clerks,*
> *You will not have the intellect for it,*
> *No matter how brilliant your abilities*
> *If you do not proceed humbly.*

But already her mind was awakened—and her curiosity aroused. For this work was indeed audacious and complex enough for the Inquisition to submit it for evaluation by twenty-one of the most eminent theologians of the University of Paris.

Ade turned the page and continued her translation. Thereafter she was captivated, caught in the dialogue between Reason and Love, around which Marguerite structured her thought: their exchanges, their arguments, their confrontations. The book whispers and then takes flight, alternating forms and cadences between rhymed prose and rhythmic prose, between interior dialogues and dramatic scenes, between vehement injunctions and lyrical moments. It is a prideful text, certainly, as ardent as the Valenciennes beguine herself, her soul thirsty for love, who was striving through her writing to achieve knowledge and understanding of the divine. It is also a deliberately obscure work, filled with complex allegories and many words with dual meanings.

Now Ade lifts her hand to pass to the next page—and flinches. Another flash of lightning outside the house, followed immediately by a crash of thunder that shakes the walls and makes her lamp tremble. It is not yet night, but she calls her servant to ask for more light, so much is she struggling to make out Marguerite's irregular hand. There is a strange contradiction between her mastery of thought and the meandering flight of her quill across the page, as if it were caught in the eddies of some internal torrent.

Distracted from her reading, Ade is suddenly surprised by an unwelcome memory. Brother Humbert leaning over her shoulder, helping her decipher a difficult phrase. She is embarrassed by his closeness. She can feel his robe rubbing against her back. She can smell him too—his own particular smell, which she knows since she noticed it at Ysabel's house. Warm, slightly sweet, so different from that of other men… and from her husband's, whose scent was close to that of the horses he rode and the wine he drank, strong and a little acidic.

She found the Franciscan much changed when she saw him on the forecourt of Notre-Dame. Older, his face hard—but with a different hardness than the one she remembered. Less angry, but more tense. He had acknowledged her with a simple nod, then walked away.

*

'We did not think we would see you again after such a long time. Is it not a little late to be claiming your due?' Ysabel had asked when he came back to the Beguinage.

'A promise never expires,' he answered simply, holding out the book he had been hiding under his robe. Ysabel could think of no reply. These days the lives of everyone in the great cities seemed to be accelerating. The rhythm of work was replacing that of the Church; merchants and moneylenders juggled due dates in order to make a profit. Nevertheless, today as yesterday, time belongs only to God, who draws it out to infinity. Pilgrims know this: a commitment made before the Creator cannot be postponed. When he starts on his journey, he does not ask when he will be returning. Louis himself left his kingdom for seven years in order to honour his Crusader vow. Whatever had happened to Humbert during all this time, he was now within his rights.

'Will you at least give us news of Maheut's family?' Ysabel asked.

'Her brother has agreed to cede part of his land to Guillebert. But that is paltry compensation. The man wants more than bastards to ensure his posterity. I doubt the affair is over.'

The Franciscan had come back two days later, and again two days after that. Ade received him in her living room, always in Ysabel's presence. Together they turned the pages of the manuscript, while he explained words and turns of phrase from the Picardy dialect that she did not understand, and discussed obscure passages with her so she would be able to translate them more accurately from French into Latin.

Then he had disappeared for a few days. When he appeared again, he brought several virgin sheets of parchment. Small in size, like those one takes on voyages or hides about one's person. They came from a magnificent skin, fine and supple, a rich cream in colour.

'Your master is no penny-pincher,' Ysabel had remarked.

'My master is dead,' Humbert replied.

Neither of the two women had anything more to say. Ade had returned to the book, and her feelings began to change.

*

She has not yet touched the vellum. She borrowed a wax tablet from the Beguinage school with the intention of preparing the lines of translation paragraph by paragraph on it, before trans-ferring the words over to the costly parchment. But to turn *The Mirror* into Latin, she must first understand it, feel it resonate within her, let its movement overtake her, and travel through the seven stages that the author claims will lead to the annihi-lation of the soul, the renunciation of the will, and fusion with God. Humbert, to whom she explained her plan, approved of it: 'This will enable us to clarify the text together before I return to Valenciennes.'

First a soul, recites Ade. *A soul that saves itself by faith and without works. That knows only love…*

The rain is pouring in waves on the roof above now, drowning out the sound of her voice:

To which nothing can be taught, from which nothing can be taken nor anything given to it…

*

The storm ends an hour later. The young woman closes her eyes that are burning with fatigue. She lets herself go, leaning back on her chair, throwing back her head to undo the knots in her neck.

Someone knocks on the shutters downstairs. Ade hears a youthful voice, a little laugh. Clémence. She gives a slight huff of irritation. The servant climbs the stairs with her heavy gait, scratches at the door and pushes it ajar. Ade shakes her head, puts her face in her hands.

'Dame Ade is resting,' she hears an instant later.

'Is she not well?'

'She is resting, is all.'

Despite the rain, Clémence lingers in front of the house whose door has been shut in her face, still holding the basket of fruit she brought for her friend, and which she did not even think to leave with the servant. Upstairs, through the window, she can make out Ade's silhouette in the flickering candlelight. She is sitting at her writing desk—Clémence knows that room from which she has been banished for more than two weeks so well that she can picture it with her eyes closed—and Ade seems to be reading, rather than resting.

Clémence's heart is gripped by sadness. And because she is still a child, and a child who has almost always got what she desired, a resentful drop of bitter poison wells up inside it too.

4

N EVER HAS SUMMER seemed so strange to Ysabel. The Beguinage is utterly still amid the heatwave that lays siege to its walls. The atmosphere is heavy with the nauseous stench from the tanneries upriver, relieved by occasional wafts of sweet fragrances from the flower and fruit gardens. The evenings are stifling and dusty. Finally, just before the passage to the following day, the sky clears. For the space of an hour, the firmament shivers with stars. Only then does the world recover its vibrancy.

The beguine senses this shift, wakes and leaves her bedroom almost every night. She has never slept very much, but with old age she is falling asleep later and later. She sometimes feels as if her body were filled with so much energy that it must hurry to spend it before death takes it away. She sits on the bench in her herb garden and gazes up at the stars like she did as a child, sharpening her vision to the point where she can detect the smallest glimmers of light, note the distances between them and the shapes they form, the creatures they make tremble in the darkness.

This night at the end of July finds her at her post once more. Three stars shine brighter than all the others, forming a vast triangle that spans the Milky Way. The world seems to hang on a fragile thread, suspended between dusk and dawn. Waiting. Perhaps like the Beguinage itself?

Within the walls, nothing is going as it usually does. For the first time, the institution has no actual mistress.

It all happened silently. After the death of Jeanne la Bricharde during the Council of Vienne, the succession process was thrown into upheaval and no decision was announced.

When the institution was founded, the superiors were recruited by the king himself. As an admirer of Saint Elisabeth's beguinage in Ghent, Louis IX looked for his mistresses in French Flanders, where they were experienced in organizing and running this type of establishment. But with time, the Paris Beguinage grew independent, and now its mistresses were chosen by their companions with the approval of the Dominicans of rue Saint-Jacques.

But this time, the Dominican prior acted first. He put no name forward, but asked the wise women of the Beguinage to kindly appoint the eldest among them as mistress while they waited for the Vienne decrees on the beguines to be promulgated.

It could have been worse, thought Ysabel at the time.

Armelle is a sensible, responsible woman who has spent the last twenty years of her life here. But she does not have the stature of the former mistresses and has long suffered from heart trouble. Bit by bit, the affairs of the Beguinage are escaping her. Meanwhile the Dominicans, anxious to protect the king's beguines, or so they claim, are tightening their control. They have made their presence felt, blocking the nomination of a younger, stronger woman who might take over from Armelle. Months go by, the heat grows oppressive, and the aged Armelle weakens, which is painful for her companions to see, and frightening too, because the mistress embodies order and security in the little world of the Beguinage.

*

Ysabel has been staring at the same point in the sky for too long and her vision has grown blurry. She lowers her eyes, sighing with pleasure as a fresh breeze caresses her cheek. It is the breath of air that announces the coming of dawn; she should go back to her room, but she feels good here. From time to time, a zigzagging shadow flits through the air and brushes past her. Bats are nesting in a niche under the chapel belltower. Ysabel is not afraid of them, and she knows they have their place in her garden, like the spiders and earthworms and all the other obscure, creeping, subterranean creatures.

In a few weeks' time, around the feast of Saint Lawrence, the firmament will be lit up by a burst of shooting stars. No doubt she will be here to watch them. How could she do otherwise? Fortunately, the Beguinage is quieter than usual. Many of her companions have gone back to their families to spend the summer days in the coolness of their country homes. Agnes, thank God, is one of them! Her cousin Geoffroy has a grand estate in Champagne.

Ysabel shakes her head as if to dispel her troublesome thoughts. For a long time now, she has had the feeling of being caught in a trap, the nature of which she cannot discern.

When Agnes first asked her to teach her the rudiments of the use of plants, she did not have the heart to refuse. The woman has assisted her for years, with ever greater efficacy, sparing her the burdens of organization and stock keeping. Thanks to the new authority she seems to have acquired she has even been resolving the small conflicts that regularly arise among the sick. Ysabel herself learnt the remedies from her grandmother, and such expertise should not be kept to oneself. But she would have preferred a different pupil.

Her assistant lacks the prime talent required for any apprenticeship, and especially one in the usage of plants—the capacity to observe: not just watching and replicating, but watching for a long time, to the point of forgetting yourself and absorbing all you see; not merely noting the ingredients of a remedy and their quantities, but also paying attention to the manner of preparing them, whether to mix them delicately or vigorously, roll or pound them with the pestle; patiently trying to get a sense, using your eyes, nose and fingertips, of the intrinsic qualities of different herbs—their heat or humidity, their strength or subtlety—in order to mix them more precisely. Agnes has not understood the essential point: every preparation is unique, and into each you have to be capable of putting an intention.

And yet, despite Agnes's lack of competence, she is now claiming the right to treat patients. She does not say so frankly—another talent she lacks!—but by suggesting that as she grows older, Ysabel will need to rest and rely on the help of someone who can care for the less seriously ill patients. Agnes, who was once so discreet, no longer hesitates to bring phials of her own concoctions to the infirmary. Thus, in the eyes of some, without Ysabel ever saying so, Agnes has become the herbalist's apprentice.

In any case, her current absence is a blessing. Agnes knows Humbert from when he first came to the Beguinage. She would certainly have come across the Franciscan during his frequent visits to Ade's house and might have recognized him. Ysabel suggested to the mistress, and to several of her curious companions, that the young woman was receiving a family friend who had come to help her prepare for a return to life as a wife. Ade has forged too few friendships within the Beguinage for anybody to spare her much thought—except maybe for Clémence. The girl has been living on her own with a servant since Agnes's departure, and she appears anxious and troubled. She is still a child, distant from her family. Perhaps Ade ought to spare some time for her. Ysabel will speak to her about it tomorrow.

To the east, above the houses leaning against the city wall, light is spreading through the sky, gradually wiping it clean of stars.

Dawn is here already.

Ysabel sighs. She ought to sleep; it does no good to worry. Humbert plans to go back to Valenciennes in August. Agnes is coming back in September for the Nativity of the Virgin Mary. Everything, at least in that respect, will go back to normal.

The old beguine rises, but before going inside, she chooses an earthenware pot and sets it in the best exposed corner of the garden. Inside she puts a fragment of crystal taken from her alms purse. The sun should soon touch it and transmit its warmth. She will come back at midday to find the crystal and put it to macerate. Imbued with the stone's force, the water will give some strength to Armelle.

5

No doubt Humbert also feels the strangeness of these summer months, but he does not admit it to anybody, certainly not himself. He has set a rigorous programme for his weeks in Paris and he sticks firmly to it. Each day, after Mass, his mornings are devoted to studying at the theology school of the Cordeliers. He listens to the masters' sermons, practises with them and receives their advice and criticism, pursuing the training he began here a year ago, and whose completion has become more pressing since the death of Jean de Querayn. Then until nightfall he reads old sermons consigned to books in the library.

Except for Tuesdays and Fridays, when, at the three strokes of noon, he crosses the city to the Beguinage.

When he arrives this afternoon, the eve of the Feast of Saint James the Elder, Ade's room is illuminated as always by the many candles sitting on her desk and in alcoves in the wall to supplement the weak light from outside. The room smells of ink and melted wax. And as always, too, as he enters, Humbert is conscious of the emanations from outdoors and his own odours exhaled from his thick homespun habit.

Ade is alone. To begin with, Ysabel, alerted by Guillaumette, would receive the Franciscan and accompany him to her friend's house. But now she seems to think her presence is not necessary. At last, she is tamed, Humbert thought the first time the old beguine left the room to go back to the infirmary. But actually, was it not he who had been tamed?

*

The ritual begins. They greet each other, then set to work, without any discussion, without asking each other anything, even how they are faring. It is a habit that dates from their earliest exchanges, when Ade was on edge, Ysabel hostile, and he—he felt like a boorish yokel violating a sanctuary.

But while the silence has remained, everything else has changed. What matters is not heard but seen: the rhythm of their movements. To begin with he stands far away from her, on the other side the room. She reads the last paragraphs she has translated. Her voice still has the softness he noticed that day when he saw her teaching, but it is more melodious now. Humbert listens to Ade's words, letting them come to him, takes one step towards her, then another, Marguerite's text a swell that carries him along. Ade lets him approach, no longer with any sign of tension. Last week she put a chair alongside hers so he could sit down, but he prefers to remain standing.

The young woman has progressed well since his previous visit, deciphering several pages and noting a passage that still seems obscure on her tablet. She reads aloud:

The Soul, says Love, is free, yet more free, yet finally supremely free, in the root, in all her branches, and all the fruits of her branches.

She stops, looks at the text, then carries on in a lower voice.

The Soul responds to no one if she does not wish to, if he is not of her lineage. For a gentleman would not deign to respond to a peasant, even if such a one would call him or attack him on a battlefield. And for this reason anyone who calls her will not find such a Soul. Her enemies no longer have any response from her.

Again she falls quiet. Humbert respects her silence, himself absorbed by what he has just heard. He has the feeling that his understanding of the text, which he already knew from having heard it read by Brother Jean and by Marguerite herself, is being renewed by Ade's reading voice, her patient deciphering. Her apprehension of the work seems guided—is she conscious of this?—by an empathy that surpasses intelligence alone.

Like other passages heard on previous days, these last sentences set him wondering. *Her enemies no longer receive any response from her.* Humbert thinks of the silence with which Marguerite opposed the men who exhorted her to yield, to confess, or merely to speak. He remembers her face—closed mouth, gaze turned inward—when she stood tied to the foot of the stake, waiting to be burned alive. Was it really obstinacy that made her act this way, as he thought at the time? Or else a detachment from herself that was so profound, and the result of thoughts so subtle, that it was impossible for him to share in them.

There, instead of the feminine mysticism he once looked down on, which consumed meaning while pretending to appeal to the mind, he is now gradually discovering a structured and scholarly line of thought. Despite the concrete images that Marguerite uses, and phrases that are sometimes tinged with courtly literature—*God, like a desired lover*—she is indeed nourished by theological doctrine. The former student recognizes themes that echo great thinkers like Gregory the Great and Bernard de Clairvaux... The dialectic that the beguine Marguerite sets up between Love and Reason is reminiscent of the university debates in which he participated during his days at the Sorbonne. There is no muddled meaning, no pathological language linked to the sensual desires that are known to exist among women.

Marguerite's book is a rigorous, soaring intellectual work.

How could he not have discerned this before now? How little he had trusted the accurate judgement of his master! What was it—jealousy?

*

Ade calls him. He moves closer again, leans over her shoulder, follows her finger as it moves over the page, feels his heart and his thoughts grow peaceful. Something in this woman Ade has the gift of calming him. Even his mother did not know how to control his wildly shifting emotions: anger, frustration, remorse. He was always agitated, never at peace. But when he is close to this young widow, so distant but not cold, the knot of tension he has felt inside him since the death of Brother Jean finally comes undone.

He ought not to have been so tardy in accomplishing his mission. But the death throes of his master had been so long and so frightful. After months of suffering, Humbert had reached the point of hoping that this man he had so loved would simply die. But in fact, was he even still the same man? In the last days, his eyes were those of a madman. His hands clung to the bar that had been fixed to the bed to prevent him from wandering as he sometimes did, stumbling, his arms stretched out before him, groping at the walls, as if to find there the sole support his lost mind could reach. Was it death that frightened the holy man? That made no sense. Or if it did, then all their lives were senseless.

At the very end, Jean opened his mouth like a nestling that holds out its beak to its mother. But he had already stopped eating. Humbert spoke to him, perhaps imagining that his voice would hold him back.

Then his heart stopped.

Autumn had come, rainy, so the routes were not propitious for travelling. Then winter, and the temptation to renounce his promise. But of course, that was inconceivable.

One day a notable guest travelling to Flanders had presented himself at the monastery. Hugo de Novocastro, one of the greatest masters of the Paris university, had been toiling for years on a treatise devoted to the end of days. The man brought with him the rumour of a strange prophecy that was circulating in the corridors and study rooms of the capital's colleges. A mysterious Columbinus, he said, probably a Franciscan, had been announcing the imminent arrival of the Antichrist.

For years, mystics and scholars of all religious orders had been issuing warnings about the end of days, seeding a vague dread in the people's minds, but Columbinus demonstrated the prospect of the apocalypse with frightening precision. In the vast echoing refectory, where the monks would discuss the news gathered from visitors and returning travellers, Humbert heard Hugo report those learned calculations. God, the prophet said, had planned the world around a single motif: the figure 7. The seven days of Creation, the seven planets, the seven spheres, the seven sacraments... And most important of all, the Seven Seals of the Book of the Apocalypse. Each seal corresponded to one of the Churches of Asia, to which Jesus in Saint John's text addressed his admonishments: Ephesus, Smyrna, Pergamum, Thyatira, Sardis, Philadelphia, Laodicea. And each church coincided with an age of the world, each with a duration of two hundred years starting from the Incarnation. Columbinus asserted that men were now living at the end of the sixth period, that of the Church of Philadelphia, and therefore exposed to the great dangers and evils that heralded the arrival of the Antichrist, who, accompanied by Gog and Magog, would come out of the abyss in 1316 to reign over the world.

Humbert had always felt a certain joy in playing at eschatological computations. More than once, following in the footsteps of Franciscans like Joachim de Flore and Pierre de Jean Olivi, he had plunged into endless speculations with Brother Jean, experimenting with numbers, which everybody knew were imbued with secret power. Those that are even, divisible and imperfect, which refer to the earthly world and to men; those that are odd, and especially the incorruptible primes, which express eternity—and even God himself. He explored all the combinations in which the union of the soul and the body, the mortal and the immortal is played out.

But this time Humbert had only one thought: he remembered the man condemned alongside Marguerite Porete on the place de Grève. The priest who called himself 'The Angel of Philadelphia', and claimed to defend her, but who in the moment of her execution abandoned her. A few days later, Humbert decided to return to Paris.

*

This Soul is supremely noble in adversity, Ade reads on.

Footsteps on the stairs outside. Humbert straightens up. Ade raises her head. Ysabel comes into the room. There is an air of vigorous exercise about her, and her face is rosy-cheeked from the outdoors. Her arrival dispels both Humbert's memories and the sweetness of the moment.

The old beguine stays until nightfall. As the Franciscan is getting ready to leave, somebody knocks at the door downstairs. Ade's servant goes to answer. All three of them hear a panicky voice: 'Is Dame Ysabel here?'

The servant murmurs in protest, but the visitor pushes past her into the house. 'Dame du Faut is asking for her. She must come right away. Juliotte has disappeared!'

6

FOR THREE WHOLE DAYS they search for the mute girl.

The morning of her disappearance, she left the shop while her companions were barely awake. Jeanne du Faut had given her permission to go to the shops at Les Halles in order to prepare a meal for the feast of Saint-Jacques. Juliotte seems to have a special devotion to the patron saint of pilgrims, though nobody knows why. But what does anyone really know about her, though she takes care of everyone?

When she was not back by Terce Jeanne began to worry. At Sext, Juliotte had still not returned. Everyone started to fear there had been an accident. The area around Les Halles market is clogged with carts and porters; barely a day goes by when a passer-by is not injured by a collapsing load or a beast of burden. First the girls from the Silk House, then the freelance spinners and embroiderers employed by Jeanne du Faut, went out two by two to look for her. First in the neighbouring streets, then further and further away.

The news spread quickly through the quarter. Artisans sent their apprentices and companions to lend help. Giacomo, alerted by the rumour, sent his servants. Marie Osanne herself went with a seller to the fish market where Juliotte used to go. But at Saint-Eustache, nobody had seen her. Nor had anyone at Les Halles, or on the wharves. When asked, the herring-sellers declared they had no memory of the mute girl. It's so busy round here! In the evening, a boy reported that he'd seen a little beguine carrying some flowers to the church of Saint-Jacques-la-Boucherie. That could be her, thought Jeanne. Two lads accompanied the boy back to the church and searched through the building and the alleys close by, but with no success.

Night fell and the watchmen were alerted. Ysabel arrived, and Marie Osanne came back.

That night nobody slept.

*

They report the disappearance to the bailiffs the next day. But nothing happens. Or rather, everything happens just as Jeanne du Faut ought to have expected.

'You let her go out alone?' they ask. 'A girl of that age?'

'How was she dressed?'

'What was her usual manner?'

'Did she tend to provoke passers-by?'

The day comes to an end, and then another. Some of their neighbours continue their searches, others give up. Giacomo asks some aldermen who are in debt to his cousin to put some pressure on the provost to organize a search. The Italian merchant comes by each morning to ask for any news. The shop remains open. Jeanne stays in her room while Maheut receives customers, folds and unfolds pieces of cloth, dusts and tidies the shelves, mops the marks left by shoe soles on the parquet floor. Everything will be clean and orderly for Juliotte's return.

On the third night, the heat that has been gathering over the city begins to shimmer. Then the storm finally bursts, with jagged blades of lightning and thunder like a galloping charger. On the morning of the fourth day, a Saturday, a woman comes to the shop, a headdress-maker from rue Beaubourg, asking for

Jeanne. The mistress listens to her talk, grows pale, sits down, and sends for Marie Osanne.

Together they set out for Saint-Gervais, wearing heavy capes despite the heat. Under the elm tree in front of the church, where the corpses of the unknown are left, guarded by a bailiff, Jeanne immediately recognizes the body of Juliotte.

When Ysabel arrives at the Silk House just before Sext, having been summoned by Beatrice la Grande, she brings with her herbs for perfuming a room of death.

*

Juliotte lies on Jeanne du Faut's bed. So small and skinny, her tiny breasts already falling back into her thin ribs, her hair thin. She was beaten, defiled in all sorts of ways, then thrown into the hole where the bailiff found her. At the bedside stands Jeanne, holding out a basin into which Ysabel dips the cloth with which she is washing the body.

Marie Osanne is present, too. And Ade. The young girls of the house will not be allowed in until Juliotte's dignity has been restored. Maheut, despite her status as woman and mother, is being kept at a distance. Told to stay in the attic with her daughter. But she is not there.

Downstairs, the door of the shop has been left ajar for neighbours who come to offer their support and to share in the household's mourning. The sound of their muffled voices rises through the room's parquet floor. The shutters are closed and the heat is oppressive. The body is already giving off the stink of a rotting carcass.

*

Despite her attention to her task, Ysabel is the first to see her. The child has slipped silently into the room. Her eyes are glazed, as if she were sleepwalking; they are shining, but she is not crying. Ade notices her, too, and steps forward, arms outstretched. Ysabel stops her. Leonor goes up to the bed, takes Juliotte's left hand in hers, loosens the rigid fingers, places them against her cheek, closes her eyes.

Down below, in the shop where she has taken refuge, far from the room where Juliotte will never sleep again, Maheut too has closed her eyes. At the back of the room, hidden from view, she rests her head against Giacomo's chest. He has slipped his arms around her; she would like to weep but she cannot. She feels only her heart pounding in her ears.

7

T HE DEATH OF JULIOTTE is like a marker on a path that stops you getting lost. A broken branch at the foot of a trunk, a few stones piled on top of each other, a rock that stands out because it looks like an animal's head... If you lose your way, find yourself teetering on the edge of a precipice wondering how you got there, you turn back—and then you find the marker.

Later, when they tell the story, some will say that her murder was the first sign, the one that heralded the catastrophes to come. But they will be wrong, because of the narrowness of their view, or the tenderness of their heart.

Before Juliotte—a twig lying broken at the roadside—there had been so many other signs, so many other milestones... The pyres built for the Templars near the Saint-Antoine gate. The miserable cleric from the Sorbonne coming to preach mortification and retreat from the world in the Beguinage chapel. The king's hunts. The expulsion of the Jews and the Lombards. The sky tinted red and saffron on the last day of January 1309. Maheut's headdress ripped off by a stranger. Marguerite's execution. But just as important were the bankruptcy of the royal treasury and the ruin of the feudal class, the devalued currency, the black coins—events of a different kind, but just as significant.

As one who pays careful attention to causality and chance, Ysabel knows this: however small our lives are, they are all part of a greater whole; the movements and the troubles of the soul depend on those of the world at large; violence does not end with its target, but rebounds onward like a pebble skipping over water, striking and striking again. Just as collective fears grow from individual acts of baseness, so great causes may be reflected in the most mundane struggles. Juliotte is dead and buried and the investigation yielded nothing. Was she chosen because she was a beguine, or simply because she was a female? It does not matter. Her fate is one with all that preceded it and all that will follow.

*

Jeanne du Faut's living room seems too small for the big Franciscan. He remains standing as usual, his shoulders hunched.

'What is happening?' he asks.

Ysabel wishes he would sit down. She has a sore neck and it hurts her to look up at him when she talks.

'Brother Humbert, I am sorry, but we can no longer receive you at the Beguinage.'

'So I gathered, but for what reason?'

His tone is impatient. He must still be smarting, Ysabel thinks, from being turned away from Ade's home and sent to the Silk House. But everything happened so fast! At least Guillaumette was able to give him a message.

'The Dominican prior is expected at the Beguinage this afternoon.'

'How does that concern me?'

'I do not wish him to know of your frequent visits.'

'Why not? Could you not present me to him as you did to Dame Armelle?'

'The prior will be less understanding—or perhaps less naïve.'

The Franciscan frowns, and protests.

'I do not understand why his visit should prevent me from

coming back another day! We have almost finished. One or two more sessions would suffice.'

Humbert turns his eyes to the bench where Ade sits, listening intently.

'We have almost finished, have we not?' he insists.

'We have, it is true,' murmurs the young woman.

Why this obstinacy? wonders Ysabel. He says himself that their work is nearly complete. She allows a brief silence to grow and then continues as if she has not heard them.

'The Jacobin is not coming today out of courtesy. He has asked to meet the mistress in order to give her new instructions. And his secretary must inspect our registers. They are tightening their grip on the Beguinage. Surely you would not wish to put Dame Ade in danger?'

The slender figure sitting near the window remains silent. Humbert turns his gaze away.

Just then, somebody knocks at the door. Ade rises. She has guessed who it is. Humbert sees a little girl come into the room. She curtsies, takes her godmother's hand then the two of them go back to the bench.

'This is Maheut's daughter, Leonor,' explains Ysabel.

The little girl is snuggling up to the copyist. With the light coming through the window at their backs, Humbert can barely see their faces, but it was enough for him to see the young woman bend down to the child a moment earlier. Now he knows the tenderness of her smile.

'I am sorry if you felt insulted.'

Ysabel's voice jerks the Franciscan from his thoughts:

'No, doubtless you are right, my visits have become imprudent. The Dominican prior's intervention serves only to confirm the rumours.'

'What do you mean?'

'According to a brother recently returned from Avignon, the pope is preparing to publish the decrees of Vienne against the beguines. The sovereign pontiff is unwell, with a sickness that gnaws at his intestines, but he seems determined to fight those who want to introduce the Free Spirit into the Church. The Dominicans are no doubt aware of his plans.'

'Should we be worried?'

'I don't know what to say to you. Nobody knows the details of the decrees. Apparently the pope was not satisfied with the initial decisions; he had the first copies destroyed and made substantial modifications. Still, people say that beguines are in danger of being abolished.'

Humbert hesitates for a moment, then goes on.

'Everything remains confused, and even contradictory for the time being. But Marguerite Porete—or at least her book—have come under discussion.'

'In what way?'

'Several Parisian theologians who contributed to her condemnation three years ago were part of the commission gathered in Vienne. They used phrases extracted from *The Mirror* to incriminate all beguines. Notably the idea that the perfect soul can take leave of the virtues.'

His final words ring out strangely in the room, which echoes with the laughter and voices of the girls elsewhere in the house and all the sounds of simple daily life. The mystical speculations that he has shared over these last weeks with Ade scarcely have any place here. The Franciscan rises to his feet, trying to shake off the malaise that is overtaking him.

'How long have you known this?' asks Ysabel.

'I learnt it several days after the death of the little... of Juliotte. I did not want to speak of it then. You had other preoccupations.

I was waiting to see how the affair would turn out. There have already been so many delays.'

'And still you kept on coming back to the Beguinage?'

'I told you, I was waiting to see how things developed.'

The explanation seems pathetic to him, but Humbert does not want, for now, to analyse the real reasons for his stubbornness.

'Well, now you see,' replies Ysabel drily. 'What are you planning to do? Insist that we keep the book at the Beguinage?'

He shook his head. 'I don't know. I am aware of the perils to which I am exposing you. But I made a promise, and so did you.'

He breaks off. Thinks of Brother Jean, of what he would have wanted. Turning to Ade, he concludes with the only words that seem right.

'I will not make use of Maheut, or her daughter, to force you to continue. It is up to you to decide now.'

8

THE FEVER THAT HAD SUBSIDED in the morning starts to rise again. Ade is suffocating, in pain; the light duvet covering her seems to crush her bones, her cotton chemise chafes her skin.

She feels a presence at her bedside. Opens her eyes, tries to fight free of the confusion fogging her mind. How long has she been lying like this? She turns her head, feels a wave of well-being go through her. Someone is mopping her brow with a cool, damp cloth. Is it Ysabel?

Ysabel has been caring for her. Yes, she remembers now… The worried look on the old beguine's face as she greets her. It was the day she came back to the Beguinage. She is freezing, despite her cloak lined with grey squirrel fur. All the coldness in the Champagne earth, the bare clay of the fields rimed with frost. The château's high-ceilinged rooms, which cannot be heated. The wall hangings fluttering in the icy draughts that blow in through the ill-fitting windows and swirl over the floor. The chapel, its stones glistening with ice. The flickering candle flames as they lay the body in the family vault. Her sister-in-law Héloise pressed her body against hers, and they trembled together.

It was there that Ade fell ill. Her brother's death five months ago came as a rude shock. He had gone out hunting one November morning and never came back. Fell from his horse and cracked his skull. Her sister-in-law had just given birth to their second child. She was devastated, and Ade stayed at her side for several weeks after the funeral, although she wanted only to return to the Beguinage. She should have waited longer rather than brave the roads in the middle of February. With her brother dead, now she was free to choose her own life, yet she felt trapped in the family château.

The cloth dabs at her cheeks now. It is already less cool.

Those frightful memories that had tormented her during her stay! She had gone to pray at Marie's tomb—her baby, dead before she ever saw her—and that of her husband too, staring at the face of the recumbent statue, sculpted in stone, the wide shoulders under the pleats of the robe, the sword at his waist... Her handsome husband. But nothing was any longer as it ought to be.

How is this possible? At her daughter's tomb, she wept. But at her husband's, she felt only bitterness.

Ade moans.

The scrape of a door somewhere, but that was in the past. A voice, women's voices. Different. Then another voice that drowns out all the others. A laugh, always the same. Faces float in front of her closed eyes. Her husband—looking at her with contempt. Suddenly Humbert is there, his lips twisted into a scowl. And then that other face, so brown it could belong to a Moor, which warbles and mocks.

'Ade,' murmurs a soft voice, 'do not fret so much, try to rest.'

*

Clémence rinses the cloth in the basin, squeezes it out and mops her friend's forehead once more, caresses her cheek, anxiously clasps her hand. The fever will pass, Ysabel says so. It's not unusual for a patient to suffer a fit like this at night... But she seems in such a bad way.

The young girl bends over, bringing her face close to Ade's. Her lips are cracked like old parchment. Clémence smells her sour breath, breathes it in, forgetting Ysabel's advice to avoid this corrupted air, but Ade moans again and turns her head away.

Clémence feels tired herself. She has slept badly for several nights now and barely ventured from her room during the day. This morning, Ysabel recommended once more that Ade be moved to the infirmary, but once more the girl refused. Agnes, always so kindly and benevolent, has been helping her. And Clémence's mother, impressed by the strength of her friendship with Ade and proud of the commitment shown by her formerly capricious child, often comes by to lend assistance too. Clémence would never admit this to anybody, probably not even to herself, but the illness has finally permitted her to get close to her friend again. She thought she had lost her last summer, believing the lie she had been fobbed off with at first, that Ade was preparing for her return to the outside world. But she had glimpsed her friend through the window several times, sitting at her desk with that Franciscan at her side. Then she had passed the man in the corridor one day, seen the expression on his face and understood that something else was going on.

After the monk's visits to the Beguinage stopped, her private lessons had resumed, but infrequently. Ade seemed preoccupied and fatigued. Clémence watched out for her on her way to prayers in the morning, accompanied her as she hurried back from the chapel; sometimes in the evening she would even watch her silhouette through the window, always bent over her desk. She would have liked to help her. But Ade never confided in her, even in the intimacy of her room. She did treat her conscientiously enough, guiding her reading and her quill with precision, but shared with her only the surface of things. The secret that Clémence had once spoken of with Agnes remained hidden.

And then there was that long absence after the death of her brother.

*

Ade finally grows calmer, her breathing more steady. Her eyes cease their rolling under her eyelids. She has grown so thin, thinks Clémence; when she is cured I will forbid her to spend so many hours writing.

The girl stands up, stiff from remaining hunched over the bed so long. Tells herself it is time to get some rest on the straw mattress made up for her in the corner of the bedroom. Gently smooths the eiderdown covering her friend. But the night breeds fears and conjures up ghosts. So of course she thinks again of the Franciscan who has come between her and her friend. Then, because she is feeling less worried about Ade, whose attacks of fever are coming less and less often, and because she fears being sent away from the room when Ade is cured, and because her fatigue makes her impulsive, she does something she has never dared before.

The room is dark and cold. The fire has not been lit for days. Clémence shields the candle's flame with her hand, skirts the writing desk and work table and slips past the fireplace. The chest is hidden away in a corner cupboard at the back of the room. She pulls away the cloth draped over it, lifts the heavy oak lid and peers inside. By the light of her candle she sees a wax tablet, covered with Ade's neat writing. Underneath it lie two cloth bundles. She reaches inside the chest and starts to untie the knots holding the cloth in place, knowing she shouldn't but unable to stop herself.

The first manuscript is a crude affair, the cover no more than an envelope of parchment backed by cloth; the other is smaller, made from a supple and creamy vellum, not yet bound. Though Ade has been teaching her Latin, she has not made good progress. But the title of this book has often been mentioned in her presence.

9

T HE CHRONICLERS CANNOT agree when the event takes place: either the Monday before or the one after Saint Gregory's day. But whenever it happens, it causes an irreparable tear in the fabric of time. Ysabel, who witnesses it, albeit from afar, might explain why: the suffering and betrayal so familiar to this century were on this occasion accompanied by unforgettable words and gestures.

The drama's first act takes place on the forecourt of Notre-Dame. That Monday sees a solemn gathering in front of the cathedral—the Archbishop of Sens, whose ecclesiastical province includes Paris, three cardinals, many prelates and canons, and the four last high-ranking Templars: Jacques de Molay, Geoffroy de Charnay, Geoffroy de Gonneville, and Hugues de Pairaud, who have been brought directly from their cells. Their Order no longer exists, having been dissolved two years ago, and its goods transferred to the Hospitaler Order, but their individual fates have not been decided. The pope has decided to take care of the matter himself, and has brought together a council in Paris which is due to announce its verdict.

Everybody expects the Templars' punishment to be life imprisonment. And since the accused have stood by their confessions—and seem determined to do so until the bitter end—the sentence pronounced in front of the great portal of the Last Judgement is in fact captivity for the four men until the end of their days. But suddenly, to everybody's surprise and for reasons that remain unclear, both Jacques de Molay and Geoffroy de Charnay, Grand Masters of the Crusader states of Outremer and Normandy respectively, demand to be heard. Rudely repudiating the Archbishop of Sens, they proceed to deny everything they had previously admitted.

They have therefore fallen back into heresy. Relapsed. They are handed over to the Provost of Paris, and the council will reconvene the next day.

But the end does not come the following day, and not in the provost's jail. Instead it happens almost immediately, on the tiny island of Javiaux, in the Seine, to the south of the royal palace. Receiving word of the developments, the king decides he can wait no longer; it is high time he put an end to the soldier-monks. A double pyre is hastily erected on what is little more than a bank of silt and sand between the royal gardens and house of the hermit brothers of Saint Augustine. There Jacques de Molay and Geoffroy de Charnay are tied together and, at the hour of vespers, burned alive.

But before that happens, the gestures are performed and the words spoken. Before all those present, Jacques de Molay is stripped of his garments until he is naked under his chemise. Without trembling, he asks that his hands be left free so he may join them in prayer. And that his head be turned to face the Virgin Mary on the façade of Notre-Dame Cathedral. Then, his face lit up by the rays of the setting sun, he speaks again. Only one man hears him, or at least claims to have done so: Geoffroy de Paris, a clerk at the royal chancellery, who is standing nearby. According to the clerk, before his death the Grand Master curses all those responsible for his and his companions' executions to misfortune and suffering. Is it the truth or did the clerk, caught up in the moment, let his imagination run away with him? It matters little. The scene is sufficiently striking that nobody will ever forget it.

Nothing is known of this martyrdom within the Beguinage—or almost nothing. Amidst all the smoke rising from the city's chimneys, nobody even notices the long grey plume of ash blown on the river breeze. The news does not reach the gate of their enclosure until the following day, when the first visitors arrive. Among them is Jeanne du Faut.

The silk merchant and little Leonor turn up just after morning Mass, an hour when Jeanne is usually to be found in her shop. No doubt she has a good reason for being here so early, but for now she says nothing to Ysabel, who greets her with surprise. Sitting opposite her friend as she works on her remedies, Jeanne shares the news she gleaned on the way, from a spinner on rue Quincampoix.

'They say the grand master was unrecognizable. An old man, his hair whitened by age and captivity.'

'Many thought him already dead before the pope convoked this council to judge him,' sighs Ysabel.

Is it fatigue? The news should come as a heavy blow, but instead she feels its impact only dully. No, decides Ysabel, it is because Leonor is here, sitting on the bench, so well behaved, gazing with interest about the old beguine's lair. It has been so long since she saw the little girl! She has barely left the Beguinage for weeks. There have been so many worries to deal with. The harsh winter that has once again filled her infirmary. Ade, who came close to death and is taking so long to get well.

'How are things at the Beguinage?' asks Jeanne.

'I don't know what to tell you. Our mistress, Dame Armelle, is holding on, fortunately. She is a fragile rampart, but a rampart nevertheless.'

'Has the Jacobin prior spoken of naming another mistress?'

'He has always shown respect for our institution, but for him, too, these are complicated times. He must think of the king, to whom he owes it to safeguard the Beguinage, of his order, which he must defend from the criticism of regular clerics, and of his monastery, where there are many who envy his position as prior.'

'And Agnes? Is she still proving so enterprising at the infirmary?'

'*You should take care of yourself,*' simpers Ysabel, mimicking her assistant's pout.

Jeanne smiles.

'Poor woman. She does not have the stature to check you.'

Ysabel does not reply but turns her head slightly to contemplate Leonor. The little girl is perfectly still and silent, as she so often is. She seems to be transfixed by an alcove in the wall, which is crammed full of flasks, bottles and uncut gemstones. Her face has matured. A triangle with high cheekbones. She does not have Maheut's vivacity, yet seems to glow with the faint light of a star in the night sky.

'What are you looking at, little one?' asks Ysabel. Leonor smiles but does not answer. The old beguine turns back to her friend.

'And how are you? You seem exhausted.'

'Don't worry, I was a little late to bed, that's all.'

Ysabel knows that she is lying, but does not press her. Jeanne has never got over the violent death of Juliotte. Nobody had understood quite how much she cared for the girl. The rumours of the beguines' special status being abolished only add to Jeanne's distress. She fears for her business and for the girls she employs. Ysabel cannot get used to seeing her so worried.

While they have been speaking, Leonor has got down from the bench. She takes a few small steps over to the alcove and stares up at it.

'Ade will be glad to see her,' murmurs Ysabel.

'How is our friend?'

'She's been up and about now for ten days or more. She was sorry that Maheut refused to bring Leonor to visit.'

'Maheut said she feared contagion.'

'And she fears it no longer?'

'To tell the truth, I did not ask her permission.'

The old beguine puts down the pot she is holding and goes over to the little girl. Tries to understand what is intriguing her so much. And then she sees it. Leonor has noticed something among the jumble of potions that should not be there.

Ysabel rises on tiptoe, takes it down and holds it out. It is cold and hard, but alive, just as it was that long-ago morning when she found it on a walk with her grandmother.

'This is a deer's antler.'

The girl runs her fingers over the antler's rough base and in between the points; it has the faded colour and rough woody texture of an old branch.

'It is for you. You can keep it,' says Ysabel with a smile. Then, turning to her friend, 'Let's go and see Ade.'

But a serious look has come across Jeanne's face. 'You take Leonor to her godmother. I will wait for you here. I have something to discuss with you.'

She lowers her voice.

'To do with Maheut. And Sire Giacomo.'

10

ONLY MAHEUT COULD EXPLAIN.

But even without her saying so, who could imagine that she would dutifully live out the rest of her life as a false widow in the habit of a beguine?

Surely not Ysabel.

The shivering pauper Ysabel found four years ago at the gate of the Beguinage, the restive young mother, the clumsy apprentice... Maheut was all of them. And she is all of them still, for, like the layers of an onion, former periods of our lives are not discarded, but covered over by later ones. But at the heart of the plant that grows, bears fruit, then wilts and withers, the bud that determines its nature remains the same. Maheut is still the girl raised so liberally by her father, too, and the runaway who knocked her husband off a horse in order to throw herself without protection into the greatest city in the kingdom. Impulsive, rebellious, caring little for the consequences her acts may have for other people, and for herself.

'I don't understand... How dare she?'

Ade stands lost for words before the old beguine. The joy of seeing Leonor again, the happy time spent together... all that is swept away by what Ysabel tells her.

'And this man! Has he no respect? In a house where he was received with kindness...'

Ysabel does not understand Giacomo's attitude, either. She can see that Maheut's strange beauty might be seductive. But he is a merchant, and his good reputation in the silk neighbour-hood and beyond is precious to him. How could he risk it by compromising a young beguine who, apart from anything else, lives with one of his partners in trade? Did he not imagine that tongues would wag? Especially these days. The weather has grown warmer this week and people have brought their chairs and benches out into the street in order to indulge in the favour-ite pastime of city folk: watching the world go by, chatting and gossiping. This is how rumours spread through the city, from neighbour to neighbour, like wildfire through dry grass.

'I have the impression that he is not accustomed to restraining his desires,' is all Ysabel says in reply.

*

Maheut has said nothing about her absence. She claimed to want to take advantage of her Sunday to rest. But while everyone thought she was stretched out on her bed, she went out. One of the girls went up to the attic and found her gone. At vespers, Maheut was still not back, and they began to worry. Jeanne du Faut was about to send out a search party when Giacomo came through the door with Maheut behind him.

'We lost track of time' was all he offered by way of an excuse.

'But where did they go?' Ade asks Ysabel now.

'They claimed they crossed the river to see the archers prac-tising at the foot of the ramparts, near the Bernardine college. Giacomo thought that this might entertain Maheut. It seems she told him that she liked to draw a bow as a child.'

'And is that really what they did?'

Ade is pale, but under her transparent skin the blood is flowing healthily once more, bringing colour to her cheeks and mouth. She seems to be getting back her strength. How to answer her? They probably did go to watch the archers as they said. But both Giacomo's initiative and Maheut's trust in confiding her childhood memories to him are signs of a growing intimacy.

'Master Giacomo came by again yesterday,' Ysabel goes on. 'He made honourable amends, confirmed that he had no bad intentions, but was simply carried away by the joy of a spring day. He wished only to please Maheut, not to sully her honour. He considers himself a friend of the household.'

'A friend would not have betrayed the trust placed in him,' snaps Ade. 'And nobody betrays trust without bad intentions! How will Dame du Faut respond?'

'What can she do, apart from sending the girl away? To forbid Master Giacomo from visiting the house would be to admit that there has been a transgression and therefore that there is cause for scandal.'

'But if he continues with such behaviour?'

'I don't believe he will. He only wanted to amuse himself. And if… if despite everything, it happens again…'

Ysabel hesitates for a moment, then declares:

'If it happens again, then we must act. We cannot let Maheut put our friends in danger.'

*

When the infirmarer has left, Ade collapses into her seat. What she has long feared has finally come to pass. She rubs her hands together, not because she is cold but rather to fan the flames of her anger: so this is how Maheut thanks those who have cared for her! She summons up old memories: the Redhead roaming around the enclosure at night, an animal from the outside, a beast in the dark. She conjures up images from the past: her flaming hair, water dripping from the long tresses onto her white skin as she washed herself in the tub, the triangle between her thighs devouring her rounded belly. With such spells Ade seeks to counter the feeling that invaded her during her sickness, and which she feels rushing into her again now. But how can you fight against a void?

It took so little… The fever was already gripping her when she returned to her husband's château to pray at his tomb. Her mother-in-law's face. Hard and cold. Like that of the recumbent statue in which Ade saw both her loved one's beauty and his arrogance. A woman dark as a Moor passed in a passageway. And suddenly Ade no longer knew why she was mourning her husband.

But what had changed? At the time, she had accepted it, forgiven him. He had been in pain. She knew she could never offer her husband a child. The doctor had told her. So he had satisfied his desire with other women, serving girls at the château, the dark one whose laughter she heard coming from the bedroom next door. A bastard was born. All men did the same. Why should she feel such rancour now?

Sometimes it seems to her that the only solid thing in her life is Leonor's love, the trust the child places in her—and now she risks losing her.

Ade paces the room in torment.

She thinks it over, trying to calm her fears. Maheut has not been thrown out of the Silk House. And if she were, Ysabel would not permit her to take away their goddaughter.

Ade feels somewhat reassured. She gives herself over to the memory of the pleasure of seeing Leonor again. It was for her sake that she came back to the Beguinage after her brother's death, rather than entering a convent as she had intended. For Leonor's sake, but also for the task she had promised to complete—and which a letter received ten days ago has made more urgent.

Calm again now, she goes to the chest at the back of the room. Already, she hears the voice that drives and gives rhythm to her thoughts. She removes the manuscript, turns the thick pages, follows the frantic writing with her finger. Finds the passage she was seeking.

> *Beguines say I err,*
> *Priests, clerics and Preachers,*
> *Augustinians, Carmelites and the Friars Minor.*

These are the lines on which she was working when Humbert was sent away from the Beguinage. Since then, she has often come back to them. There is such solitude in these words. And courage too. A courage that nobody can deny the Valenciennes beguine possessed, for it was measured on the execution pyre. Was that why, to her own surprise, when the Franciscan gave her permission to abandon her task, she simply replied: 'I will finish what I started'?

The young woman shifts the desk into the daylight and chooses some new leaves of parchment, which she fixes upon the writing case. Copying makes for lengthy, tedious work. Carefully tracing the lines and margins that will serve as guide, trimming and retrimming her quill, forever dipping it in the inkwell. Writing with her hand poised in mid-air, till her fingers grow numb and her wrist is stiff with fatigue. Trying to keep the script legible while varying the thickness of the letters, making some smaller and some larger, playing around with blanks spaces and abbreviations, all to make the text fit the rulings on the page as exactly as possible... But the words she is writing possess magical power, they are means by which the Word is transmitted, the mount in which its jewel is displayed. Ade knows she must remember this and take care.

In his letter, Humbert said he would arrive around the feast of Saint James the Lesser. She has just enough time to finish.

She takes up her quill and rests its nib, which she has split so it will draw a strong line that suits Marguerite's style, on the parchment. She catches the smell of the ink, and, at the same time, the sweeter scent of the Franciscan bending over her shoulder.

Does she realize? Marguerite's *Mirror* is reflecting a new, different image of herself back at her.

11

THE SUN THAT SHINES on Paris at the end of March 1314 also warms the Hainaut. But in the lands of the north, just as in the capital, the wind and rain return before the end of Lent, to scourge the land and its inhabitants. In the Franciscans' garden, the fine Easter flowers lie broken and soiled with dirt, the festival of light wallowing in the mud.

Like everybody else, Humbert feels the interminable greyness of these days, which seem to snuff out the life in each of the monastery's rooms, darkening corridors and cells, plunging the chapter hall and refectory into gloom—even the library, despite its wooden panelling and the warm presence of books. Only the majestic darkness of the church, brought into relief by candlelight, can resist the lifeless melancholy of the world outside.

On the Monday after the Low Sunday after Easter, he lingers in the sanctuary as the faithful troop noisily out of church. Coming down from the pulpit, he stands for a while with his hands crossed over the front of his habit. He has always appreciated this place whose austerity suits his own: the stark simplicity of the vast nave, its harmonious proportions, the five wide arcades that branch off from the central nave, linking it to the lateral aisles and giving the space a sense of unity and solidity, the pillars soberly surmounted by abacuses and capitals sculpted with twining greenery. The only decoration on the pulpit itself is formed of simple twisted columns and the face of a green man, whose forehead, temples and beard are tangled with the stylized foliage of a tree. Situated near the choir, on the church's southern side, the pulpit allows the preacher's voice to reach the whole congregation, carrying all the way to the church doors, while the sacredness of the sermon is underlined by its proximity to the altar. The solemnity of this place pleases Humbert more than the hubbub of the grande place of Valenciennes or the market stalls or any of the other busy spots to which the Franciscans' apostolic mission has often sent him to spread the new word.

The final words of his sermon still echo in his ears. Whatever mood he is in when he begins, preaching always plunges Humbert into a state of concentration and fills him with an overwhelming feeling of elation. The carefully chosen words, the flow of the sentences, the gestures that he matches to their rhythm, using his hand just enough to emphasize a point without gesticulating wildly, the tone of his voice, gentle but strong... His whole being, body and soul, is animated by the force of his thought. But when he finishes, it is as if a heavy, leaden cloak has fallen onto his shoulders. He feels crushed by fatigue and discouragement.

*

There is no lack of work to be done at the monastery. Following the teaching of Saint Bonaventure himself, the Franciscans usually establish their communities in dynamic cities where money and believers are plentiful. Valenciennes, built at the confluence of the Escaut and Rhonelle rivers, just at the spot where the latter becomes truly navigable, is one of the most industrious cities in all of Flanders. Linked to Tournai, Ghent, Antwerp, and beyond them to the North Sea, it is dominated by a powerful merchant guild. The Franciscans also play their role in the city's busy commercial life, maintaining strong ties with the various craft confraternities, hosting meetings of master drapers, wool-workers and dyers at the monastery, taking part in processions of the confraternities' patron saints, and thus gaining an influence over the running of the city, and dozens of surrounding villages.

Just as all his fellow brothers do, Humbert contributes to the monastery's affairs according to his own talents. The prior is pleased to have permitted his training in Paris. The Franciscan's abilities as an orator are now known throughout the region. His preaching wins the monastery both believers and donations, and Humbert is regularly invited to stay in establishments that are connected to the Order, and his reputation as a learned man has led him to the tables of the city's wealthy merchants. But he is often gripped by ennui—and like now, by a dizzying sense of loneliness.

He misses Brother Jean so much! Their stimulating conversations, the affection the old man showed him, of which Humbert only understood the true value after his death. Then there was the example he provided. For Brother Jean, learning was not something done for its own sake: it inspired a spirit of solidarity in accord with his Order's ideals. Guided by him, Humbert had found a way of giving meaning to his life. The master's death has left him empty, hollowed out by his own impatience, regrets and frustrations. The freedom of the mendicant friars, their activity in the world, which had attracted him to the order after his parents were ruined, today seems to him like a handful of rye tossed to a starving man.

*

Outside, the fog shrouding the monastery has turned to drizzle, and the drizzle is growing heavier. It beats against the stained-glass windows of the choir in fierce gusts. The winters get harsher and longer ever year, thinks Humbert, and the springs colder and wetter. The harvests are dwindling; there is talk of a new famine. Rumours of the impending apocalypse seem more plausible than ever.

What would Brother Jean make of it all? The heavens and political affairs seem in gloomy accord with each other. The monetary problems that have struck the kingdom have only worsened the sense of insecurity. The impoverished and desperate are flocking to the monasteries in ever greater numbers. A wave of discontent is sweeping the countryside and beginning to affect the minor landed nobility, who have organized themselves into leagues to claim what they believe is due to them. The war between Frederick of Habsburg and Ludwig of Bavaria for the title of Holy Roman Emperor is sowing further unrest. The century's majestic progress seems to have been stopped in its tracks.

The weakest, as always, are the first to suffer. That is what Jean de Querayn would say.

*

Humbert lets his arms fall to his side and shakes out his rangy frame. He is disappointed with himself, worried about the lack of mastery he exercises over his thoughts. For he knows where they lead him; they always go back to the same place.

He goes back up the nave, past the side chapels that line the lateral aisles, stops at an oratory blazing with candlelight, which flickers on the marble face of a Virgin. Seated in the crook of her elbow, the Infant Jesus stares up at her as if trying to pierce her mystery. Humbert looks at her, too, but the grace of her features, the tresses that flow down her neck, only worsen his troubles.

He has held the thought of Ade at a distance all these months, but for the last three days he has been unable to do so. Ever since that letter arrived from the Cordeliers. By one of those coincidences that the devil is capable of arranging, Humbert was the first to come across it—he sometimes helps the prior, whose eyesight is weakening with age, with his correspondence—but by now the news from their Parisian brothers has thrown the whole monastery into turmoil. After many delays and postponements—so typical of this sickly pontiff—Clement V finally published the decrees of the Vienne Council against the beguines on 21st March 1314.

Their special status is on its way to being abolished. The decree severely condemns their communal way of life, their habits, which resemble those of nuns, and the privileged relationships they maintain with certain friars. By all these practices, it is alleged, the beguines are dishonestly sowing confusion, passing themselves off as nuns when they follow no rule and owe obedience to nobody, and in fact continue to manage their own property. The decree also criticizes them for engaging in theological speculations that risk leading simple people into error. On top of the pope's disciplinary sanction comes a series of doctrinal articles that define the supposed heresy of the beguines. Mixed in with the whole tirade is criticism already made elsewhere of the Free Spirit and even the Waldensian movements, for such faults as disobeying the Church's commands and refusing to pray, fast, or stand in reverence before the Eucharist.

The humble piety of the majority of beguines, their life of work and charity, scarcely merits such accusations. Brother Jean foresaw all this, and some of his companions—including Humbert himself—had thought his worries exaggerated, yet he was right: any faith not controlled by the Church now risks condemnation. Any manifestation of secular piety considered too liberal is regarded with suspicion. Alarming news has been arriving recently from the Germanic regions, where laywomen affiliated with the Franciscan order are being violently attacked. Indeed, over and above the beguines, it is the Franciscans who are the power-hungry clergy's true target. Accusing the beguines of heresy is a way of compromising the brothers who are in charge of their spiritual conduct.

Humbert closes his eyes and presses his hands to his face, trying to dispel the anger contorting his features. When he opens them again, the smile of the Virgin at the Child, altered by the wavering shadows, suddenly seems gentler and sadder. He turns on his heel. Impatience has gripped him, and he refuses to fight it. He goes back to the central nave, striding more violently than he should in such a place, trampling the funerary slabs of the wealthy merchants and nobles of the city that pave the church entryway.

A rainy gust slams the door shut behind him.

12

THE FRANCISCAN ARRIVES in Paris just as the scandal of the king's three daughters-in-law breaks. Marguerite of Burgundy, the wife of Louis, Philip the Fair's oldest, is accused of having taken Philip d'Aunay, a Norman knight attached to her husband's retinue, as a lover. Blanche of Artois, the wife of Charles, the sovereign's youngest son, is accused of having done the same with Gautier d'Aunay, the knight's brother. Blanche's sister, Jeanne d'Artois, is accused of having known about these liaisons and said nothing.

On that Friday, as Humbert passes through the city gates in the fine carriage of the Valenciennes cloth merchant Sir Jean de Castel, the two seducers confess under torture to having committed the crime of adultery for three years running, including on holy days and in holy places. Two days later, they are flayed alive on the public square. Their penises and heads are cut off and their bodies dragged to the gibbet where, stripped of all their skin, they are hung by the shoulders and arms. Later a bailiff, as well as dozens of servants and nobles in the entourages of the king and his daughters-in-law, are put to the question and executed in turn, some drowned, others hanged in secret.

The people of the city, although used to the horrors of the day, are shocked by such violence. With two of his sons, including the heir to the throne, publicly cuckolded, of course Philip could not let the affront go unpunished. But the savagery with which the punishment was applied speaks more loudly than the offence itself. Despite the king's austere lifestyle and the penitence he inflicts on himself, evil has entered into his very dwelling; the king now sees himself as the last rampart against sin, an avenging angel.

*

Humbert and Ade have heard whisperings of the scandal, if not the details, but do not speak of it. When he knocks on the door of her house, the day after his return, she is not expecting him. He, on the other hand, has had time to prepare himself for the meeting. Still, he is shocked by the gauntness of the beguine's features, the hollowness of her cheeks, and more disappointed than he ought to be when at first she keeps her distance from him. Yet she soon comes to greet him, holding out her hands like a friend. And he no longer regrets his imprudence in visiting.

The prior of Valenciennes was surprised at his request to bring his trip to Paris forward; the date had been fixed for the beginning of May. But Humbert was able to convince him: Jean de Castel, whose family has strong ties with the monastery, was going to the capital for business and had agreed to take Humbert with him. His journey would be both quicker and cheaper this way. Humbert would also be able to consult their Parisian brothers on the best attitude to adopt towards the beguines in future. The pope's decrees had been published but not yet promulgated, so the Franciscans of Valenciennes did not yet know how much danger they were in, but still it was possible to take certain precautions.

As soon as he arrived in Paris, letting himself be guided by the impulse to which he had surrendered himself, Humbert sent a letter to the mistress of the Royal Beguinage.

'I do not know if Dame Armelle remembered my name, but as soon as she saw that the missive came from the Cordeliers it must have done the trick,' he explains now. 'She wrote straight back granting me permission to visit you.'

'I am relieved to hear it,' Ade says.

Yes, she has indeed grown thinner. Her robe hangs loosely over pointed shoulders and a hollow belly. Even the perfect oval of her face is changed, the flesh hanging loose despite the tightness of her wimple.

'You seem unwell,' whispers Humbert.

'I was, but I am in good health now. How goes it with you?'

'Well, thank you.'

They fall into a tense silence. What more is there to say? They have never spoken of themselves before, Humbert realizes. Perhaps he ought to have warned her of his visit, but he feared she would suggest they meet at the Silk House. He remembers his last visit there with displeasure. The cramped, crowded room, the voices and laughter of the other women so close by, their curious glances when he left the building with a heavy tread. There was that little girl too, whom he has often thought of since, though he does not know why. Small and slender, but so composed. She sat at Ade's side, huddled close to her. Not like a child seeking protection, but like a friend who gives it.

His hostess watches him and waits. Finally, she is the one to bring the conversation around to where it must go.

'I am sorry, but I have not completely finished the work you entrusted to me. I was not expecting you so soon.'

'Do not worry. I am in Paris for several weeks. I can wait.'

Opposite him, the young woman lowers her head. The veil of white muslin wrapped about her hair slides down onto her cheek and lifts slightly when she speaks again.

'Despite everything, I have spent much time at my desk these last days. There remain only a few pages to complete.'

'I am grateful to you.' Humbert would like to say more, but nothing seems appropriate. He is troubled to learn that Ade worked so much while she was ill, and conscious that he is to blame for her fatigue. A door bangs shut somewhere outside. What is he waiting for? He should leave.

'I will be at the Cordeliers,' he says. 'You may send me word there when it is time to come and collect the manuscript.'

He makes a step towards his hostess, as if to take leave of her, but Ade does not move. She seems deep in thought. Then, suddenly, she rises briskly to her feet and stands in front of him.

'Would you like to do as we used to?'

Humbert does not understand.

'Shall we read the text together? The final pages that we did not have the chance to work on before your departure?'

'I cannot stay very long,' he murmurs.

A few minutes later, it is just as it used to be: Ade sitting at the work desk with Humbert leaning over her shoulder.

13

'I WON'T, ADE. I WON'T!'

Clémence's eyes are full of tears, her cheeks burning, her nose running.

She practically forced her way through the door. Ade only had time to hide the book in the chest. The parchment she was working on is still on the desk, the pages held open by two paperweights. The ink is still wet, the quill strokes shining on the matte vellum. Ade moves in front of the desk in an attempt to hide it, but Clémence does not spare it a glance. Instead, she throws herself at Ade, wrapping her arms round the older woman's waist, pressing her cheek against her bosom. The girl came rushing over without a cloak. Her robe gives off a sour smell of stale sweat.

'Clémence, calm yourself.' Ade tries to loosen her grasp. 'What is happening?'

'It's my father!'

'You are hurting me,' Ade protests, pushing her back more firmly. 'Take hold of yourself.'

Clémence finally lets her go. Ade takes her by the hand and leads her into the bedroom.

'What happened to your father? An accident?'

'Oh, Ade, no… it is not that.'

'Then what?'

'He wants me to leave the Beguinage.'

'It is not the first time he has said so. Why are you so distressed?'

'He wants to sell me!' she cries in a shrill voice.

Ade sighs and puts her arm around the girl's shoulder, trying to master her own impatience. She did not need this interruption; she is sufficiently troubled without it.

'Tell me, but please calm yourself or I won't understand a thing.'

Clémence's chest heaves and trembles against her own. Her hair under the veil is as neglected as the rest of her body, her greasy locks hastily tied up. She is nothing like the girl everyone in the Beguinage knows—always so well-cared-for, coquettish even. What could have happened to her? Ade has not seen her in a while. Clémence has knocked on her door once or twice, but she was so busy that she did not want to be disturbed. And since Humbert's visit, she needs peace and quiet more than ever.

'My father came to visit just now,' the girl eventually replies. 'He declared that he had waited long enough, that I was of an age to enter society. He gave me three weeks to prepare.'

'Was your mother with him?'

'Yes, but what difference does that make? She follows her husband's lead in everything!'

'Why do you say he is going to *sell* you?'

'It's because his business affairs are going badly. I am not stupid, I've heard the talk. He wants to marry me to one of his merchant friends.'

'Are you sure?' Ade asks gently. 'Maybe he is just concerned about your future?'

'But I do not want to leave!'

She is becoming hysterical again.

'Be reasonable, Clémence. You will soon be eighteen years old.'

'You don't understand, you will never understand! I want nothing to do with a husband, I want to stay near you.'

Ade lets her arm drop from the girl's shoulders. All of a sudden, she is filled with a profound weariness. Clémence has so little control over her emotions. What she feels for Ade is only infatuation, the admiration of a young girl for a grown woman. She has the same urge for recognition that Ade herself felt in her younger days, the same desire to be chosen. She remembers how a smile from the Benedictine nun who supervised her writing lessons would send her into transports of delight, so deeply did she venerate her. But every age has its needs and its duties. Clémence is a child no longer, though she behaves like one.

She must respond. She knows what she should say. It is obvious. Yet Ade is too honest not to hear how the words sound in her mind. How can she lecture the girl? Is she free of confusion herself?

She shudders, and Clémence, still waiting in silence, pressed against her friend's side, feels Ade trembling—and begins to hope.

*

It was almost nothing. A new softness, an intensity in Humbert's eyes. She wanted to find a way back to the strange complicity that they had known last year. She has missed those times spent together, though she can not bring herself to fully admit it. After fearing Humbert at first, during the hours working with him on Marguerite's text, she had let herself be overcome by the subtlety of his mind and the brilliance of his thought. He too had been surprised at her rigour as a reader, her comprehension of *The Mirror*, the precision of her translation. Two minds contemplating each other. Ade had never known an intimacy of this kind.

But when they were reunited almost two weeks ago, another atmosphere had taken over.

Had she changed, or had he? They could no longer find the same harmony; there was a tension between them now, a feverishness. Ade's voice wavers—but perhaps that is just because of her illness? She is still getting her strength back, after all. Humbert fetches her some water to wet her throat; their hands brush as he hands her the goblet. He is no closer than before, but the space between them is heavy with his presence. Time passes, the room darkens. She longs for the relief of his departure, but hopes he will stay a little longer.

Since then, he has not left her thoughts.

*

'Ade…'

A whisper in her ear. Clémence is worried by her long silence. Ade becomes aware of the body pressed against hers, moves away and gets to her feet.

'I don't know what more to say to you, Clémence.'

The sentence is spoken wearily, but to the girl's ears it sounds like a door slamming shut.

'You could talk to my mother. Try to persuade her. She trusts you.'

'You said yourself she follows her husband's lead in everything.'

'And Dame Armelle?'

'I expect she will accede to your father's wishes.'

The bed bangs on the floorboards. Clémence stands bolts upright, facing Ade. Her eyes are burning again, but this time with anger.

'So you won't do anything? This is how you care for me?'

'I do care for you, Clémence. But I don't know what you want from me. I have answered you in the friendliest and wisest way I know how. Surely you don't expect to spend your whole life in the Beguinage? There are other commitments waiting for you, and other pleasures, too.'

Then, thinking to soften the girl's pain, as unreasonably as she is behaving, she adds: 'We will be able to see each other, Clémence. You can come to visit me, and I will do the same.'

But these words, instead of appeasing the girl, rub salt into the wound.

Clémence starts to walk away, pauses in the doorway and turns around.

'You are humiliating me, Dame Ade. I took care of you for weeks. I mopped your brow and washed your body. This is how you thank me! With the promise of a visit!'

'Clémence, I beg you.'

'I hoped for so much from your friendship. I thought we could share more than chattering about life here. Those books, for example, and those scholarly conversations that you seem to love. I worked so hard to learn. But no doubt my mind is not sufficiently elevated for yours. You prefer to keep your fine intelligence for others! And to send me to join the flock of good wives. So be it.'

She is already going down the stairs. But as she goes, she throws over her shoulder:

'Oh, and don't act so superior, Ade. I know what you are doing.'

14

T HE CATASTROPHE COMES from an unexpected quarter.
Like a bowstring drawn by an archer, its power has been
growing little by little. But it is the tender hand of a young girl
that lets fly the arrow.

More than two weeks after his earlier visit, Humbert returns
to the Beguinage. As he passes through the gate, he is aware
that this is one of the last times he will come here. When Ade
welcomes him into her home, she knows that the next time he
crosses her threshold it will only be to take away the manuscript.

This situation affects what follows—and how they are with
each other that day. Like the distance that they have imposed
between themselves out of prudence. They now know the power
of that: every detail of their encounters will be dredged up time
and time again by their starving minds; every gesture and glance
will be deformed as if put under a magnifying glass; every word
will be charged with the weight of those that were left unspoken.

Humbert lays down his cloak, runs his eyes over the last pages
of the translation. Ade has spent even more time composing
them than the preceding pages. For almost a year this task, so
often interrupted but always resumed, has set the rhythm of her
life. She now fears losing it.

They keep far away from each other, she standing near the
window, he bent over the writing case. She watches him. The
high forehead, the straight eyebrows, the deep line above the

nose, which slices like an eagle's beak across his angular features. It is a tense, ascetic face. And yet the lips are full and generous.

The Franciscan silently mouths the words that Ade has written. His eyes, like those of a sailor transfixed by the motion of the waves, slide down the downstrokes and climb the upstrokes, noting a weakness in the parchment here, a scratch in the vellum there. Each letter is a movement and he can see the copyist's hand in every one: her dexterity, her carefulness, her gentle rigour.

Ade does not need to hear the words he is reading. She knows them all. Marguerite's whole book, its dialogue and its argument all lead to this point, this ardent apotheosis: the song of the Soul reaching its own annihilation, reaching the absolute freedom where it is sitting mingled with that of God.

> *I have said I will love Him,*
> *I lie, for I am not.*
> *It is He alone who loves me,*
> *He is, and I am not;*
> *And nothing more is necessary to me*
> *Than what He wills,*
> *And that He is worthy.*
> *He is fullness,*
> *And by this I am impregnated,*
> *This is the divine seed and true Love.*

Humbert closes the notebook. What does he mean by this gesture? He himself does not know. He goes over to Ade, takes her hand between his, brings it to his lips. She feels her legs weaken, her body give way, lets herself fall against the chest that receives her.

On the other side of the passageway, Clémence is at her window. And she sees them.

For a week now the girl has kept to her room, saying she is ill. Hoping, without admitting it to herself, that her friend will come to see her. But Ade did not come. Only Agnes.

The days went by. Her neighbour did not so much as ask how she was. Her anger returned, but not the kind of furious, invigorating feeling that surges up, strikes out and is then soothed. Instead she felt her rage dwindling in the emptiness of loss. Gradually, the need to see Ade began to overshadow everything else. Clémence would soon be ready to apologize, even to take back her words with a smile if she had to. One more day and she would do just that. She was already feeling excited, almost joyful at the prospect. And then that very morning she hears footsteps outside, somebody knocking at Ade's door. She opens the window and sees him. He has come back, the Franciscan who is the cause of everything.

When the two shadows mingle, the feeling of betrayal is so violent that it takes her breath away.

*

After that, everything happens so quickly! Agnes comes back from the infirmary, sees Clémence distraught, questions her insistently. She has never been capable of keeping a secret—her mother was always telling her: 'Learn to keep your mouth shut, girl!' She tells her everything. The writing desk, the manuscript in the chest, the friar. Agnes asks more questions, which the girl barely hears; she is hot, feels like crying, is already afraid, but it is too late now, is it not? She has told somebody. Agnes reflects, looks through the window at the sun still high in the sky. Then she says:

'Clémence, get your cloak.'

15

LATER THE GIRL will replay the scene many times in her head. Each word, each gesture, and the actions that followed them. What she should have done, what she shouldn't have said.

But it is too late. Agnes's cousin Geoffroy was seated opposite her in a dark wood chair. His skull shaved almost to the skin, his face held bolt upright above his collar, the rigidity of his body accentuated by the stiffness of his white robe. He is still young, with regular features but skin pitted with smallpox scars. The girl tells her story once more, her tone less assured, less heated than before. She is tired from the walk from the Beguinage, oppressed by the silence of this gloomy room, the walls lined with great oak armoires.

'This Dame Ade, has she been at the Beguinage for long?' asks Brother Geoffroy.

'About ten years,' answers Agnes.

'How does she comport herself?'

'She lives very discreetly, takes little part in communal life.'

'Has she shown signs of excessive or demonstrative faith?'

'I would not say that. But how can one know what she does in the secrecy of her room? She spends most of her time there, especially in recent months. Is that not so, Clémence?'

The girl lowers her head.

'And this Franciscan, do you know him?'

'No. According to Mademoiselle de Crété, he had already visited, and more than once, last summer. But I was absent at the time…'

'That is true,' confirms Clémence. Then she adds in a whisper, 'But he came before too.'

She had not told Agnes this. She says it now because she senses confusedly that the man opposite her does not mean well, that his attention should be deflected away from Ade. She did not want things to take this turn, she hoped only that the Franciscan would be sent away, and that Ade would be reprimanded and made to give up the work that takes up all her time and attention. That everything would return to the way it was before.

'When?' Geoffroy asks curtly.

'A long time ago now. I had been in the Beguinage for a few months; Dame Jeanne la Bricharde was still with us. She was the one who introduced us to him. She was showing him around. Ade did not know him then, I am certain.'

'La Bricharde?'

The Dominican is surprised. Everyone in the room knows that the mistress is buried close by, in the church.

Agnes shoots Clémence a confused glance. She also seems unsettled by the turn the conversation has taken. The girl frowns, focuses on an image that surfaces from her memories.

'He was from the North,' continues Clémence. 'A very tall man, black hair.'

No, Agnes has not forgotten. The friar looking for the redhead, and Ysabel lied to him. But the thread of events escapes her.

'Are you sure it was he?'

'I am sure. I recognized him the instant I saw him.'

'Where did he come from?' demands Geoffroy.

'He was looking for an acquaintance from Valenciennes,' answers Agnes. 'I suppose he came from that town.'

Geoffroy breaks his rigid pose, strikes the arm of his seat with his hand. 'Valenciennes! Like that beguine! She had supporters there. Even in the Franciscan monastery!'

The Dominican stands up. He is tall. Clémence thinks of her father; when she resists him, he intimidates her with his stature. But Geoffroy's authority is of another kind. Cold and hard.

'This is a serious affair. I'm sure you are aware that certain Franciscans are suspected of dabbling in the heresy of the Free Spirit. If that is the case with your man—and I suspect it is, given what you have reported to me—we must act. As a preaching friar he may be spreading erroneous and forbidden ideas. Not to mention that he may have other followers within your community. Since Jeanne la Bricharde herself frequented him...'

'But, cousin,' cried Agnes. 'Not her, you knew her!'

He brushes away her protest with a wave of his hand. He has forgotten Clémence now and looks only at his cousin.

'Jeanne la Bricharde had a high opinion of her role. As for me, I was always hesitant about the Beguinage, you know that, Agnes. The king did us the honour of giving us the supervision of it, but for too long your mistresses and companions have acted as they wanted. I do not think it good for women to be in sole charge of their fates. Nor that they purport to be educated, although that is growing more common in our days. A beguinage is no place for religious debates. What you have just told me only makes me more convinced of my point of view.'

The ugly marks pitting his skin have paled and grown larger.

'What do you mean to do, Geoffroy?' Agnes whispers.

'The Franciscan Order, like ours, benefits from pontifical exemption. The matter falls within the purview of the Inquisition. I am going to have to refer him to it.'

'The Inquisition...' Agnes hesitates. 'I did not think the matter could go so far. Perhaps the prior of the Jacobins would prefer it to be treated with more discretion. He might simply send Dame Ade away and warn the Franciscans about their brother's misconduct. Their shame would be sufficient punishment for the both of them.'

'A book banned by the pope's emissary is circulating in your Beguinage and you want us to close our eyes? A woman is seduced in the Royal Beguinage and you speak of warnings?'

'That is not what I was suggesting,' murmurs Agnes. Her voice is subdued. Clémence feels fear gnawing at her belly.

'I am sure that the prior will agree with me,' Geoffroy goes on, 'but do not worry, I will not act imprudently. Go back to the Beguinage. It is late. Tomorrow morning, I will come myself with a witness and we will visit this Dame Ade. We will see what she is hiding.'

*

Night has fallen. A horn rings out from the watchtower of the Châtelet. Clémence clings on to the side of the cart that is taking them back to the Beguinage at a pace, rattling over the cobblestones, jolting with every crack in the road. She is freezing, her body stiff with cold. As she alights from the cart, she slips in a puddle, but cannot bring herself to take the arm Agnes holds out to steady her. As soon as they are through the gate she runs to the house. An old woman pokes her head out of her window, worried about noise at such a late hour. But Clémence does not see her. She sees only the light in Ade's window.

A few moments later, Ysabel hears a knock at her door. She opens it to find the girl wrapped tightly in her cloak, her face tense with distress.

16

As AUTUMN REDDENS the forests where he has brought down so many stags, now it is the hunter's turn to drop to his knees. He hunches over, panting, and collapses to lie on his side, his head and crown resting in the dirt.

Nobody knows what King Philip the Fair is suffering from. The doctors are confounded. Neither his pulse nor his urine gave any sign that he was ill or in mortal danger. But the sovereign feels the end approaching and asks to be taken to Fontainebleau, so that he may die in the place of his birth. He gives his eldest son his final words of advice, threatening him with a curse if he does not follow them. He receives the sacraments before a large audience, then takes his last breath in the thirtieth year of his reign, the last Friday of November 1314, the eve of the Feast of Saint Andrew.

Philip leaves on the throne a son who is incapable of producing a legitimate heir: Marguerite, his adulterous wife, is imprisoned in a freezing cell, hair shorn and shivering in a ragged chemise. With any luck she will not survive much longer. The king is also abandoning a ruined kingdom beset by unrest and rebellion. Merchants are complaining about the constant manipulations of the currency and the taxes levied for a military campaign in Flanders that was halted even before the first battle was fought. Meanwhile the nobles, the traditional supporters of power, are tired of seeing their prerogatives flouted by the agents of the crown—all these jurists, bailiffs and magistrates, these judges and financiers who have taken their place and pillaged their coffers. So, the nobles have organized into leagues in Champagne and Burgundy, Forez, Ponthieu and Artois...

Nevertheless, the king is buried with the customary honour and solemnity. After the state funeral at Notre-Dame on the twenty-fifth day of the moon, the body is brought on a litter to Saint-Denis, dressed in an ermine mantle and covered with cloth of gold, bearing the crown, sceptre and hand of justice. His whole body is buried near his forefathers, except for the heart, which at his request is removed to be interred in the Dominican convent at Poissy that he founded.

*

The great bell of Notre-Dame tolls long that day, echoed by every bell tower in the city. The solemn sound fills every neighbourhood, every street. A deep, unending vibration that sets walls and people aquiver. Even huddled in her hiding place up under the eaves, Maheut can feel it.

The Silk House is deserted, the shop closed. Jeanne du Faut and the girls have gone out, like most of the city, to line the route of the funeral cortege. Only Maheut does not have permission to attend the ceremony. She has only just dragged herself out of bed and is not yet dressed in her robe. She is in her chemise, her hair hanging loose. She can feel it warming her skin through the rough cloth of her garment. It is more than a year now since she cut it. Since the day of another cortege, that of the kings of France and England who processed by torchlight along the same Grande rue Saint-Denis that the king's body will be carried along today. Her hair came loose that day too, a lock of it dangling from her headdress. '*Bellissima!*' Giacomo had said, just as he had of Leonor a few minutes earlier. Then he took her hand in his.

Now the curls snake over her shoulders and breasts, flow over her belly, falling all the way to her waist now, looser than before. Maheut takes a lock in one hand and plunges a comb into it with the other, taking as much comfort as she can from the feel of the warm, living mane under her fingers.

Everything is so sad here! Even without the tolling for the dead outside, the atmosphere would be funereal. The house has changed—she has barely been able to recognize it these past few months. Or rather, she barely recognizes Jeanne du Faut. The mistress has been snuffed out, like a dancing flame that dies down and shrinks, till only an ember remains, and soon just ashes. First there was Juliotte's death. Then the threats to their community. The death of Pope Clement was announced in April and the promulgation of the Vienne decrees again postponed. The beguines all thought they had won a brief respite, but some people were already taking advantage of their weakened status to criticize their privileges more openly. Linen weavers and silk spinners accused the women, who were exempt from having to undergo apprenticeships, of unfair competition; the guilds demanded that their activities be limited.

'If we do not work,' complained Jeanne, 'they accuse us of living off gifts and begging and of diverting money from the truly poor, while we are young and strong enough to provide for ourselves. But when we *do* work, we are exposed to all kinds of criticism and denunciations.'

Finally came the scandal that rocked the Beguinage itself. Now Ade is gone, and Ysabel no longer comes to visit.

The silk work is still done and done well, and the clientele still satisfied, but in the bedrooms and the attic workshop the girls' cries and laughter are stifled now, as are the songs the embroiderers used to launch into whenever they stopped to stretch their fingers.

The comb snags. Maheut pulls the handful of hair away from her bust to get at it better. The cold pinches her nipple, making it stand out under her chemise. She ought to get dressed, but she already feels like she is suffocating. It isn't just from being shut up in the house for a couple of days, it's this whole life, in which every gesture must be held back. Jeanne has become so fearful, constantly telling the girls to watch how they dress, how they walk, to make sure they don't talk too loudly. If she could, she would tell them to blend in with the shadows in the alleys.

The novelty of this place has gone now, along with the relative freedom that allowed Maheut to find some pleasure when she arrived in rue Troussevache. Everything weighs on her, including the city, with its stale air, high walls and narrow passageways. A cage for her already shackled body. When did she last feel a fresh breeze on her skin?

'If you wish,' Giacomo had said, 'I will take you with me. You can shoot your bow as much as you want, and ride horses too. You'll see. I have a large estate, with green pastures that stretch up into the hills for you to gallop through. The horses love that. My animals are all very happy. You know, I have a stallion the colour of your hair.'

Maheut shakes her head, pulls the eiderdown from her bed and wraps herself in it. Of course, he is not the man she dreamt of as a child. A cloth merchant! But what is she herself today? A runaway without rank or money. Of course Giacomo is kind, flattering and well-mannered with everyone he meets—that is his job, after all—but still she recognizes a strange freedom in him, a vitality like her own. He loves all that Maheut has been forced to hide for so long: her red hair, the flamboyance of her soul. And he tells her so.

The letter is hidden under her mattress. Maheut didn't think she would hear from him again. After their escape to the archery butts—how they had run! People had stared but she hadn't cared a bit—he had promised to send word. They'd had such fun together! She had not laughed like that since her childhood. He could have taken advantage of the situation, her head was spinning, but he had merely put his arm about her waist in an alleyway corner. Then he had told her about his country, his house, the wife he had lived apart from for years.

After that he had come to the Silk House only once more, to conclude his business there. Jeanne treated him amiably enough: it was important to show that nothing serious had happened, to protect her reputation in the neighbourhood. Giacomo had not said a word to Maheut during this visit, but only shot her one of the rapid, intense glances she knew so well. The look that had touched her from the beginning. When he looked at her, he saw everything, just like when he examined all those pieces of silk and could detect the slightest defect, the most discreet repair. He could see whether she was happy or tired, noticed when she changed her headdress. One day he noticed a scratch at the base of her fingernail. He was the only one to have understood the depth of her distress when they had brought back Juliotte's body.

She thought he would disappear after settling up with Jeanne. But then, at the beginning of the week, came this note, passed to her in secret by an errand boy. Maheut tried to slip away from the house but was caught and punished. And now she cannot decide what to do.

*

She hears the door fly open downstairs. Raised voices, inside now. A rattling of pots and pans from the kitchen. They are preparing a meal, no doubt.

The stairs creak. Light steps patter up the ladder to the attic. The door is pushed open. It is the little girl.

She is kind, thinks Maheut. She knows I am shut up in here. 'Come,' she says and holds out her arms.

Leonor comes closer, climbs onto the bed. She sleeps there now, at her mother's side. She has shot up since the spring so that she no longer fits in her cot, and the laundress who has taken Juliotte's place in the attic refuses to let her share her bed. Maheut does not complain. Leonor is still just as quiet, and she has grown used to her soft body.

She opens the eiderdown she is wrapped in and pulls the child in close. Leonor lets her. She still barely speaks. The women of the house had worried about her reaction when Ade stopped coming. But the child has asked nothing about her absence, nor shed a single tear.

Giacomo said he was ready to take her, too. He made no promise except to take care of them. Now it is up to Maheut to decide what she wants—and what she is prepared to risk for it.

17

I T IS TOO LATE, thinks Ysabel. She holds out the phial of wine she was allowed to bring, but he barely swallows a mouthful before setting it down and letting his head fall back against the wall. He is thinner, of course. His beard is unkempt and his hair has grown over the circle of his tonsure. It falls over his forehead and ears now, and she can see it is turning grey, as are his eyebrows. But it is not so much the physical transformation that makes him unrecognizable. It is the air of sluggishness about him, the total abandon that slackens his features, the lifelessness of his eyes.

'How did you get in?' he asks eventually.

'A few coins were enough to sway the guard.'

'You should have saved your money.'

'I did not want Advent to go by without visiting you.'

'Advent,' murmured Humbert, his eyes still closed, 'the time of change.' His voice is husky, catching in his throat. '…The time of winter and darkness, of seeds sleeping under the earth. Of flowers of hope and fruits of love both ruined…'

'But after which,' whispers Ysabel, 'thanks to the birth of Christ, comes the time of renewal when the dawn breaks, the plants grow and bear fruit.'

She sighs, sits on a little bench that the guard set out for her. Humbert is not chained, they have left him free to move. He sits on the floor at the foot of his mattress, leaning against the wall in a corner of his cell. A bare foot protrudes from under his robe, the toes swollen and the nails blue.

'I know the four periods of the liturgical year as well as you,' Ysabel goes on gently. 'And like me you know that, just as with the seasons and the hours of a day, they form a circle, ceaselessly repeated, a cycle that is always renewed. Do not yield to despair.'

The Franciscan does not react. He sits like an animal hiding in its lair, hunched in the darkest depths of the earth, no longer fighting, merely waiting for the end to come and its body to grow stiff. He seems so far away. How can she bring him back?

'Despair is a sin,' she says again. 'It turns man away from God and deprives him of his senses, of his awareness of the mire in which he lies and of the devil who leads him to hell.'

Humbert's eyes are closed, but a droll smile stretches across his lips. He finally leans forward, away from the wall.

'You would have made a good preacher, Dame Ysabel. You know how to use the right words...'

He coughs. It tires him to speak. A malady of the lungs, no doubt. This is not the worst of dungeons, the beguine thought when she arrived at the small underground cell reached not by a trap door but down a narrow staircase. But the place is ice cold. The walls are lapped by the waters of the Seine outside and drip with moisture. The air is heavy with miasmas of mould and rubbish, and the stink of the overflowing latrines.

'Are they feeding you?'

'Dry bread and water.'

'Perhaps I might...'

Humbert shakes his head.

'Don't concern yourself with that. Instead tell me why you are here. This is the behaviour of a friend. I did not know that you were one.'

'I came at the request of Dame Ade.'

'Ade?'

That laboured breathing again.

'She wanted me to tell you of her gratitude.'

'For having put her in danger?'

'For what you did afterwards.'

'Did I really have a choice?'

'You could have fled.'

'I could have.'

'Instead of which, you presented yourself to the Inquisition.'

'Is that not what you expected of me?'

Ysabel does not answer, but stands up with difficulty. The bench was obliging her to sit in a crouched position which hurts her legs. Now she leans against the wall, beneath the cell's sole window. The opening is placed so high in the wall that you cannot see anything of the outside world through it, but at least it lets some daylight, however weak, into the cell. There is nothing worse than living in permanent darkness. It drives many to madness.

She turns her eyes away from Humbert, and wonders: is he right? Was she hoping he would surrender when she asked for the package to be taken to him, along with a letter, just after dawn?

When the catastrophe unfolded, Brother Geoffroy had arrived when Mass had barely finished, with another Dominican, a commissary from the Inquisitor. Ysabel was at Ade's house when they knocked on the door, led by Agnes, her face strained under her wimple, her eyes downcast. What a degrading scene! Her friend's room searched, her chest opened and the books inside strewn over the floor. They read the letters from her sister-in-law and late brother out loud, picking over every little word, before confiscating them. Ade just let them get on with it, giving monosyllabic answers to their questions. And of course, Geoffroy lost his temper at that.

When he threatened Ade with taking her before the Inquisition, and that girl, too, Clémence de Crété, who had waited so long to denounce her, then of course Ysabel hoped that her letter to Humbert would attain its goal. She did not appeal to his charity but to his honour—and she did so deliberately. Because she knew that there lay his weakness and his pride. She spoke of Ade, whom he had exposed to danger. Each of her words was carefully weighed, and nothing is more poisonous than words.

Today, she still has no regrets. She feels compassion at seeing him so weakened, but no regret.

*

'How is Dame Ade?'

Humbert speaks softly, trying not to provoke his cough.

'She was very shaken. They interrogated her and then threw her out of the Beguinage.'

'Will they go after her?'

'The Inquisitors exonerated her due to the weakness of her sex. Your declaring that you had seduced her into doing your will was the best way of protecting her... You conducted yourself nobly.'

'And now you find me in a very noble condition.'

With a wave of his hand, the Franciscan indicates both the cell in which he is imprisoned and his own person. Something has broken in him. He already had a harassed, hounded look, but until now he has stood tall against his opponents.

'What will happen now, Brother Humbert? Has the date of the trial been announced?'

'The Inquisitor was not satisfied with my testimony during the interrogation. He sees my zeal for *The Mirror* as a sign of heretical practices. He does not believe in my innocence.'

Ysabel lowers her eyes. Like Humbert, she knows what this means: months of imprisonment, perhaps torture, to drag the truth from him.

'I cannot get them to feed you better, but I will ask if remedies can be brought to you.'

'They will no longer be of much use.'

The old beguine bends over, kneels on the stony ground. She takes the Franciscan's arm—which stinks of muck and urine—and presses her thumb against his wrist. The pulse is slow and weak.

'You see,' says Humbert. 'You ought to be concerned with my soul rather than my body. That is what I am trying to do now.'

'Are you succeeding?'

'With difficulty. My old master has been visiting me often recently. Day and night. He died in torment, and I fear he did not find rest in the afterlife.'

'Perhaps it is the weakness of your body that creates the illusion of his presence in your mind.'

'I do not know. Brother Jean was kind to me during his life, but his ghost is severe indeed.'

'And why do you think that is?'

'I put the community of women he so esteemed in danger. And I failed in the mission he entrusted to me before he died.'

Ysabel is still kneeling close to him. She searches for the right thing to say.

'You spared us the worst by giving yourself up to the Inquisitor and surrendering Marguerite's book to him. Now it is you who must endure the greatest suffering. As for the translation, do not worry… You have kept your promise to Jean de Querayn. Clémence de Crété hid it in her room. And now an acquaintance—somebody we trust—has it in her hands. A woman who is leaving for Italy. I asked her to take it with her and she will do it. She is indebted to me.'

'So, all is well.'

Humbert lets himself fall back against the wall. Several crude drawings have been scratched into the plaster by his head, the work of former prisoners: a crucifixion, a tournament, some writing too, names perhaps. The light is too feeble for Ysabel to make them out clearly.

'You know,' Humbert rasps, 'what seems to be the most… how to say this… the most terrifying thing, is to die for having defended a woman and a treatise that I so despised. I sometimes wonder whether the whole thing was a trick of Satan.'

'This is not Satan's work,' sighs Ysabel.

She looks at him and again asks herself how to go on. He is hunched over like a wounded beast once more. Is he in a fit state to understand what she is about to tell him? But they will probably never speak again after this day, and her words, if he understands them, will enable him to face what comes with his eyes open and clear.

'You have played your role, Brother Humbert, just like Geoffroy and Agnes, Clémence, Ade and I have played ours. Nevertheless, the events that led to your fall are beyond the power of any of us to control. They come from far away, from the depths, the very guts of our world as it changes and grows. They are many, but they all point in the same direction.'

She lifts her eyes to the skylight where the daylight trembles like a reflection on water.

'They are pulling us into darkness. Brother Humbert, you have merely been one more messenger bearing an oft-repeated warning. Night is falling on the beguines.'

18

Y SABEL WAITS FOR EASTER to pass and spring to get under-
way before leaving the Beguinage. She is getting too old for
uncomfortable journeys like these, on muddy roads, with your
horses forever at risk of getting bogged down or swept away by a
river in full spate. She shares a travelling wagon with an alderman
going to Provins. He knows all the best stopping places on the way,
the inns where they can rest safely. In her saddlebag, she carries
various restoratives, provisions, and a knife protected by a sheath,
a gift from her first husband, for cutting the apples which are so
good for revitalizing a body worn out by the trials of the road.

The journey should take four days. Ysabel's companion proves
not to be loquacious. Most of the time he sleeps. The cart's chassis
is suspended on leather straps, which do something to cushion
the rattling and jolting of the wheels, and sometimes Ysabel even
nods off herself, caught in the long rhythm of the journey, which
removes you from that of daily life as surely as hours spent in
unmoving prayer. But most of the time, she stays awake, drinking
in the flood of sensations and images flowing around her. The
land here reminds her of the country she crossed to reach the
Beguinage from her family's estate. A vast undulating plain of
waving wheat and oats, hills fringed with vines, flocks of sheep
grazing on the fallow land, where the yellow grass of winter is
giving way to new growth. The countryside ordered by the hand
of man, fruitful and harmonious.

The little girl at her side is just as avid, staring about them, wide-eyed. It must be the first time, Ysabel thinks, that her gaze has been free to wander without running up against a wall. For a while, she planned to simply take Leonor with her to the fields where she gathers her harvest, beyond the gardens of the marsh. The child had seemed fascinated by her collections of herbs and stones. But things have turned out differently. Perhaps it is for the best…

In any case, it is a pleasure simply to watch her, as the cart rolls on to the rhythm of the horses' heavy tread, through villages and past watchtowers, stopping in farm courtyards where they restore their strength with an egg and a draught of thick, creamy milk. Leonor never seems frightened. Her face has grown rosy from the fresh air already, and the hair escaping from her headdress has turned golden in the sun. Even her eyes have taken on a new colour, a clear green. She looks more like her mother than ever.

Did Maheut hesitate before leaving her behind? Ysabel still wonders. She showed no regret. When she left Leonor at the door of her house, she was already dressed for the road.

'Do you know what you are doing?' Ysabel asked. 'When that man has had enough of you, you will find yourself on the street again. You will have lost everything.'

'I have already lost everything,' was Maheut's simple reply.

'Not your salvation.'

'I will pray for my salvation when I am as old as you.'

The girl stood there with Ade's doll in her arms and a bundle at her feet. Waiting. Maheut knelt down and hugged her tightly.

'Ysabel is going to take care of you, my girl,' she had said. 'It is for your own good that I'm not taking you with me.'

She gave her a kiss, and then she was gone.

*

Ysabel weighed her decision for a long time, but with every league the horse-drawn wagon covers her concern grows. She is conscious of her responsibility to the child and to the mother who entrusted her to her care. Leonor has already suffered so many losses; she fears exposing her to yet another. Should she have left her at Jeanne du Faut's house? The silk merchant was prepared to take her in. But her brave friend Jeanne is now too fragile a support for a young soul to cling to. So Ysabel tries to comfort herself by thinking of a lesson learnt from her grandmother: even the driest and most depleted soil can produce green shoots, but it will certainly never do so if nobody plants a seed in it. She must trust in her instinct, have hope for the future, and plant the seed.

On the third night they stay at an inn in Provins. She sleeps badly despite the comfortable mattress, and getting up in the morning, before lauds, proves difficult. The two women travellers leave at dawn, huddled together against the cold. Soon the town's solid ramparts are mere dark shadows on the horizon, before they disappear completely. The horses pass by fields of the fine sheep whose wool is used to weave the blue cloth of Provins. More fields, more villages, and then there are only two leagues left.

The sun has climbed to its zenith when they arrive at the foot of the château, a forbidding fortress built on the lip of a valley. The drawbridge is lowered, the horses' heavy iron-shod hooves ring out on the wood, the cart sways. Leonor clings on to the cart's leather covering and stares up at her godmother, looking afraid for the first time. Ysabel smiles back at her, feeling light-headed with fatigue.

Now the cart has arrived in the grassy lower courtyard. A valet approaches with a little boy at his side, waving a wooden sword in the air.

'Who are you?' asks the boy.

A figure appears behind them. A young woman dressed in a robe of azure blue, bearing an infant in her arms. Further off stands another woman wearing a robe of the same colour but a darker shade. A white veil floats over her shoulders.

Ysabel gets down from the vehicle, holding Leonor by the hand.

The woman who was standing behind the others comes to the fore, lifts the child's fingers and presses them to her mouth.

*

'When did it happen?'

As the afternoon reaches its end, Ade and Ysabel walk in the garden beneath the keep, sheltered from the wind by the high walls but open to the south. The air is perfumed by the first flowers and milder than it is inside.

'The fifth Sunday of Lent,' answers Ysabel. 'The guard found him on his mattress in the morning.'

'Did he suffer?'

'His lungs were congested and his heart weak. His body gave way…'

'So, he did suffer.'

'I would not lie to you by pretending otherwise, but God was merciful. He spared him a long and difficult imprisonment.'

'I had hoped…'

Ysabel slips her arm under Ade's and holds her close.

'I had hoped that he would be permitted to go back to his monastery and remain confined there until the trial.'

'The Inquisitor is a Dominican and the Dominicans have supervision of the Royal Beguinage. They did not want to take the risk of the affair unleashing even more rumours. For them it was best if Brother Humbert was forgotten at the bottom of his cell.'

'So, he was found guilty even before being judged.'

'He knew he would be, Ade.'

A child's cry rings out at the foot of the walls. The little boy runs about, swiping at imaginary enemies with his sword. His mother laughingly calls him over, Leonor at her side.

'How did things go at the Beguinage after I left?'

'Visits were banned for several weeks, except with the prior's authorization. Only women who could show they had outside work to do had the right to leave. The Dominicans conducted an inquiry, questioned the sisters.'

'Were you yourself threatened?'

'My age and my husband's name protected me, although Agnes tried to implicate me in the affair.'

'Agnes?'

'She thought she could reach me through you, but she did not get much benefit from her denunciation. She left at the start of Lent with some story about a sick relative and never came back. I fear she will end her days in some hermitage.'

'I have no pity for her, I admit, even if I do not understand why she was punished.'

'Agnes is not very intelligent. She let herself be manipulated by her cousin, an ambitious man who I am sure will have the highest office among the Jacobins one day. No doubt he was hoping that this scandal would make the current prior appear negligent. It is unwise of him to weaken his monastery in this way, but he has too much support to be held to account. Still, they had to find someone responsible for the scandal. So, Agnes was sacrificed.'

The two women leave behind the vegetable plots and pass under an arbour that leads to the little garden that Ade's sister-in-law Héloise has planted about the château's chapel. Ade walks unsteadily, but she seems less fragile than Ysabel feared. When she left the Beguinage, after the humiliation of the search and Humbert's arrest, the old beguine feared for her life.

'How do you feel, Ade? You seem to have got back your strength.'

'Héloïse makes me go outside each day.'

'Are you going to stay with her?'

'She asked me to do so a few weeks ago. But that was not my plan. I wanted to retire among the Benedictines... You know I have been planning that for a long time.'

'And now?'

'Now? Now Leonor is here, thanks to you.'

'So, you have changed your mind?'

Ade shakes her head.

'Do not press me, Ysabel.'

She slips her hand from under her companion's arm, moves away, then adds in a whisper:

'You know, we did nothing wrong.'

'I know.'

*

A few minutes later, when Ade has gone, the old beguine lingers in the garden. Pointing up from fleshy stems, irises are already spreading out their petals. The flowers of the rainbow, thinks Ysabel, shining with every colour from blood red to the yellow of the sun. These ones will be blue, dusted with violet. Then the peonies of Pentecost will bloom, then the lilies too, and then the roses that will perfume the altar for the Assumption.

As she goes back towards the door that leads to the living quarters, she sees Héloïse. The young woman is alone, spinning around and calling: 'Jean, Leonor!' Her voice echoes like laughter from the walls of the keep.

The children have climbed to the top of the ramparts, the boy showing the little girl the way. They duck out of sight. Ysabel takes a few steps and tries to make out where they are. She sees a shadow move. It is Leonor, poking her head up. Now she gets to her feet. She has seen the forest from above, and a bird flying over it. She spreads her arms, lifts them, and moves her agile hands, making them glide through the air like wings.

Ysabel stands with her feet planted on the freshly mown grass, breathing in the good smell of the manure from the nearby stable and the hay held in the barn. She contemplates the girl, and smiles. Perhaps the seed she sowed has already broken through the soil and begun to grow.

AUTHOR'S POSTSCRIPT

The Vienne decrees are finally published in 1317 by Clement V's successor, John **XXII**, under the name *Constitutiones Clementinae*. The beguine status is condemned and banned, but the text ends in an ambiguous phrase: it is not prohibited, the pope specifies, to 'pious women, whether they have taken the vow of chastity or not, to live honestly in their dwellings and there serve God in a spirit of humility'.

In the years that follow, many communities in northern Europe profit from this 'escape clause' and become subject to the goodwill of local authorities, to the benevolence of their bishop, and to the support of donors. Everywhere, enquiries are hastily organized to ensure beguinages are following orthodox teaching. Some institutions resist, others see their goods confiscated or are forced to submit to new rules.

In Paris, where the *Clementinae* circulated in November 1317, the reaction is swift and severe. Some chroniclers report that the Royal Beguinage is closed. 'The beguines no longer sing, the beguines no longer read,' wrote the canon Jean de Saint-Victor.

*

In the name of his ancestor Saint Louis, the new king, Charles IV, successor to the short-lived Philip V, takes the Beguinage back under his protection, but gives it stricter regimentation. Nevertheless, the Beguinage—like the House of the Capetians and the whole kingdom that are soon to be swept away by the Hundred Years War and the Black Death—has begun its decline.

By 1470 the buildings have fallen into ruins. Only two women still live there. In 1471, Louis XI transfers them to the Franciscan community of the Daughters of Ave Maria. The last beguines join them. In 1485 the Poor Sisters of Saint Claire, a strict and rigorous order, is established in turn in the free women's former Beguinage. The archives of times past are not preserved and the memory of the Parisian beguines disappears.

Five centuries later, as I tried to follow the tracks—so faint—that the beguines left behind, I discover this notice published in 1994 in the Newsletter of the French Association of Ecclesiastical Libraries, by the medievalist Geneviève Hasenohr:

> *Manuscript sought…*
>
> *The Mirror of Simple and Annihilated Souls, by the beguine Marguerite Porete (–1310) a major text of medieval mysticism, is currently known only in its original French, in a single error-strewn manuscript copied long after the author's death (in the late 15th / early 16th century) and held by the Condé Museum, in Chantilly.*
>
> *However, the manuscript's first editor, M. de Corberon, claims to have had private access, in 1955–7, to a much earlier manuscript (perhaps even from the 14th century) which … was apparently in the possession of an order of nuns—French-speaking but established outside of France—who preferred not to make their name known…*
>
> *Given the importance that Marguerite Porete's work has taken on, for the history of spirituality as well as that of the French language, might these nuns be willing to make themselves known and allow a trusted philologist access to their precious library?*

To my knowledge, the request has remained unanswered to this day.

—ALINE KINER, 2017

AUTHOR'S
ACKNOWLEDGEMENTS

My thanks to historian Yann Potin for checking my manuscript with such goodwill and attention to detail.

To medievalist Pierre Prétou, who guided me through the complex workings of justice in the Middle Ages.

To art historian Anne Egger for her ever-judicious remarks.

To Sébastien Barret and Francesco Siri of the Institut de recherche et d'histoire des textes (IRHT) for their clarifications on medieval manuscripts.

To Cluny Museum for its warm welcome and for its marvellous collections, particularly staff members Axel Villechaize, Béatrice de Chancel-Bardelot, head conservator of the gardens, and Florence Margo-Schwoebel, in charge of the document archives.

To the Saorge monastery.

To all my female readers, for all the words shared.

To Liana Levi and Sandrine Thévenet for their confidence in me.

Finally, my deep gratitude to Isabelle Desesquelles, who hosted me so generously in her writing retreat, De Pure Fiction. It was there that my beguines found the beauty and love of books that allowed them to blossom.

TRANSLATOR'S NOTE

Unfortunately Aline Kiner died not long after this novel was published and so I never had the opportunity of working with her. When I first read this 2017 best-seller in French (*La Nuit des Béguines*) at the suggestion of my friend Bella Glicksmann and then followed in Kiner's footsteps down these narrow Marais streets, there was still almost no mention of the Paris Beguinage's existence anywhere in the capital's museums and libraries. The fact that there was no memory of a 'City of Ladies' in late medieval Paris testifies to the darkness of the night into which the beguines were plunged by repression, as recounted in this novel. It was the American medievalist, Tanya Stabler Miller, who reignited interest in the Beguinage with her *Beguines of Medieval Paris: Gender, Patronage and Spiritual Authority*, published in 2014. Aline Kiner was inspired by such modern research to reimagine this community of relatively free women, and to construct her plot around the fate of the mystical treatise written by Marguerite Porete, the only medieval author to be executed for a book (in fact, for *The Mirror of Simple Souls*).

I would like to thank Tanya Stabler of Loyola University in Chicago for her help with my translation of this novel, undertaken during the Covid pandemic, for answering innumerable queries, allowing the publisher to use her map of medieval Paris and for providing an English bibliography. I also want to thank two women from my medieval studies seminar, Janice Lindsay and Denise Rankin, who commented on the first draft, and other friends who read the novel in French or in my MS.

The context of Kiner's novel is a time of great socio-economic change in the late Middle Ages, the Valois monarchy's struggles with the papacy over the conduct of the Inquisition and repression of heterodoxy. The targets were the Templar Order, of course, but also this community of "free women" from all kinds of backgrounds who were seeking alternatives to the binary choice between marriage and the cloister, as Tanya Stabler Miller put it. As the novel closes, looming on the French horizon are the Hundred Years War and the coming of the plague. The curse on the Iron King, indeed.

As for the 'free women', the beguine model persisted into the modern era in the Low Countries and is now enjoying a revival, as modern women seek new ways of combining spirituality with communal living and working. Readers interested in this background should consult Tanya Miller's *Beguines of Medieval Paris* as well as the other works recommended under Further Reading. Readers interested in contemporary beguines can turn to www.beguine.link.

FURTHER READING

Bennett, Judith M. and Ruth Mazo Karras, eds., *The Oxford Handbook of Women and Gender in Medieval Europe* (Oxford, 2013)

Böhringer, Letha, Jennifer Kolpacoff Deane, and Hildo van Engen, eds., *Labels and Libels: Naming Beguines in Northern Medieval Europe.* (Turnhout: Brepols, 2014)

Field, Sean L., *The Beguine, the Angel, and the Inquisitor: The Trials of Marguerite Porete and Guiard of Cressonessart.* (Notre-Dame, IN: University of Notre-Dame Press, 2012)

Field, Sean L., "On Being a Beguine in France, c. 1300", in Letha Böhringer, Jennifer Kolpacoff Deane, and Hildo van Engen (Eds.), *Labels and Libels: Naming Beguines in Northern Medieval Europe* (pp. 117–133). (Turnhout: Brepols, 2014)

Field, Sean L., *Courting Sanctity: Holy Women and the Capetians.* (Ithaca: Cornell University Press, 2019)

Grundmann, Herbert, *Religious Movements in the Middle Ages: The Historical Links between Heresy, the Mendicant Orders, and the Women's Religious Movement in the Twelfth and Thirteenth Century, with the Historical Foundations of German Mysticism,* tr. Steven Rowan. (Notre-Dame, IN: University of Notre-Dame Press, 1995)

Hallam, Elizabeth M. and Charles West, *Capetian France, 987–1328,* 3rd ed. (Routledge, 2019).

Lerner, Robert, *The Heresy of the Free Spirit.* (Notre-Dame, IN: University of Notre-Dame Press, 1972)

Lerner, Robert, "New Light on the *Mirror of Simple Souls*," *Speculum* 85, pp. 91–116. (2010)

Makowski, Elizabeth, *"A Pernicious Sort of Woman": Quasi-Religious Women and Canon Lawyers in the Later Middle Ages*. (Washington, DC: Catholic University of America Press, 2005)

McDonnell, Ernest W., *The Beguines and Beghards in Medieval Culture: With Special Emphasis on the Belgian Scene*. (New Brunswick, NJ: Rutgers University Press, 1954)

Miller, Tanya Stabler, "What's in a Name? Clerical Representations of Parisian Beguines (1200–1328)". *Journal of Medieval History* 33: 60–86. (2007)

Miller, Tanya Stabler, *The Beguines of Medieval Paris: Gender, Patronage, and Spiritual Authority*. (Philadelphia: University of Pennsylvania Press, 2014)

Minnis, Alastair and Rosalynn Voaden, eds., *Medieval Holy Women in the Christian Tradition c. 1100–c. 1500* (Brepols, 2010)

More, Alison, *Fictive Orders and Feminine Religious Identities, 1200–1600*. (New York: Oxford University Press, 2018)

Newman, Barbara, "La mystique courtoise: Thirteenth-Century Beguines and the Art of Love", in *From Virile Woman to WomanChrist: Studies in Medieval Religion and Literature* (pp. 137–167). (Philadelphia: University of Pennsylvania Press, 1995)

Piron, Sylvain, "Marguerite in Champagne", *The Journal of Medieval Religious Cultures*, 43: 135–156. (2017)

Porete, Marguerite, *The Mirror of Simple Souls*, translated & introduced by Ellen Babinsky, Paulist Press, 1999. NOTE: All quotations from *The Mirror of Simple Souls* are taken from this edition. Babinsky's introduction includes a history of the manuscript versions.

Roux, Simone, *Paris in the Middle Ages*, tr. Jo Ann McNamara (Philadelphia: Pennsylvania University Press, 2009).

Stauffer, Robert and Wendy R. Terry, eds., *A Companion to Marguerite Porete and* The Mirror of Simple Souls (Brill, 2017).

Strayer, Joseph, *The Reign of Philip the Fair* (Princeton University Press, 1980).

Van Engen, John, "Marguerite (Porete) of Hainaut and the Medieval Low Countries", in Sean L. Field, Robert E. Lerner, and Sylvain Piron (eds.), *Marguerite Porete et le Miroir des Simples Âmes: Perspectives Historiques, Philosophiques et Littéraires* (pp. 25–68) (Paris: Vrin, 2013).

AVAILABLE AND COMING SOON
FROM PUSHKIN PRESS

Pushkin Press was founded in 1997, and publishes novels, essays, memoirs, children's books—everything from timeless classics to the urgent and contemporary.

Our books represent exciting, high-quality writing from around the world: we publish some of the twentieth century's most widely acclaimed, brilliant authors such as Stefan Zweig, Yasushi Inoue, Teffi, Antal Szerb, Gerard Reve and Elsa Morante, as well as compelling and award-winning contemporary writers, including Dorthe Nors, Edith Pearlman, Perumal Murugan, Ayelet Gundar-Goshen and Chigozie Obioma.

Pushkin Press publishes the world's best stories, to be read and read again. To discover more, visit www.pushkinpress.com.

THE PASSENGER
ULRICH ALEXANDER BOSCHWITZ

AT NIGHT ALL BLOOD IS BLACK
DAVID DIOP

TENDER IS THE FLESH
AGUSTINA BAZTERRICA

WHEN WE CEASE TO UNDERSTAND THE WORLD
BENJAMÍN LABATUT

THE WONDERS
ELENA MEDEL

NO PLACE TO LAY ONE'S HEAD
FRANÇOISE FRENKEL